W9-BGO-798

PLAYING IN THE LIGHT

PLAYING IN THE LIGHT

A Novel

Zoë Wicomb

THE NEW PRESS

NEW YORK
LONDON

I gratefully acknowledge the support received from the Arts and Humanities Research Council (UK). I am also indebted to the Civitella Ranieri Foundation, New York, for a wonderful residency in Umbertide, as well as to Alice and Johnnie Green for kindly making their cottage in Galloway available to me.

© 2006 by by Zoë Wicomb

All rights reserved.
No part of this book may be reproduced,
in any form, without written permission from the publisher.

Requests for permission to reproduce selections
from this book should be mailed to: Permissions Department,
The New Press, 38 Greene Street, New York, NY 10013

Originally published in South Africa
by Umuzi, an imprint of Random House (Pty) Ltd, 2006
Published in the United States by The New Press, New York, 2006
Distributed by W. W. Norton & Company, Inc., New York

ISBN-13 978-1-59558-047-4
ISBN-10   1-59558-047-6
CIP data available

The New Press was established in 1990 as a not-for-profit alternative to the large, commercial publishing houses currently dominating the book publishing industry. The New Press operates in the public interest rather than for private gain, and is committed to publishing, in innovative ways, works of educational, cultural, and community value that are often deemed insufficiently profitable.

www.thenewpress.com

Book design by William Dicey
This book was set in Caslon

Printed in the United States of America

2 4 6 8 10 9 7 5 3 1

102506 B+T $24,95

3 6150 0245309 0

*I*t is on the balcony, the space both inside and out where she spends much of her time at home, that it happens. A bird, a speckled guinea fowl, comes flying at a dangerous angle, just missing the wall, and falls dead with a thud at Marion's feet. Amid scatter cushions and a coffee tray and the smell and roar of the sea, it lies on the brown ceramic tiles. There had been the usual squabbling, angry flapping and circling overhead, and then a heart attack in mid-flight, she supposes. Still warm with rage but undoubtedly dead, her bare foot decides. Marion bends down to check the eyes, bloodshot and staring, and the distinctive feathers, by no means as fine a plumage as it appears from a distance.

There is silence overhead. Will the others, the enemies, line up on her balcony wall to pay their respects? Should she withdraw? She would like to toss the bird onto the communal gardens below, but she is squeamish about touching it; and besides, its landing is sure to be seen by someone who would calculate from the trajectory precisely which balcony it's been hurled from. Someone with the correct respect for property, who may well ring her doorbell, bird in hand, to return the fowl to its rightful owner. That someone would have to hold it by its feet, head hanging, so that the feathers billowed, the guinea fowl declassified by the ruffling of its black-and-white patterned plumage. Marion reaches for a shawl from the back of the rattan chair, spreads it on the tiles, rolls the bird over with her foot – it is surprisingly heavy – and wraps it in a shroud of sage green. Fortunately it is Thursday, cleaning day. She leaves the girl a note asking her to take the parcel of bird away. One never knows what uses such people might have for a dead guinea fowl.

A respect for property is precisely what this new luxury block on the beachfront at Bloubergstrand can guarantee. Residents are more than happy to pay for smartly uniformed attendants who monitor all and sundry entering the grounds. Every car owner must stop at the barricades to fill in a form recording the names of driver and passengers, registration number and purpose of visit. Security – you have to pay for it these days, especially if you are a woman on your own. No point in having a glorious outlook on the sea, with the classic view of Table Mountain on the left and Robben Island on the right, if you are not secure. Here, your property is inviolable.

Marion's apartment is modest – she has no need for more than one bedroom – but the flat is the fulfilment of an adolescent dream. There is a tingle of recognition when she flicks through *Home and Garden* magazines and her interiors seem to spring from the glossy pages. Thus the leather sofas arrived not with stiff, creaky newness, but with matt familiarity, settling into her home as comfortably as tabby cats. Or the four-poster bed, a house in itself, into which she can retreat from the larger one when she needs the cocoon of draped muslin after a hard day's work, the noise of the world dampened to a distant hum. She remembers distinctly when she first saw such an astoundingly luxurious thing: subtly lit photographs of a country house in an English magazine, and a bed that was hardly an item of furniture. Rather a bower for an egte fairy princess, who would lie for a hundred chaste years in gauzed limbo, waiting for the world to change into a better, a more hospitable place. Marion knows that the bed is extravagant, foolish perhaps for such a small flat – but what the hell, she deserves it, this marker of her success.

But lately, the four-poster has turned against her. There have been times, propped up with her magazines, when something buzzes in her ears, a sense of swarming that grows louder and louder, even as the sunset, which she can see from the bed, curls in serene pink and gold across the horizon and the cool Atlantic laps at Robben Island. Then, for a moment, she seems to gag on metres of muslin, ensnared in the fabric that wraps itself round and round her into a shroud from which she struggles to escape.

There is no point dwelling on such moments. From her bed, Marion can look out at the sea, at the speckled guinea fowl that strut the roofs below or perch on chimney pots, and take pleasure in this haven from the hurly-burly of work. The attacks are not serious, last for no more than a couple of minutes; it is just that she is tired, over-worked. An intimate friend might say that such a palaver is enough to warrant therapy, or at least a dismantling, a disrobing of the bed. But she has no such friend; there are no gatherings of young women who giggle and bare their souls and call themselves girls. And Marion has no truck with therapy. She despises those who do: indulgent, effete, English types, who do not know how to roll up their sleeves and get on with things. Why spend money and time to discover the obvious: that as the only issue of older parents, she had a peculiar childhood; that her parents loathed each other; that her mother, like all mothers, was responsible for her insecurity?

Besides, she has come round to thinking that this is simply the human condition – even for men. Marion has advanced in the world precisely because she presses on. The strangling effect of muslin will simply have to be overcome, will necessarily fail in the face of her no-nonsense approach. If creatures must fall out of the sky to die at her feet, so be it. She is not superstitious; she attaches no significance to such things. And since she never sees the cleaning girl, whose wage is left on the table, she will never know what happened to the bird. Here by the cool waters of Bloubergstrand she'll stay, with her heart-tugging postcard view of sea and mountain, even if her father does whine about it being so far away. Of course that is precisely why she has chosen to live here, miles from Observatory.

It is not that she does not love her father. He is an old man past the fury of manhood. The frown on his forehead has set into folds she calls interesting, folds that balance the craters on his cheeks and those around the sagging mouth. But there is an uneasy edge to their love, a fringe of cloud that perhaps is necessarily there between father and daughter. For all his jolly banter, Marion now recognises in his facial lines the guardedness, the hesitation that must have been there all along: he is

3

a boer trespassing in the city, where the bucolic is mocked; he is wary of ambition. Marion supposes that it is due to humble roots, to lack of education, to the barefoot childhood on the farm from which he escaped to Cape Town, where he would never be comfortable.

Thankfully, her mother is dead, has died a self-willed and efficient death, and after that marriage of bitter bickering John has become her dear Pappa. He likes being called that, Pappa, which in his family is what you call your grandfather, but her old Pappa too is long since dead. His family members, unlike other people's, all disappeared into the jaws of the city or died young or, for all her father's easygoing bonhomie, fell out with him years ago. Family! he used to exclaim elliptically, shaking his head and pulling a face that she could not interpret. As if between the thought and the utterance he had changed his mind, so that his expression hovered somewhere between distaste and regret. Nowadays, threatened with extinction, he whines, My beauty, my Marina, what about some grandchildren then for your old Pappa? In spite of himself, because he turns away immediately to complain about a shoelace or a pain in his chest, and she knows that he is embarrassed, that he does not really mean it, does not really want to be plagued by children crawling all over him like insects.

It is Saturday afternoon when Marion visits her father. She remembers to include in the food basket some walnuts, dried apricots and biltong. These are delicacies that John Campbell still thinks of as special fare: the stuff produced for a livelihood on the farm in the Karoo, but which the family was barred from eating, except at Christmas time. Except for what the brothers stole from the loft on lazy Sunday afternoons, pocketfuls taken to the mealie field, where they would lie hidden between rows of maize, chewing, and checking the lengths of their penises.

In the cramped tin-roofed terraced house in Observatory, he often thinks of the old farm: the house with whitewashed walls and black window frames; the loft, which stretched the entire length of the roof, with

4

its black wooden door. All the farmhouses had woodwork painted in gracht green. Why not theirs? Why had he never asked his father? But his father was a man of few words, a man without letters who refused to answer questions. Or perhaps knew none of the answers.

Why do we have an English name?

Why, why why? his father mimicked. Is that all you can say? Ask no questions and you'll hear no lies.

Yes, he thinks often of the house, of Ma and all the brothers, whose names he sometimes finds himself chanting: John, Pieter, Karel, Paul, Roelf and Dawid, in descending order and starting with himself – otherwise how would one remember all of them? And their adorable sister Elsie, slap bang in the middle.

Kembel, that was what the officer at the Traffic Department wrote down when John first said his name; and John, who could read and write perfectly well, knew that it would be a mistake to correct a man so dapperly turned out in khaki – yes, those were the days before the airforce-blue uniform. Why fuss over a spelling that made not the slightest difference? Or if it did, if that was all it took to turn him into someone new, a man of the city with prospects, who was he to complain? The name could easily be corrected later without offending the officer.

John has a special ear for traffic. Which is not surprising, given that his working life was spent on crossroads and traffic islands, appreciating the sounds that he came to identify as one might the separate instruments in a symphony. That, for the young man from the Karoo, was the essence of the city: a symphony of sound, of people chattering in Afrikaans or English or, in their neighbourhood, switching smartly in mid-sentence between the two; of buses, bakkies, cars and lorries. He loved the cheeriness of electric light licking at the slopes of Table Mountain, and especially the red, green and amber of robots that governed all that circulation of traffic. To be a traffic cop is to be at the very source of the movement and sound of the city, to know your way about its veins and arteries and to feel the power of the beast between your thighs: the gleaming Harley-Davidson. And with pristine white gloves to guide motorists through the harmonies of weaving and crossing and finding their way through the traffic. At night, at home, when the silence of the house where Helen crocheted and he browsed *Landbou Weekblad* became oppressive, he would summon the music of that roar, hear the muted sound swirling about until it seemed to emanate from the centre of the room, from the fresh arrangement of artificial blooms replaced on Friday evenings by the flower company.

But Helen brought an end to that pleasure. In the specialist trousseau shop that she managed, a chic customer spoke of her future mother-in-law's vulgarity, her pride in the plastic bouquets, to which Helen nodded in a flush of embarrassment. Helen called the company to have them removed; she wanted them out, ruffled doily and all, and did not even hear John's objections. Her head kept on nodding like a mechanical toy; she said over and over that it had been a mistake, only a mistake. No, she had no complaints about the quality of service, she said to the saleswoman, and no, she definitely couldn't wait until Friday. And then Helen's voice grew shrill and hysterical as she threatened to put the flowers in the dustbin that instant, so that a coloured chap on an inferior motorcycle arrived within half an hour to take the arrangement of sweetpeas, roses and crisp green ferns away in his delivery box. Only then did she stop nodding.

John shuffles along the passage, idly trailing his left hand along the wall; he will not acknowledge that he needs the support. Damn, he has left his stick on the stoep, and anyway, who would have thought he'd have to go again? The last trip to the lavatory had turned out to be a false alarm, a waste of time; and now, just as Marion is about to arrive, his bladder is letting him down once more. There is no time to go back for the stick. He is sure that he can hear her car rising above the sounds of the city. Nowadays, John insists that he has a gift for identifying individual cars, for which he is grateful – it distracts from waiting. That is what he does, how he gets through time. He waits for Saturdays when Marion comes, or for the occasional phone calls during the week when she might announce that she'll be popping in, or that she is on her way, by which he has come to understand that she has only just thought of coming, and that there will be long minutes of hunting for keys, of finishing a cup of tea, of finding in her cupboard treats to bring for him or stopping at a shop for a packet of biltong or mebos, while he waits patiently through slow time. But with his special ear for traffic, he picks out precisely the sound of her car as it approaches the robot in Main Road; he can tell from the screech of wheels whether she is waiting at a red light before turning, or whether she is slowing down on the green, slipping into second gear in order to turn into Burns Road.

For sure, it is Marion's Mercedes shooting along Main Road; and then the sound becomes steadier as it slides into the clippety-clop of horses' hooves. No more than a boy he is, holding the reins, his lithe body tense on the wagon kist as they negotiate the narrow, winding road of the Swartberg Pass. High black peaks cast higgledy-piggledy shadows across the road. The horses are not happy; the adolescent boy coaxes and encourages, especially his favourite, Bleskop; he steers them expertly round the treacherous cliffs with the sheer, sheer drop on the side from which they shy, shaking their heads and snorting with fear or perhaps resentment. While he holds the reins, Pa chews on a twist of tobacco, pretending not to keep a watchful eye on the boy's hands, on the fitful horses. Pa spits his confidence in an arc of brown tobacco juice that plummets to the valley below. He is pleased with himself; he has negotiated a better price this time for the tobacco harvest, and they are returning to the farm not only with provisions for the winter months but also with a good roll of banknotes. The provisions are carefully ticked off on Ma's list. A bag of sugar beans, of course, Pa had argued, snatching the list from his hand as if he could read; and John, not having the courage to insist, was forced to agree, even if Ma's clear writing said samp, not beans, of which there is still half a sack in the loft.

God steers them by an invisible rope from heaven, hauling them up into the high peaks. To God they must seem pitiful, like lizards that without his guidance would slide down the rock, clinging for dear life. Pa says it is a good thing to be reminded of their insignificance, to be humbled by the mountain. The stillness of the barren black rock is awesome; the sound of horses' hooves cuts into it like colour. At the top of the mountain, they stop for black coffee and hunks of buttered bread. Now John can look at the scorched aloes clinging to the side of the road. Their blackened candelabras wave feebly, crookedly in the breeze, and he cannot imagine them red as the flaming of horses' hooves.

Marion's car coming to a halt only yards from the front door catches him out before the descent of the mountain pass. Panic rises, for he has been standing for some time over the lavatory bowl. His bladder is letting him down; it is finished and klaar. Ag please almighty God … The words tumble out before he can stop them. He reprimands himself: it isn't right to speak to God of such things. He gives the old tollie a shake while kicking backwards with his left leg to close the bathroom door. Ag, come on now, he cajoles, tugging at the wayward old organ, summoning a trickle that no sooner starts than stops again. He hears Marion rap at the front door.

Pa, Pappa, she calls, his Marina, with the voice of a mermaid; and just then, when he's distracted, an arc of piss passes across the seat onto the cracked tiles at the side of the bath. Womanish tears threaten to spill from his eyes as he shakes the useless old tollie, begging for the dribble to stop. Should he be sitting down on the lavatory like a woman? And why must the child shout so loudly? He is certainly not deaf. Next thing she'll come barging into the lavatory. But he calls out in an apologetic voice that he barely recognises, Won't be long. Clumsily he swipes at the piss with paper. It's no use, he knows she'll find him out; she is also her mother's child.

Although she never uses it, Marion still has a key that she's kept since childhood, when she let herself into the house after school from a string around her neck. Safe as houses in those days, to be alone, playing in the garden, as long as you didn't answer the door to the hawkers. She and her best friend Annie Boshoff, who was sometimes allowed to visit after school, stifled their giggles as the hawker shrilled his wares when he thought no one could hear: Aartappels 'n ui-we; lekker lekker ui-we, maak die stokkie stywer.

On the narrow stoep she lingers over a potted geranium. As a child she hated their street, the terraced houses so close to the pavement, where families distinguished themselves from their neighbours by painting their doors in violently clashing colours. As if, returning from work in the evenings, tired and absentminded, they feared walking into the wrong house, and so relied on grass green or acid yellow to trigger recognition. Then, she'd dreamt of a row of houses in uniform white-wash, with woodwork graded from east to west in slowly deepening shades of green, from the palest hint of apple to traditional Cape-Dutch gracht green. She'd imagined her father, unable to distinguish between the subtle shades, stumbling into the Van Zyls' where, according to his philosophy of making the best of things by covering up with chatter, he would settle himself comfortably at their dinner table and plunge into jokes and anecdotes, without her mother's Don't-speak-with-food-in-your-mouth.

Marion would have preferred to live above the Main Road, close to Annie Boshoff. Those verandahed stoeps, edged with broekielace, were wrapped around at least two sides of the houses, so that people could spend all day outside in the ambiguous space between private house and public street. From there you could see the sweep of Table Bay, the masts of ships and the clutter of the docks, and then, across the glint of water, the white sands of Bloubergstrand. At Marion's house, with the mean, verandahless strip of stoep that slipped without as much as a path straight into the street, they kept indoors, even in summer. Her mother urged her to keep out of the sun. Did she want to end up like mad Mr Moolman across the road, who was burnt pitch black like a coloured and who stood in the mornings on that strip of concrete in his vest, if you please, doing his exercises? The child watched him through the lace curtain, could hear him pant as his torso bent left, right, left, right, his chest covered in a pelt of black hair. Then he stretched luxuriously and sniffed like a hungry animal at the salty sea air drifting up from Woodstock beach, before going indoors for his breakfast.

She pinches off the dead leaves of the geranium, sniffs for the scent, but the wind has already risen and there is only the smell of sea air blown inland. Marion probes gingerly with a finger. Yes, it is quite dried out, the soil is coming away from the sides – damn, she's ruined her newly varnished nail. It is not like her father to neglect a plant, but the truth of the matter is that he no longer cares: only the single pot remains on the stoep. Determined to revive his interest in gardening, Marion had bought him a book with lavish illustrations. He'd paged dutifully through the colour plates before leaving it on the coffee table, where it still lies. Sometimes he remembers to pretend that he's been reading it. Then he speaks volubly, boasts like a boy about growing beans eighteen inches long – he has returned to the imperial measure of his youth – and red dahlias the size of saucers.

The lace curtain at his bedroom window is bunched up into the right corner, so she is able to look in. Her parents were always meticulous, neurotic really, about curtains: drawing them before switching on the lights, careful about keeping them neatly in place during the day. It is not that she cares for lace curtains; rather, Marion is alarmed by her father's growing forgetfulness, the slide into someone she doesn't know.

The window brings a memory of a cold winter's evening, with rain falling heavily, noisily, like dead locusts onto the stoep. Her mother stepping out of the bedroom, wearing John's too-large corduroy trousers. The look in her eyes made them both start, a bold look of defiance as she did up the last fly button and swaggered across the room before returning to the bedroom door, where she assumed a coquettish pose. Their eyes followed her. John said with an uneasy chuckle, Just as well no one'll visit in such terrible weather. Then, as she mimed with poised fingers the smoking of a cigarette, her bottom lip pouted to exhale smoke, he said, Okay Lenie, that's enough now. Get dressed.

Helen's voice was that of a film star, husky and scornful. Campbell, you're no longer on the farm; this is the city. I won't be a plaasjapie here, and you know better than to call me Lenie. It can't be a sin to wear trousers, because nowadays, here in town, you'll see smart, respectable women wearing slacks. What's the point of working hard, of building a new life, if your husband is determined to be backward, a poor white? she said bitterly.

The child winced at her unfairness. They were surely not poor whites, and besides, if she didn't want to be a tannie it wasn't Pappie's fault.

They didn't stop shouting until Marion looked up and pointed to the curtain, so close to the street, that had not been drawn. Which made them rush to the window, bumping into each other, the question of trousers dissipated in the panic of being on display. Marion cannot remember when her mother changed back into her dress.

John takes so long that Marion lets herself in. She brings along the key in case he's laid up in bed, although he says it's nonsense, that he has never, not even with last year's vicious flu, taken to his bed during the day; such weakness he would resist to the bitter end. Yes, I know, she said, but there's always a first time. That's where you – then she corrected herself – where *we'll* all end up, flat on your back with your mouth hanging open, staring wildly into space.

He heard not only the replacement, but then also the loss of the tactful *we*, and felt afraid of the old man she imagines: he whose mouth hangs open, who stares into space.

At last he can tuck away his useless tollie and zip up. Marion is in the kitchen unpacking a Woolworths bag of fruit into a cut-glass bowl she takes out of the cupboard. Does she not realise that the bowl, beautiful as it is, is too heavy for him to lift? Guavas too. He sniffs appreciatively, remembering the tree that pressed against Ma's kitchen window. But he says nothing. As he stumbles about looking for his stick – Jisso, where on earth did he put it? – she flings open doors, windows, complains about the smell, the stuffiness, so that the southeaster, gearing up as usual at this hour, sweeps through the house. The smell of sea rushes right into the kitchen, and Marion stops scolding for a moment to plant a cool kiss on his pate.

Marion often has a late lunch with her father on Saturdays. Today, she prepares a light meal of poached kingklip and vegetables. He complains about not having potatoes, so she cuts a slice of bread and admonishes, You have to watch your weight, Pappa, remember what Doctor said about your heart.

So this reversal is what it all boils down to, he thinks resentfully: you insist that the child should eat the right food and then, before you know it, the years have flashed by and the child in turn, believing that she knows better, invents a diet for you. This is just plain old bullying, he says. He sulks and does not eat the slice of bread she has buttered with margarine. He hasn't asked for bread; it is potato that he wants. What kind of a meal is fish without potato? How can butter from God's cattle be bad for one? And who has lunch at two o'clock in the afternoon?

Marion says that she'll leave some prepared dinners from Woolworths in the fridge. You mustn't shop at Woolworths, he says, it's too expensive. She takes from her cooler bag a bottle of Zonnebloem, still cold. He sips from his glass with something of a grimace and complains that he doesn't like wine; it's cheap stuff that bergies drink. He takes a good Oude Meester brandy, not to excess of course, but a tot in the evening makes for a very nice sleep.

Cheap stuff? Marion repeats. She has admonished herself to be patient, but that commodity runs out without warning. Well, let's not waste the wine on you then, and she puts the cork back with a decisive press of the palm. It's no good trying to civilise you. Then she says, by way of making up, Okay Pappa we'll take a chair into the garden for you; the place needs tidying up.

It is a good-sized garden for so small a house, and private too. She struggles with fork and spade. Really, it is no garden any more. The bougainvillea in the corner has all but taken over, the weeds in what once was a lawn are ankle high; but the old man will hear nothing of a gardener. Does she think he's not capable of doing it himself? Besides, what's wrong with a few weeds? If things get out of hand, he'll certainly tend the garden. John does not understand this urge to fight nature. I grew up in the veld, he says; I don't mind things going a little wild.

Her foot lingers on the haft of the spade. Christ, is ageing really like this? This is nothing short of a change of character. Her father might as well tell her that he's taken to robbing banks. He's forgotten his youthful obsession with gardening: dahlias, marigolds and Christmas roses, whose colour he would doctor with doses of potassium to get the correct shade of blue. Along the left wall he had a row of runner beans, their scarlet flowers towering over the rest. Cook it yourself, her mother would say to his offering of beans; and he would cajole and cover up with a jingle about beans bringing a blush into the cheeks of his girls.

Marion explains patiently that nature means not only weeds, but also mice, rats, snakes even, who'd have no regard for the threshold of the back door. She will send round a gardener next week, she says.

But he'll have none of it. They kill you in your own garden, hack your head off with your own blunt spade. Haven't you seen in the papers?

Ag Pa, she sighs. I'll send the man who does the grounds of our block. Plaatjie's reliable; he's been with us for five years now. But John is stubborn in his old age. No, he says, these kaffirs of the New South Africa kill you just like that, just for the fun of it.

Should she resist this slippage into slovenliness and bring Plaatjie anyway? How is one to know what to do? What is good for him?

He stumbles back into the house, to his seat by the window where he can gaze at the comings and goings through the lace curtain. A young woman in a shrunken top is strutting up and down, puffing furiously at a cigarette, her roll of brown belly trembling. Is she muttering to herself? Has she lost something in the street, a ring perhaps? He leans forward to look and his elbow catches the curtain at the very moment that the girl looks up. She tosses her bleached yellow hair and snarls, Fuck off dirty old man; mind your own fucking business. So that he retreats hastily, pulls back the curtain and sits far back in his chair, shaking with rage and terror. Yes, this is what it boils down to: the young terrorising the old. No respect, he mutters, and a flash of his former self on the traffic island in Long Street, in his uniform, giving white-gloved directions, comes to his rescue then goes again as he staggers out of his chair.

Marion is about to leave when her cellphone rings. It is the armed-response people. The alarm at the office has gone off, and a sinister voice assures her that they are on their way to investigate, guns at the ready. Jesus, why ring her when they should be getting on with the job of catching the bastards? What can she do with the information? Sometimes she wonders if the nation is not being taken for a ride, if the people who work for armed response are not themselves responsible for all the break-ins. Organised crime indeed. While armed response is messing about on the phone, the bastards are no doubt sauntering out with all five computers. Don't they even wait until it's dark any more? The office had been cleaned out only six months ago; Marion would want a life for every computer taken.

She fights the tears that try to well up; she doesn't want to hear the inane words of comfort that her father would resort to. Fortunately John is somewhat deaf and it's easy to fob him off.

She doesn't know that he has made the correct inferences from her terse replies on the phone, that he knows all too well what is going on, but that since lunch, the world has become too much for him, and so he gratefully accepts her assurance that everything's fine. They sit in silence. For what can she do, what can he do in the face of all this greed and violence, these senseless killings, the anarchy into which the country is slipping? Thus moved by his own helplessness, his inability to protect his darling child, he lets on after all: This country is going to the dogs, he says, wringing his hands. To think how hard we fought, took up arms for a decent life, for a country of which we can be proud …

Marion stares at him in amazement. Is he losing his marbles? But Pappa, she says, you've never supported the liberation movement. What on earth are you talking about?

He pushes back the frail shoulders and, once more the reservist soldier fighting for his country, tugs at the imaginary uniform. Sis man, he says with indignation, I'm not talking about that lot, about terrorists. Remember Sharpeville, remember the kaffirs here on our own doorstep in Langa? Well, I was one of those who volunteered as a reservist to defend South Africa against the blarry Communists. Oh, your mother was proud of me alright; she always liked a uniform. But all in vain, hey. Look what's happened: kaffirs and hotnos too lazy to work, just greedily grabbing at things that belong to others, to decent people.

How could I remember Sharpeville, she says, I was only just born. But there is no point in talking politics with him. He is of that generation that cannot think themselves out of an imagined idyllic past, especially not the past that has shaped him into a man of the city, a jintelman.

It pains him, he says, to see how things are going to pot, to think of the good old days now all in a heap, collapsed, but in his confused politics he has also somehow collaged the rehabilitated image of Nelson Mandela into that past. Also a jintelman, he says, how it must pain that poor man, seeing the country go to the dogs.

Marion jingles her keys. It is a sound that makes loneliness rise, that reminds him of the first fearful weeks in the team of traffic cops, so he straightens his shoulders and sits up bravely. Ja-nee, he says, you'd better be going. Is my mermaid going dancing tonight?

Dancing at her age – what an idea. But she says brightly, Yes, because that will make him happy. But first I must just drop in at the agency.

Armed response has come up trumps: there is only one broken window. Shot them down like flies, Marion hopes, then revises the thought – she wouldn't like to trip over dead bodies. She might as well stay and get things done; and besides, she likes being in the office when everyone has left and the place is hers to potter about in, as she cannot do in the presence of others. On the pad on her desk is a list of tasks for Monday morning that she might as well get started on; but she is restless, perhaps because it is getting on for Saturday evening in a city decanted of people – people who are readying themselves for the elusive pleasures of the night. There are times when Marion wishes to submit, just once more, to the idea that there is a live, warm heart to Saturday night; that it is incumbent on all under the age of, say, forty to go out, aglow with hope, in search of that throbbing heart. She hums the Tom Waits tune. Johan, her last attempt at a boy-friend, had given her the tape, the very best thing in her meagre collection; perhaps she should get herself more Waits.

She stares wistfully at the telephone until the moment passes. It may be well to stumble upon such a thing, the chimerical heart of Saturday night; but only too aware of the triple bypass that beckons, she fears that she is past it. A good night's sleep, that's what she needs.

There is, however, no rush to go home; she'll carry on pottering for a while. She rearranges the silk magnolias on the filing cabinet into a new clay pot. Thank God that someone has thought of modifying the old potbellied style into this tall, asymmetrical shape. She has always disliked ethnic style, its slavish devotion to the past, when Christ knows that no one, nothing, can do without revision.

Her eyes sweep across the room, taking in the improvement, but then she notes that the shelves have been tampered with. It is only natural that people should want to impose their taste, their own aesthetic on their environment, by shifting a desk or placing the brochure stand at a particular angle. But to rearrange the books and trophies on the glass shelves – MCTravel, one of the few independent companies left, has won a couple of prizes – is intolerable, although possibly done without thought. She doesn't care who the culprit is; she will not say anything. All that matters is that things are returned to their rightful places, for that surely is her prerogative: determining where things go. As for the individual desks of her staff, she would of course not interfere. Neatness is all that is required, although she had to draw the line at Tanya's pink teddy bear, facing out to leer insipidly at clients. Now the bear sits sulking on a cabinet in the kitchen, where Tanya offers it an apology every day for its banishment, equally irritating, but at least out of public sight.

This evening, the order of glass and chrome and matt-black furniture is subtly undermined by something else, which she can't quite put her finger on, a whiff of something that makes her stop to sniff for an explanation. But it is not a smell; there is nothing to identify, so perhaps she should go home. It is after six o'clock when she switches off her computer. Leaning against her desk, she surveys her little kingdom, checks again for that which might have escaped her; but no, on the surface at least, order has been restored. She is not given to hunches and feelings, but wonders all the same if it is something to do with Brenda. The terrible thought of looking in the drawers of Brenda's desk occurs to her, but she restrains herself; there is no evidence of anything irregular. Give them a pinkie and they'll grab your whole hand, her mother always said. But that was the kind of prejudiced stuff her parents were prone to, the nonsense with which that generation burdened themselves. Perhaps it is not so surprising that things have been different since Brenda's arrival, which after all coincided with old Mrs Chester's retirement.

Brenda Mackay is soft spoken, soothing even, unless that is just the musical lilt of her Cape Flats accent, but at times there is something of an ironic edge to her voice that is unnerving. Irritating, too, is the way she has that idiotic cleaner and tea-girl, Tiena, eating out of her hand, so that that one would serve her immediately after Marion. Then Brenda, with impressive diplomacy, would wave Tiena along: no, she couldn't stop for tea just then, she'd have to finish this or that urgent matter first. Or she would produce her own herbal tea bag, needing only a cup of boiling water that she'd get herself. In just a moment, and she'd wink at the stupid girl, whose hand would fly to her mouth to suppress a giggle.

This morning, Brenda asked if she could take next Friday off. She'd like to go away for a long weekend. An opportunity has arisen, she said vaguely. Then she swiftly changed the topic, chattered at length about the problematic contract with Farnley Foods, perhaps out of embarrassment, for Marion was brief, said no, Friday was far too busy. Marion would have liked to oblige, but it's true, Fridays are impossible, especially in the afternoons, when the place buzzes with young and old alike, those who, faced with yet another dull weekend, with the reality of their humdrum lives, decide that they need to travel. This is what couples seem to do on Thursday nights, anticipating the weekend tedium, the elusive heart of Saturday night: they plan a trip, and then it simply can't wait till Saturday. Marion smiles indulgently at such faith in the efficacy of travel; she has never subscribed to it, which she believes is why she runs the business so successfully, free of the illusions of travel and its supposed freedoms. Naturally she is pleased about others' enthusiasm for travel, and her father marvels at this to-ing and fro-ing that puts the honeyed bread on her table. Her parents have never travelled, except for the original journey taken by so many at the time – the one-way train ticket from platteland to town.

Would Brenda not like to have the Monday off instead? Ag no, Brenda laughed, it doesn't matter; she hadn't even thought about going away until last night. And what's more, the weekend here in town promises to be full of action: two parties and a dance to choose from, and a kwaai ou, a friend of a friend, who's more than happy to be her partner. That buffoon, Tiena, who was clearing away the cups, crowed and cackled loudly, then scuttled out with a scowl of self-rebuke.

That's one of Brenda's redeeming qualities: she doesn't sulk, always makes the best of things. In fact, it is altogether a cheerful office, for which Marion is happy to take credit. No, no one sulks. Even Boetie van Graan is only very occasionally bad-tempered. Boetie's desk is adorned with a photograph of his wife and two children in a hideous frame – turned to face the customers, what's more, as if to declare his unavailability or to protect himself against predatory women, which patently is redundant. The photograph, Marion imagines, was a gift from the wife, as he calls her. If only she had the courage to turn it around, which surely was what his wife had in mind.

Marion felt a twinge of guilt about Brenda. The girl has turned out to be reliable and conscientious; she's never missed a day, even coming to work when she had that dreadful cough and had to be sent home. Come on, she said, take Monday off; take yourself away somewhere nice.

No, really, Brenda said, I'm not in need of a break. It's just that a ge-leentheid has arisen. Marion looked at her, puzzled. That's what we call it in Bonteheuwel, Brenda explained, and translated: A geleentheid is an opportunity ...

Yes, of course, I know, Marion said impatiently. I'm Afrikaans; I know what the word means. It's so irritating that people think I'm English be-cause of my name. It's only in the office that I speak English.

But Brenda carried on regardless: You go on a trip not because you have a desire to go to such or such a place, but because an opportunity arises, a geleentheid. Which means that word gets out about someone going somewhere, and that he has a spare seat in his car or bakkie. It's like Fate. Suddenly you realise that that's exactly where you ought to go, where you'd like to go. Nothing to do, of course, with the fact that someone, whether out of altruism, thrift or ecology-mindedness, has let it be known that he has a spare seat. Not that you'll ever hear the news from the geleentheid itself – the person who offers the lift is himself known as the opportunity – no, there must be uncertainty, a circulation of rumour whose source cannot be pinned down, an intermediary who spreads the word. In fact, if you approach the geleentheid yourself, there'll be much humming and ha-ing and pensive nodding, as if the idea had just been planted, or as if he really can't be sure that a nice, quiet, private trip, just him on the open road, would not be preferable – so he'll agree to let you know later. After a decent interval, he'll send a message saying yes and then the delicate business of a financial contribution can be broached. So you see, the geleentheid is a complex business that works best with an intermediary.

Marion had only just noticed Brenda's bent towards the pedagogic.

All this talk, talk, talk, Boetie chimed in, you talk too much, man. Just you watch yourself travelling alone across the veld with strange men.

Brenda looked at him pensively. That's how she carries on, suddenly falling into silence, turning abruptly to her work and saying not a word until lunchtime. Which makes the rest of the office, who had been listening and laughing, return to business.

When Marion first announced to her staff that things were tight, and that when Mrs Chester retired she planned to replace her with a young coloured girl, she was not surprised at Boetie van Graan's scepticism. It was to be expected: he was not as enlightened as the rest of them. But when Brenda arrived, a slip of a girl who looked no more than sixteen, he did the right thing. Times were changing and he certainly was not going to be left behind. Boetie shook her hand warmly and said, Brenda, very pleased to meet you. I'm Mr van Graan and I hope that you'll be happy here.

Brenda smiled her wide and innocent smile, nice teeth she has too. I'm so pleased to meet you, Mr van Graan, with just a hint of emphasis on the *you*; and, holding up her palm in anticipation of a protest, Please call me Brenda. I've been brought up the old-fashioned way, to respect my elders – my people are from the country. And I'm here to learn, so I hope I'll have the benefit of Mr van Graan's experience in the travel business.

That Boetie is a youthful twenty-eight-year-old seems to escape her, and she never misses an opportunity to use the Mister. It is irritating, but again, anticipating irritation, Brenda herself raised the problem of the lack of a respectful second-person pronoun in English. A nuisance, hey, she said. Here in South Africa we should invent our own equivalent for the Afrikaans U.

Now you're talking, Boetie said enthusiastically. We ought to take the initiative and show the people overseas that there are decent ways of going about things.

Mr van Graan, Brenda would say, would Mr van Graan please cast Mr van Graan's expert eye over this document? In fact, I'll leave it for Mr van Graan to deal with. And she skips over to his desk to dump on him something that she clearly finds tiresome.

How does the girl manage to tread so delicate a boundary between respect and mockery? Her speech is melodic; she knows just how and where to linger over a sound. A deep one, that Brenda. She has obviously calculated the level of love in the office for Boetie and knows where to draw the line.

That morning, Brenda was planning, without a trace of discontent, the schedules for the weekend. Then she rose to stretch – there seems to be a problem with her back – looked out the window at the birds on the rooftop and rubbed her eyes. Perhaps there is not much sleep to be had in the townships.

Where was it you wanted to go? Marion asked. Perhaps another geleentheid will arise at a more convenient time. You mustn't be afraid to ask, hey.

Clanwilliam way, centre of citrus fruit and rooibos tea, Brenda mimicked. No, I promise not to be afraid to ask. My word, how these fat guinea fowl fight on the roof. God, they'll surely fall to their deaths, look at that one struggling to keep its foothold. Really vicious they are, fighting as if over money. And then she laughed, Oops, nope, they're having sex. Sorry, Mr van Graan, I don't mean to be disrespectful, but I believe that's really what they're doing. Mrs van Graan and the kids okay?

Yes man, thank you, Boetie said. That woman of mine is now stubborn, hey. Last night we had this argument about Elvis Presley and Roy Orbison. She said it's impossible to choose, but I say, no, you must choose.

Brenda laughed. Why? Why do you have to choose between Elvis and Orbison? Those guys are long dead, so it makes no difference who you prefer.

Nonsense, everybody must choose. It's a question of commitment; you have to take a stand, that's what I always say. Nail your colours to the mast.

You mean, if you sit on the fence then you shouldn't be surprised to be shot dead by a passing Casspir.

That's now the trouble with you people hey, always wanting to drag in the politics of the past, said Boetie, turning back to his computer.

$\mathcal{E}$ver since Marion can remember, her father has called her his meermin, his little mermaid. Because she was a child of the sea, he said. But it was he, the young man from the Karoo, who loved the sea, who marvelled at all that water surging around the Cape, and whose idea of taking out the lovely Helen was not to sit in a bioscope but rather to walk by the water, his arm around her slender waist. Why then did he not learn to swim? He cannot say. Except, except, he stumbles, out of respect: one should not take water for granted, treat it any old how; there are lessons to be learnt from water. Which brought a snort of disgust from Helen.

Marion does love the sea. Johan thought that she was simply responding to the name mermaid, that in her unhealthy relationship with her father she had adopted a second-hand fascination with the sea. That was the kind of nonsense Johan talked, and when she finished with him after only two months, his parting shot was that she was cold blooded, a plain cold fish, her father's mermaid. If she feels lonely on a Saturday night, she only has to remember what a relief it is not to have Johan and his half-baked psychology around.

On Sunday morning, Marion rises at dawn to drive to the fishing village on the coast where she rents a cottage. A pity she hadn't thought of going on Saturday. She will stay the night and leave directly for work on Monday. The morning is exquisite. When the sun is well risen, she has to stop for tortoises carrying their ancient carcasses across the gravel road. In spring, the road is flanked by fields of Namaqua daisies that bring the tourists, who drive absurdly slowly to admire the garish colours, but now in April there are not many people about. Here on the lagoon, the Atlantic is not so cold – she may even swim – but sitting in the sun with her magazines, an extraordinary tiredness, a laziness, washes over her. She is content to walk on the sand, to sit and doze all day on the beach and watch the tide come in, watch the water lap at the fine white sand, nibble at the lengthening shadow of the cliff growing greedier and greedier until it roars its hunger into the cavities of rocks.

She took the cottage after Helen's death, a place where she could bring her father who, for all the acrimony of that marriage, grew silent and brooding with grief. The sea revived him. Soon he knew everyone in the village, drank brandy with the fisher families who, he assured her, were decent white people in spite of being burnt black by sun and wind. Who would have thought, he said gleefully, that there are white people living without water and electricity. The vile long-drop lavatories sent him off into nostalgic reminiscences about the farm in the Karoo. Sometimes she left him there all week; she had fantasies of leaving him there forever, driving back to town unburdened, free of family. Now that he is frail and does not want to leave the house, Marion does not come as often; she doesn't have the stomach for the long-drop. She ought to give up the cottage, but it is not costly, and occasionally, at times like this, she is grateful for somewhere to go.

In the evening, as the silken blue of the sea turns to grey, Marion sits in the doorway watching the fading light – the signal to animals that it is safe to come out. There is much activity in the scrub, and she turns her eyes from the water to focus on cute little dark shapes scuttling between bushes. Then a shiver of horror as she realises that they are rats. They sit poised for an age at the edge of one bush, nervously inspecting the world, then race along what she had not previously noted to be a miniature pathway to another bush. But more often than not the journey is aborted: the rat stops, alerted by something or other, then scuttles back to the original bush. There it twitches nervously, waiting for the coast to clear before rushing out again. After two or three such attempts, the creature finally reaches its destination, only three metres away, where it tugs hastily at a twig before racing back in the same fearful fashion to its home. Presumably it is building a nest.

Marion shudders at the thought of a nest, so close by, where rodents copulate and dozens of filthy little rats come to life. She is torn: she leans towards sympathy for the hazardous lives they lead, for their vulnerability, for the terrible reputation they have earned themselves amongst humans, and yet the revulsion cannot be overcome. The rats do not vary their paths, do not think of shortcuts. She watches one sitting in its doorway, summoning up the courage to make a run for it. The bush shivers with its fear, even though there appears to be no danger at all. No birds of prey sweep overhead, there is no hissing of snakes, but Marion can almost feel the panic-stricken heartbeat of the creature. She is transfixed. Adrenalin rushes through her veins and she finds herself silently cheering the creature on, applauding its successful arrival at the bush. The twig it finally secures is tiny, hardly worth the effort; it cannot measure up to the fear or the courage required for that hazardous trip. What kind of life is that – to be burdened with such timidity? To have to overcome so much in order to achieve so little, to be the object of such irrational fear and loathing? Marion drags her chair indoors and bolts the door before lighting the paraffin lamps.

In the grey light of dawn, she checks the bushes, and yes, the path is indeed there, well trodden by a million rat journeys, terror imprinted in their timid footprints. Now of course they are hiding, twitching at the sound of her investigations. Marion stamps her foot in disgust: a proper fright is what they deserve. Then she sets off for town, for the office.

Next weekend, she will be in Stellenbosch, on a course for managers of small businesses, a follow-up to the previous month's session on Delegating in the New South Africa. Which is something to look forward to. She has an idea that it is a question of key-words, fancy new ways of talking about well-worn ideas, but the charismatic Geoff Geldenhuys, director of a national company that has moved headquarters to Cape Town, is not to be dismissed. Striking in every respect, he popped in for the plenary session, rolled up his sleeves and plunged right in. Good posture, too, for what she imagines to be a near-forty-year-old, and a way of acknowledging the intelligence of others that is particularly rewarding. She may not have liked him calling her words interventions, but he nodded appreciatively, and throughout held his head high and his shoulders back, which is salutary in this climate of slacking and slouching.

There is virtually no traffic on the road. Marion twists the mirror and glances at herself fleetingly, pats her hair and kisses her lipstick before turning it back. Ahead, Table Mountain looks splendid, and as she approaches the City Bowl the sunrise paints the polluted air with streaks of gilded pink and orange. In another hour there will be a nicotine-brown cloud in the blue sky.

Blue Monday. That's what they called it at school, but Marion loved going back to the classroom after a weekend at home, where the silence was relieved only by bickering. Even then, she believed that the first day of the week signalled the possibility of starting again, of a peekaboo of newness, of finding her parents blinking in the daze of a brand-new friendship. Still it surprises her: a new week, and her team reluctant, yawning and dragging their feet as if she were a tyrannical boss. That is why she arrives early with chocolate croissants and makes a pot of coffee, warms the creamy milk, bustles about energetically to ward off the Monday blues. Issuing vigorous instructions instead may well do the trick, but no, as Geoff Geldenhuys says, it is best to go with the times, and this is the time of the new: a time of hypersensitivity that requires you to recognise the special needs of others, to don your kid gloves, to tread gingerly in the New South Africa.

Marion cannot accuse the opportunistic layabouts of Cape Town of being late risers, of suffering from Monday blues. The streets are already dotted with ragged people wiping the sleep out of their eyes, buffing their begging bowls, gearing up to bully and abuse the law-abiding citizens who will not be taken in by them. She is equally impatient with the idle rich, women of leisure who, like people of the townships, stretch out in the sun. It is the hard-working middle class that she admires, which is to say people like herself.

And why should she not be proud of her achievements, of the firm she has built from scratch? MCTravel, the name she gave to her little place at the edge of the central business district only seven years ago, still gives her a thrill; she sees in the crisp new gold lettering with the flourishing tail to the L a salutary reward for her hard work. It was after the management course, which had given her such a surge of energy, and ja, she was not afraid to say it, a renewed pride in her own success, that Marion had the facelift done. How she enjoyed telling people: it will be all chaos next week when I have my facelift, before explaining how it was the frontage of the building that was looking shabby and was about to be given a new lease of life. Not that there would ever have been chaos in her office, but there is pleasure in using a phrase that in its inappropriateness underlines so boldly the clockwork precision of the business.

She smiles at the impression the facelift story must have made, which means that the right corner of her mouth lifts ever so slightly, like that of her father and of his father before him, and so on, generations of Campbells, she supposes, going back to the old snowbound days in the Scottish Highlands, passing on the involuntary muscle movement to the men in the family. It is a pity that there are no photographs of her ancestors, something to do with relatives having fallen out with her father, a family feud of sorts, but John assures her that the giveaway lift of the corner of the mouth betrays the deep-down Campbell good humour, with which Marion, although a woman, is as well endowed as any.

The window cleaner is doing the last drag of his wiper with a concentrated pursing of the lips that makes him look foolish, like a monkey, Marion thinks. Driving slowly past, she can tell that he too takes pleasure in the new plate-glass with the fine lettering. Which pleases her. She did not take kindly to Brenda's suggestion – unsolicited, of course, and surprised Marion was too that the girl felt she could comment on the place needing a new name – that MCTravel sounded stuffy and did not match the snazzy new look.

Oh yes, Marion smiled, and what might you have in mind?

So that Brenda said hurriedly, Oh I don't know, but being pressed and mistaking the smile for encouragement, she finally shrugged and stuttered,

Worldwide Travel or Magic Carpet or something, which made Marion throw her head back in mirth. The girl has no sense of tradition, no understanding of the pride one takes in one's achievement.

But she must not be harsh on Brenda; indeed, she had been most understanding when Brenda, a hardworking girl herself, had confessed only weeks after her arrival to a lie on her application form. Jobs were hard to come by; she hadn't thought that an Honours degree would stand her in good stead for a clerical job in a travel agency, and so had not mentioned a qualification that could only prevent her from being considered. Brenda had lifted an uncharacteristically pathetic, tearstained face to her employer: she had a mother to support, a brother to get through college; if Marion felt that she could not be trusted after her lie, she would of course understand.

Marion had peered deeply into the girl's township eyes, almond shaped and velvety, bovine black, and wondered about the confession. Why now? She could think of no reason not to be gracious, not to forgive the girl, who had after all the necessary computing skills and was undoubtedly an asset to the business.

Dry your eyes, lovey, she'd said kindly. It won't do to tell lies, but let's put all that behind us. No need for you to feel guilty any longer, let's just carry on as if nothing's happened. She deliberately didn't ask what the degree was in; that would have had quite the wrong effect. And if by any chance Brenda had had a pay rise in mind, the opportunity to ask had been soundly squashed.

As Marion turns to park the car, two ragged men rush towards her, vying for her attention. Talking simultaneously, they guide her into the space with melodramatic gestures. Piet Skiet, who has minded this parking lot for more than a year, is not there; no doubt he's been bumped off by these two unsavoury creatures.

Look, she says quietly, I'm not looking for a space; this parking bay belongs to me. No need for you to show me in, or to do anything at all.

See, Madam, the short one says, I'll look after the car for you, you can't just leave a Merc like that here among the city thieves. Someone's got to protect it, I mean this is mos a good getaway car. The other one tries to brush him aside, but staggers somewhat. Drunk, or from the dilated pupils, probably stoned. She'll be damned if she's going to tip these skollies for hanging about her car. You can't go anywhere nowadays without a flock of unsavoury people crowding around you, making demands, trying to make you feel guilty for being white and hardworking, earning your living; and of course there's no getting around it: hundreds of rands it costs per month, being blackmailed by the likes of these every time you park your car. And then the impudence of watching as you get out, watching as you lock the door, willing you to feel uncomfortable about your own belongings.

She turns to look just before crossing the road to the office; the short one is leaning against her car, laughing and pointing at his rival. There is a loud report of what sounds suspiciously like a fart. But she hastens to reassure herself: they wouldn't dare, not within her hearing; they need her tip.

Christ, to have to negotiate such nonsense before you even get to work. Say what you like, but five, ten years ago, before the elections, when things were supposed to be so bad ... well, the city wasn't a haven for ragged people standing around and harassing car owners. Not that Marion was a verkrampte kind of person; no, she'd never really supported apartheid. Even though she voted for the Nationalists, she knew deep down that those policies were not viable. But what could one do, short of joining the hypocritical English voters and betraying your own? Now she understands only too well that the past was a mistake, that things are better now, for instance, things like tourism. She certainly can't complain about the boom in travel; it's just that these layabouts catch you off your guard so early in the morning.

The window cleaner is already off his ladder, and she gives him a friendly pat on the back. Smart new window, hey, she says, encouraging his assent with a broad smile.

No sooner has Marion unlocked the door than Brenda is there right on her heels, a good fifteen minutes early. Which somehow takes the wind out of welcoming everyone with warm croissants and the smell of fresh coffee, but ag, never mind. Brenda, bright as a button, does not appear to suffer from Monday blues, and she can't very well resent the girl for being early.

There is nothing more tedious than listening to other people's dreams. And despite knowing this, knowing that a dream is only of interest to the dreamer – who inserts it into the puzzles of her own life, hoping it will throw its feeble light over her peevish questions, her half-hearted attempts at making sense of the world – Marion has a perverse urge to tell her dream to these people in the office, people whom, strictly speaking, she barely knows. Funny how the same word is used, given that dreams are nothing like the things we say we dream about in our waking lives. Now that would interest the others: Marion's dreams of a green Jaguar or a boyfriend, although she has her doubts about the latter.

Marion behaves like someone who doesn't know that you are exposed by your night dreams, that people will shake their heads or wink at each other when your back is turned. She does not try to stop herself from telling. There is perhaps the hope that, in the telling, the dream will release at least some of its meaning; that details inaccessible in silent recollection will reveal themselves to shape a skeletal narrative.

Marion tells of a house in a green valley; the house seems to pulsate with light. She is walking towards it. She can see the loft with its black wooden door, against which a rickety wooden ladder leans. The house is long and narrow, with rooms running into each other like train carriages. Like a nagmaalhuis: an economical design for the up-and-coming, who built little two-roomed houses in villages where they stayed over for the monthly celebration of Holy Communion. As they prospered, they would add extra rooms.

Boetie is distracted by the discussion of nagmaal houses. It's the lack of design that makes such buildings possible, now there's a thought, he says. Although the adding of rooms would perhaps be a problem for the loft?

Yes, surely, the nagmaalhuis can't expand forever; once a loft is built on top the building will have to stop, Marion says.

Not so, Boetie opines, a loft can be extended, like a house.

Tanya, who is keen on dreams, wants to know more. That problem must maar be left for the architects, hey. What happened in the spook house?

In the dream, Marion wanders through the house. It is still; there is no one. But in the kitchen there is the smell of coffee beans just roasted and the palpable absence of a woman who threatens to materialise, first here and then there, someone who moves between a central table and a black Dover stove, a darkening, a thickening outline perhaps, but no, then the air thins out, swept into uniformity. Marion keeps going out to the stoep to get away from the shape of the woman, but cannot tell whether it is the back or the front of the house, and so must return indoors. In the telling, it would seem that this is the key to the dream. If only Marion could ask the dark shape who eventually settles on the bench with her coffee, an outline of an old woman who has not quite materialised, who does not speak and who does not want her to speak. And then Marion falls asleep right there in the kitchen, on the bench.

Brenda, who hadn't appeared to have been listening, says, Is that it?

Marion nods, embarrassed. Tanya tuts, raising her eyebrows.

So then in your sleep you dream that you fall asleep? Like the house you dream of, stuffed inside the house where you lie dreaming? Now that's significant, Brenda says, that's what you have to concentrate on.

Marion wants to say: Like the long house of my dream that is stuffed inside the house where I live, that in turn is stuffed into the four-poster where I lie dreaming, but no, that is the wrong way round, and besides, she can't decide if Brenda is making fun of her. So she shuts the box file with a decisive click and swivels her chair to reach for another. Tanya starts telling of a recurring dream she has about a train, or perhaps it's a bus; actually she can't remember any more. She supposes one should pay closer attention, perhaps write down the dream as soon as you wake up.

Marion's is a recurring dream, even if there are minor variations. The most significant of these, which happens only a few days later, she feels compelled to tell. Perhaps to confound Brenda's theory, since the focus is clearly on doors. This time, all the doors and windows are shut; the woodwork is painted black. When she looks up, the loft door bangs, although there is no wind. She climbs up the ladder. Her mother is at the foot of the ladder, pleading with her to come down, giving the ladder a gentle shake to frighten her. But Marion carries on; she climbs the ladder because there is no other course to follow. When her head reaches the height of the loft door, she pushes it wide open so that a broad shaft of light falls across the floor. An old woman sitting on a low stool is illuminated; the light falls on a white enamel basin on her lap. Her face, sunburnt and cracked like tree bark, is framed by the starched brim of a white bonnet. She is surrounded by a sea of peaches, their shrivelled halves drying on sheets of brown paper. The old woman is busy, does not look at her. Her hands are sorting through peaches in the basin; her eyes are fixed on the task. Marion waits to be invited into the loft, but eventually gives up and starts going down the ladder, one foot guardedly following another in a backward descent so that the old woman disappears slowly in bands of darkness.

Boetie and Tanya shake their heads; no one says anything, and that is her cure. Why does she tell them these dreams? Marion might as well blab about the panic attacks she has in her muslin-covered bed.

Perhaps it is the woman in the dream who triggers the memory of their girl, Tokkie; she should not say girl since Tokkie was already an old woman, hence her mother's unusual indulgence. Tokkie, a family servant, had looked after Helen when she was a child, was part of their family so to speak, so that although Marion imagines she was too old to do any cooking or cleaning, she came once a week to see them and keep an eye on things in the Observatory house. She seemed to spend most of her time in an old wicker chair in the backyard, but first she would take the liberty of lining the frayed seat with the shawl of multi-coloured squares she had crocheted for Helen from scraps of wool. There she sat shelling peas that rattled into a pot, or holding between her knees an enamel bowl in which egg whites were beaten into peaks of snow. Ah, she would sigh contentedly, slipping off her shoes and wiggling her feet, it's so lovely and cool here in the shade. Tokkie could peel an orange in an unbroken spiral that Marion rearranged into a whole to fool her father. The old woman fed the little girl segments of orange with the membrane removed. Waste not, want not, she said, nibbling at the peel, from which fragrant citrus oil spurted.

Marion had no doubt that Tokkie loved her, spoiled her rotten as her father said. She couldn't wait for Wednesdays, when the roly-poly old woman would settle into her chair and haul the little girl up onto her lap, onto the special apron embroidered with flowers that she called her Garden of Eden. The pocket, into which the child would burrow her fist, was in the shape of a tulip chalice: red, with a touch of yellow on the edge of the petals. Tokkie would squeeze her tightly, stroke her hair, cup her face in the wrinkled black hands – angel child, she'd murmur – and sometimes, as Marion lay curled up like a baby in her lap, feed her cake dipped in coffee from a spoon. She said that Marion was her darling kleinding, her beauty, her sweetest heart.

Marion was about five years old when Tokkie died. Her mother held her and wept tears that left muddy rivulets down the pink pancake make-up. Her parents argued in hushed tones, but she heard them alright. They didn't like each other, even then, and Marion's hands would fly to her ears to block out the sound – not knowing meant that she wouldn't be able to take sides. This time, the argument could not be contained in the large sagging bed. At the kitchen table, Pappa said in sad dominee tones that they ought to go to the funeral. He should mind his own business, Helen said, Tokkie was hers, belonged to her family. Tokkie would appreciate any sensible decision she made, which was more than could be said for Campbell. It was plain folly to go to the funeral, to that little house in Kensington where her family were, subject the child to such things. Marion said that she wouldn't mind a little house in Kensington at all, that she loved Tokkie, that she was Tokkie's sweetest heart, but her mother wouldn't hear of it. They would have their own private mourning at home, she said. Helen made it sound like a party, a special treat, but on the day of the funeral nothing happened; they didn't speak about it or put their arms around each other. Marion found Tokkie's apron on the hook behind the kitchen door and stood on a chair to get it. She stole with it to her room, where she crept under her bed, wrapping herself in the garment the more to touch Tokkie's aged smell of orange and wood smoke.

Her father said that God would not forgive them for not going to the funeral, but Marion's friend Annie Boshoff said that that was kaffirboetie talk. There was no need to go to a servant's funeral, no matter how old or wonderful she was. Annie did not understand that Tokkie was much more than a servant, that Marion was the old woman's very special little person, but there was no point in explaining.

Helen stayed in her bedroom, robed in the multi-coloured wrap, by then a blanket, since Tokkie had added crocheted squares over the years. She said it was nonsense to speak of God and forgiveness: that was how the world was, and she knew that Tokkie had the biggest heart, which held no grudges and had no expectations. And then her face crumpled, her eyes red with tears, and all in slow motion clutched the robe as choked animal sounds escaped from deep down in her stomach.

$\mathcal{T}$he private room that leads from the office serves as storeroom, as well as kitchen and sitting room for those who work at MCTravel. There is a kettle and a microwave oven. A number of chairs in matching covers are clustered around the coffee table where they eat their lunch. All except for Tiena, who disappears over the lunch period to wherever cleaners and tea ladies go, swallowed up by the crowds of workers who congregate at street corners or under trees in search of shade. It follows, then, that you need to be fairly gregarious to be a cleaner or tea-lady; there is no room for timidity or quietude if you have to fling yourself into the melange of workers, cracking the occasional joke in order to find your place within the group. And then you can't just sit there with a mouthful of teeth and hope for the best; that is a privilege you have to earn, having paid your dues with banter. Brenda, who knows this from her weekend and holiday jobs as a student, fears for foolish Tiena, who is not the world's best hand at banter. Never mind: she may have won the others over with her expression of permanent surprise, or her giggling through a grid of fingers, pressed modestly to her mouth, that don't quite cover the passion gap between her front teeth.

Poor Tiena, she ventures. Marion says that she's mistaken, that some people prefer to hang about like that in groups; it's probably a question of being or having learnt to be more sociable. Than? asks Brenda, but perhaps too quietly: Marion, whose back is turned, does not reply. She may or may not have heard.

Marion has in fact given Tiena permission to stay in the yard if she wishes, there is a bench under the tree, or, if it rains, to have her lunch in the kitchen with the rest of them. Why does she now find herself unable to say that? She doesn't know whether it is embarrassment about having given thought to Tiena's situation, or about the proviso of rain, but surely the girl *would* be more comfortable in the yard. Marion is irritated that she has allowed herself to be interrogated by a slip of a girl, an employee.

The kitchen is a comfortable room with primrose-yellow walls. Marion knows how to make a place look homely: she followed a recent style feature in *Cosmopolitan* to the letter, right down to the shallow earthenware bowl of pebbles on the coffee table. The coffee table is a wooden chest that doubles up as a halfway station for brochures that can't yet be thrown out, but it is covered with a red and ochre kikoi to achieve a rustic look. The staff take their lunch in two shifts. Marion usually stays for no more than the ten minutes it takes to eat her salad. Today, Tanya de Wet is off sick and so Brenda finds herself on a lunch shift with Boetie, whose Tupperware of leftover bredie is spinning in the microwave.

Brenda's back is stiff after hours at the computer. She raises her arms, holds the stretch, then bends down slowly to touch her toes. Ten times, while Boetie stares at her rump, over which the cloth of her trousers strains as she bends.

Boetie frowns in concentration, as if it reveals something about himself, but who knows what thoughts that rump inspires. He may just as well be thinking of the Alsatians raging in his backyard, of how he was too late this morning to feed the beasts. Hannelie was cross; these days she is often cross. She does not like the dogs, but what does she know of a man's responsibility for safeguarding the home? A garden would be nice, she says regularly, instead of a dustbowl littered with dog shit, which is of course a hint that the yard is not cleaned often enough. Boetie unfolds his newspaper, tosses the grey jersey from the arm of the chair onto the table, and sinks with a sigh of well-being into the large armchair that he considers his. The chair, in spite of its new cover, is old; it deflates, hissing loudly to accommodate him. Boetie addresses the doubled-over body, Are you making tea?

Brenda, drawing herself up, says, No, it's too hot for tea, but if I change my mind I'll let you know.

Milk and two sugars, he says from behind the newspaper.

Brenda does not reply; she retrieves her jersey and stands at the window with the garment swinging from the hook of her thumb.

Jesus, what is this country coming to, Boetie exclaims. Look, this poor girl, shame – not bad looking either – she calls a taxi to take her to the airport, nogal a conference on violence in Johannesburg, and guess what: the taxi arrives – now there's a miracle in itself – but it's tailed by another, and when the driver gets out he's shot dead by the other one, whose friend jumps out to drive off with the dead man's vehicle. All on this poor girl's doorstep, and her looking on, stranded, with a suitcase in each hand. So this is what democracy has brought us, hey, he sighs. Just chaos and violence, that's what we can thank the new government for. In this country, you'll get killed for the twenty rand in your pocket.

Brenda does not move from the window. She hears herself asking in an unnaturally quiet, measured voice, And you don't think you should take any responsibility for it?

Boetie leaps out of his chair, flinging aside the *Argus* as if it had uttered the offensive words. Me, *me*? he splutters. Are you out of your mind? This is your lot, killing each other and causing mayhem; nothing to do with us.

Really? You don't think that years of oppression and destitution and perversion of human beings, thanks to the policies that you voted in, have anything to do with you?

Boetie wags his finger. Now listen here: first of all, I never voted for apartheid...

No? No, of course not, Brenda interrupts. It's impossible to find a person in this country who voted for the Nationalist Party. God knows how that phantom called apartheid came into being all by itself... and then of course it was F.W. de Klerk who woke up one morning to recognise the evil ghost for what it was and tackled it single-handedly. Look, since we're talking about morality, would it not be more honest to say that you didn't know any better, that you didn't understand the implications of accepting jobs and salaries that others were barred from, a choice of schools and places to live and play that discriminated against others, that came at the expense of cheap labour, of those who didn't have the vote? Or shall we say that apartheid somehow just gave birth to itself, just popped like an uninvited guest into the constitution? Still, it is nevertheless the case that in those good old days all you fine people who didn't vote for it enjoyed the benefits, led the lives of Riley in your houses with swimming pools and servants who cleaned up after you.

Now listen here, I've never had a swimming pool. You should see my house ...

But Brenda shouts him down. Oh no, it didn't occur to you *then* to be disgusted by the state of the country; it didn't occur to you then that such decent, law-abiding living was immoral, unacceptable – she curls her small fingers in the air around the word decent – or, for that matter, that you should fight the system that had so miraculously established itself.

Boetie is red with outrage. So now it's okay to kill someone for twenty rand? Is that what you're saying?

As if remonstrating with herself, Brenda frowns and looks fixedly ahead, then sits down. She says quietly, Ten rand, five rand, what does it matter. You couldn't imagine yourself then as one of the underdogs, so foolish, hey, to expect you to take that leap now, to imagine yourself one of the downtrodden who expected more from the end of apartheid. Why not try another question: if you were in a position where twenty rand would make such a difference, would you perhaps kill for it?

The point is, says Boetie, these people are just bladdy greedy. Those criminals don't need the twenty rand they kill for.

And why do you think they've become so greedy?

Don't know. And then he says again, Listen, I didn't vote for nobody, and my bladdy house, Jesus I deserve better ...

Marion comes in quietly and whispers, That's enough. We can hear you two out there, and anyway, I've told you that politics is not allowed in this office.

Brenda is unable to stop herself, although she does lower her voice.

Oh purr-leeeze, so white people didn't vote for the Nats, okay. It must have been ghosts then.

Marion hisses, That's enough. I mean it. No politics in this office, not even in here. Do you understand?

She can't believe the impertinence of the girl. But Brenda says meekly that she's sorry, that she doesn't know what's come over her, that she really would prefer not to have discussions like this.

Boetie snorts, then he says by way of making friends, How about that cup of tea then?

Brenda is angry with herself for rising to the bait. She does not usually speak out: there is no point in talking about these things. It is not possible for people from the different worlds of this country to talk to each other. But today her temper is not good. She blames her sleepless night, listening to her mother tossing and sighing, the horrible rumblings of the old lady's stomach in the heat of the night. They are no longer allowed to open the windows, not since her mother's heard of how the skelms wrench out the flimsy burglar bars as if they were knitting needles. At least they will not put their fists through the glass, she says, these godless people are cowards at heart.

The room in which they eat their sandwiches is separated from the office by a doorway without a door. Boetie had once suggested a bead curtain, but Marion will have none of it. The desks inside are arranged in such a manner that customers can see nothing more than the out-sized poster of the Greek island: it fills the doorway entirely, so that the Mediterranean with its gleaming white hilltop village seems to lie just there, beyond the office. Transparency, Marion said, it inspires confidence – eating a quiet sandwich can't give offence; it shows we've nothing to hide. And like the estate agents say, the smell of coffee gives a nice, homely touch that puts people at ease. She didn't, of course, have in mind Boetie's leftover mutton bredies, but decided against saying anything about it. As long as the back door is left open the smell should not be a problem.

At tea time, she says again that arguments in the background are not good for business. That's not what their customers want to hear while they're trying to fix up their holidays, trying to get away from precisely this kind of tedious nonsense. She would like to say: kidding themselves that it is possible to get away.

$\mathcal{I}$t is not exactly a phobia, that is too extreme a label, but Marion does have an aversion to travel. Why would anyone want to see the world from the discomfort of a suitcase? Let alone the dubious hygiene of hotels. These holidays that she enthusiastically arranges for others seem like nothing more than hard work, negotiating a foreign language and rushing about to see the sights in two or three short weeks. Could such an experience, in the final analysis, be any more pleasurable than see- ing the world on film or television? She supposes that it's all part of the contemporary fuss about authenticity. No, she has to confess that even travelling in this country doesn't seem at all desirable, even in a good car with air conditioning. The dusty dorps are hateful and the business of being inspected by hoteliers, questioned about what you're up to, where you've come from, where you're going, all in the name of friendliness, makes her feel uncomfortable, as if she has no right doing what she does; or worse, as if there were another layer of meaning to what she says and does, a meaning that others have a right to probe.

She once heard a couple in the Mount Nelson, very respectable they were, talking about an innocuous-looking woman who was filling her plate with smoked-salmon sandwiches. Well, the well-groomed wife said, raising thin arcs of eyebrows, a second round of sandwiches, as if we don't know what *that* means. Marion's eyes had followed the woman in question. She ate with relish, but daintily, and Marion, unable to make any inference from what seemed to her simply a case of a healthy ap- petite, could not bring herself to have another helping. Which was a pity, because that was the joy of tea at the Mount Nelson: mountains of sandwiches and delicious cakes. That is, after being smartly saluted by the men in pith helmets guarding the gates, which makes you feel that you deserve your tea, that greed is not an issue.

He has simply asked where she was holidaying this year, as one's hairdresser might when an uncomfortable silence falls in the salon. It is their third date.

Geoff Geldenhuys watches her intently as she speaks, surprised at how she is carried away by her aversion to travel. All he suggested was that they might drive out to a wine farm sometime, although that would hardly count as travel. But he'll hold back all the same; Marion Campbell is clearly not as easy-going as she appears to be. They have been to see a film in Claremont and are having dinner at Alibi, his favourite Italian restaurant. She is reluctant to discuss the film. It was okay, not her kind of thing, but she will not be pressed on what her kind of thing is. Geoff is not used to difficult women, has no time for complicated people or pretentiously sensitive types: he cannot understand why people can't be jolly, make the best of things and enjoy themselves. He'd been so sure that Marion was a sensible, straightforward woman. Wouldn't have done so well with the business otherwise, so perhaps there is no need to take too seriously her tirade about travel. Besides, women are in the habit of saying things just to be contrary. How could anyone not enjoy the delights of a new place? Geoff finds her disturbingly attractive, a hint of Italian perhaps; he believes that her caution, her unadventurousness is a posture, an attempt to appear aloof.

The lasagne he has recommended arrives, and he passes her the parmesan. She won't have any? But parmesan is essential, the very best thing, he says, kissing the bunched tips of his fingers in a gesture that she considers uncharacteristic, if not downright embarrassing. Marion wishes that he wouldn't persist, holding the bowl before her. She can't bear the sight of it. She hates remembering her first visit to an Italian restaurant, dining with her first date at university, a moneyed, bohemian young man, Wayne or perhaps Shane, who showed her how to use a fork and spoon and whose longish blond hair required constant flicking out of his eyes. The waiter brought to the table a bowl of pale, vile-smelling parmesan.

The memory is embedded in another that won't be shrugged off: she'd heard her mother cry out, so she'd rushed into their stuffy bedroom. John was doing something to Helen's feet – doing the weird things that grown-ups do behind closed doors. Beside the enamel basin of water in which her mother's feet were soaking was a heap of crumbly, greyish yellow. She rushed out in disgust.

In the restaurant with Wayne, it had taken every fibre in her body to fight the tide of nausea. Then, she had neither heaped it onto her tagliatelle nor succumbed to disgust; rather, she had practised resistance by squaring up to the offending bowl of parmesan, looking at it directly. Which was a pity, since it had made her miss the charming gestures of the young man who, peeved by the lack of eye contact, by what seemed an astonishing lack of interest in what he had to say, had not asked her out again.

Geoff is talking to the waitress in Italian. Grazie signora, he says, and tells her that their panna cotta is the best in town. So, they have moved on from parmesan, but he is an Italophile; he wants to know whether Marion shares his enthusiasm. His trip last year was amazing. Pity about the rand being so useless these days, because there's nothing like savouring the delights of old Europe.

Marion knows how to be civil. She knows the names of museums and churches; as travel agent she knows the sights that can't be missed, and so asks after the queues at the Uffizi, the piazza in Arezzo, the subsidence in Venice. Last year, she remembers, was the Venice Biennale – does he like contemporary art? No, not really, he says, mostly a case of the emperor's clothes, and she is grateful for that. But otherwise, he proves her theory that there is no need to travel. He has no more to tell than what she has read in brochures: a wonderful wall around this city, a colonnaded piazza in that. Which puts her at ease, makes her laugh at his jokes and enjoy the wine all the more. He tells her of the beaches in Italy where families take their old folks. Old women in sagging bathing costumes from which flesh hangs like dough risen over its pan; the spectacular cellulite of matrons in bikinis, who nevertheless step boldly across the sand. Yes, there's a price to pay for the delicious pastas they make at home from scratch. It is difficult to know whether he speaks with admiration or disgust. Marion is no fashionable waif. Should she not have eaten pasta? Should she be worrying about her weight?

And then he tells of the old folks in Viareggio who dress up in the late afternoons. Oh yes, there is a clearing in the wooded park in the centre of town where a band strikes up after the siesta, and like something out of dreamtime the old folks in evening dress all but sleepwalk into each other's arms and waltz away the sizzling hours, so that the very day seems to unwind in slow motion, the ice cream sliding sensuously down your hand as you watch. A different attitude altogether to old age, he says. Actually, it made him feel lonely, watching the old in one another's arms. And that, he says triumphantly, you won't get from brochures.

No, she concedes, but it won't be long before it is included in some guide book as one of the town's attractions, and then the good folk of Viareggio will feel obliged to dance through the heat, for that then will be their tradition, what they'll be known for, what they are supposed to do. Marion wonders if they don't mind the spectators, the open-mouthed young people whose fine Italian ices melt as they stare. She can't bear the thought of her own father being gawped at as he waltzes like a bear through the forest. She would rather talk about the vagaries of the stock market.

They go often to Alibi; it becomes their special place. Marion would like to know whether he has ever taken anyone else there, before her, that is, but she cannot ask. Although they go out together quite often, it doesn't amount to what nowadays is known as seeing each other. Marion has made sure that parting at the end of a date is friendly but swift; she doesn't want to rush into anything. She loves being out with him, walking where a woman would not walk on her own, seeing Cape Town anew, but no, not like a tourist, rather the familiar place rinsed by rain into brightness.

You've never been to Steenberg? Geoff shakes his head in amazement. Surely it doesn't call for such incredulity. No, she says parodically, I've never been to Steenberg, the oldest wine farm in the Cape, nestling in the shadow of Table Mountain with crystal mountain water snaking through the vineyards.

Ag no, seriously, he laughs and takes her hand, it's the best Sunday lunch imaginable and on such a lovely warm day you'll love it. He is a man of action: he doesn't ask, but immediately makes a reservation on his cellphone. We're lucky, he says, there's a cancellation, so let's go. They have only just met for a walk in Kirstenbosch, where Geoff seems to know the names of all the plants. There is no time to go home to change, but it doesn't matter, it isn't formal – and besides, he says, she looks lovely, as always. He's still holding her hand. In the guileless yellow sunshine, under a clean blue sky, the world is clear, straightforward, and it feels right to be led by a man who is no less than a tree, sturdy and rooted, in spite of his enthusiasm for travel.

They stroll through the aromatic terraced gardens of Steenberg – he has taken her hand again – and listen to the strains of the jazz band, coloured men in suits and bow ties bent to their instruments ... or black men, she doesn't know what people call themselves these days, now it's one thing, then another. But it is a combination that she finds stirring, the sober suits and the raunchy music. They sip nectar from the oldest wine farm in the country. Light shimmers on glass, bounces from the starched white linen, and no, today she does not want a sunshade, wants the brightness of the world as it is given. Is it because Geoff has on another occasion said she looked pale, that she should spend more time out of doors? A Cape more beautiful than the brochures, Marion mocks. But Geoff has come to understand that mockery is a veil for pleasure.

We should dance, he says, and her hand freezes; she wouldn't dream of it; she feels conspicuous enough as it is. She tries not to look at a large, noisy table at the far end, where people are rising to dance. But when she raises her eyes again, squinting in the brightness, someone waves through the noisy laughter. It is Brenda, who has remained seated.

Geoff is enchanted. Shall we join them?

Marion raises her eyebrows. Certainly not, whatever for?

Then he asks whether she wouldn't like to send over a bottle of wine to Brenda's table. Certainly not, she says again in a squeaky voice. With rising panic she hears herself saying the same Certainly not for the rest of the day, over and over again.

The food is very good, even if it is a buffet, and the beauty of it is that you can have as many helpings as you like, Geoff says gleefully. He is ravenous, and when he returns with a second helping, it transpires that he walked into Brenda in the dining room; he thought it only polite to introduce himself. Brenda is celebrating her birthday, he explains; her party are friends of the band. Perhaps a bottle of wine would be appropriate after all. Marion does not say, Certainly not. She finds his attitude pathetic; she says that she hopes they will not argue about something that has nothing to do with him. To smooth over the disagreement, they drink an expensive bottle of wine rather quickly, and in spite of everything, of a further attempt on Geoff's part to persuade her to dance and his diagnosis that she needs to be brought out of herself, each deems the day a success.

Marion has had a bad night, waking twice with buzzing in her ears, wrestling with the swaddling drapes of her four-poster, so that when she wakes again to birdsong, to another summer's day at the end of May, she is exhausted. The sky is turning from the pink of dawn to sapphire blue. She drinks her coffee on the balcony; the air is unseasonably balmy. Below, the sea lies still and mirror smooth, precisely the blue of the sky into which it melts on the horizon – except for where finger-wagging Robben Island perches sternly on the water. She can't wait to get to work, away from the puzzling disquiet of her home.

At the car park, she waves distractedly at Solly, one of the new car minders, who mutters something about her to his mate. He guides her into the space with extravagant gestures, but Marion does not respond to his buffoonery. The telephone rings as she gets in. It's not Geoff, even though it's already Friday and he hasn't yet been in touch. It is her father, who complains that he hasn't seen much of her. She ought to be sympathetic: she too is of that worldful of people peeved by the absence of another. John is confused. He speaks of seeing her for lunch today, so that she has to say several times that it is only Friday, that she will be at work.

You work too hard, my little mermaid, he says. Pappa will come with you to the coast, how about a weekend at the cottage, hey?

She says no, she has too much to do, she'll come for lunch tomorrow.

Yes, of course, he says, tomorrow is Saturday, but remember, Marientjie, that mermaids are made for tumbling in the sea, not for turning into harders in sunbaked offices. At which he laughs uproariously.

Ever since she can remember, her father has been fixated on mermaids. There is a story, a fairytale, she isn't sure of the details, about a mermaid who gets mixed up with humans and who may well have come to a sorry end, but she doesn't think that they read children's books on the farm. When she was little, he made up stories about fabulous creatures with torsos that tapered into glittering fishtails, and who with their siren-songs lured sailors to their islands, from which the lucky men never returned. A watery kind of Luilekkerland. Robben Island, he'd say, was such an island. Shush, close your eyes and you'll hear the sea, the whooshing of water over the rocks. And if she concentrated hard with her eyes shut tightly, a mermaid would rise from the water, tossing her long tresses. Then, tumbled by a wave and with a flick of glittering fish-tail, in a crystal spray of water, the creature would disappear again. Thus they summoned mermaids and compared notes on the behaviour of the creatures they had conjured up – always the shy rearing of the head, the mournful expression, the opalescent sheen that intensified into a glittering tail.

And how, the child asked, does the baby-soft skin of the torso turn into fish scales? John explained that it is gradually transformed: the mother-of-pearl skin graduates slowly, imperceptibly into the real thing, into hard, glittering scales that whip through the waves.

Marientjie was his very own meermin, with her long light-coloured hair that waved like the sea. He warned her of the dangers of cutting her hair, of how the modern cropped Jezebels of the city would come to various sorry ends. I'm a mermaid with a fishtail, the little girl sang as she struggled to bandage her legs together.

Her mother snorted, even as she helped to wind the cloth into a bound tail. It's Campbell's nonsense that prevents him from getting on in life. No good being half woman and half fish, half this and half that; you have to be fully one thing or another, otherwise you're lost. Mermaids are the silly invention of men who don't want to face up to reality, to their responsibilities, the fantasy of losers who need an excuse. I've been led astray by a mermaid, Helen mimicked in a plaintive voice, casting an accusing look at John. And see, she said, now you're all bound up, you won't be able to move.

But it was lovely to lie there, her head on her arm, as still as a mermaid, with her hair spread on a rock far out at sea. As the tide receded, Marion crawled and reached for her book, content to read until one of them came to unwind her bandages and turn her into a girl once more.

Walking along the shore at Sea Point, the little girl threw tantrums, refused an ice cream: she would eat not a morsel until she saw a real mermaid. They're shy, her father said. They can be seen only when the sea is really rough, when they can hide in the foam.

Ashamed, said her mother, as they should be, of being neither one thing nor another. No one likes creatures that are so different, so mixed up. Marion practised walking like a mermaid, shuffling along with her legs pressed together, imagining her feet fused into a fin. Free, without awkward genitals, she had no need to pee.

Marion feels a flash of sympathy for Helen, her down-to-earth mother who died so young of cancer, exasperated by John's childishness. It could not have been easy to be born dirt poor, and Helen had pulled herself up by her own bootstraps. How infuriating it must have been to be married to such a romantic, and how puzzling that a level-headed woman should have chosen the wrong man. The sympathy fades as Marion remembers the weight of their marital misery, the gloom and silence of her childhood, the air of restraint, as if the very plaster were giving its all to prevent the house from exploding.

A girl's got to make the most of her good points and you're a lucky tanner, Tanya says of Marion's cheeks, turned a healthy brown after the weekend sun. She, Tanya, just goes bright red in the sun and peels by the next day; she supposes it's the Irish blood, although that was only a drop or two from her maternal grandmother. Pink looks good with a pale skin, so it does, her grandmother always used to say, and the old people from over there, say what you like, they knew a thing or two.

Marion ought to have known that her Lovely-day-the-pink-suits-you would set Tanya off. Tanya may be wonderful at her job, but has to be led like a horse back to the business of exchange rates and travelling schedules; she has no understanding of the conventions of small talk, of the idle remarks of an employer intent on no more than friendly relations.

Thank God for Boetie, who pushes back his chair triumphantly. He has good news. Guess who's reached the target for the month already, with still a couple of days to go? Marion all but slaps him on the back, and Tanya, with a meaningful nod at Brenda, who stares distractedly ahead, says that this is what the office needs: good cheer.

At lunchtime, Marion picks up the *Cape Times* – must be Brenda's – from the coffee table. On the front page is a large colour photograph of a young woman, taking up a quarter of the broadsheet. Marion doesn't usually bother with newspapers. The tired old politics of this country does not divert her. She has no interest in its to-ing and fro-ing, and is impatient with people in sackcloth and ashes who flagellate themselves over the so-called misdemeanours of history, or with those who choose not to forget, who harp on about the past and so fail to move forward and look to the future. The telephone rings in the office. She casts aside the paper and pricks up her ears. Will it be Geoff? It is a nuisance, waiting for him to ring. She cannot believe that she, Marion Campbell, a grown woman with a successful business, is brooding obsessively about a man.

Brenda does not call out for her; it is a client. The girl's voice goes up and down, companionable and soothing, but professional. Would the client know that she is coloured? But as soon as the thought enters Marion's head, she chastises herself: she doesn't mean anything by it, doesn't mean to listen in on Brenda. Thoughts that enter one's head: where do they come from? Are they lost, looking for somewhere to lodge? Have they strayed from someone else's head? These days, her thoughts often appear to be not her own, are quite alien. Marion holds Geoff responsible for the strangeness. She hates the fact that she has regressed to adolescence; waiting like a young filly for him to call corrupts and distorts a sensible woman. She must pull herself together.

The newspaper on the table is folded into a quarter, framing a face: the photograph of the woman fills the entire space. The paper has been hastily cast aside, thrown across the prawn salad that Tiena has fetched from Woolworths. Marion is not hungry. Reaching for the salad, she dips her head to read the caption below the photograph: Patricia Williams's ordeal at the hands of the Security Police. Another TRC story: that's all the newspapers have to say these days – endless stories of people's suffering in the bad old days. There is something arresting about the face: the eyes look directly into hers. The full lips, from which a story has freshly issued, have barely come to rest for the photograph; the mouth reveals a quiver of outrage and indignation. Marion scoops up the paper and tosses it onto Boetie's chair, but then she picks it up after all, folds it hurriedly, carelessly across the face and stuffs it into her bag.

The first mouthful of prawn salad tastes strangely metallic; she cannot bring herself to eat it. It was Geoff, she thinks, who said that many people develop allergies or intolerances to seafood as they grow older. That would be a blow, a terrible thing, since there are few things as delectable as prawns or crayfish. So much for growing up as a mermaid, although mermaids, it occurs to her, should not eat fish: that would amount to cannibalism. Her mother had developed a seafood allergy shortly before she died so unexpectedly, before they could bury their differences, as people say mothers and daughters invariably do. But it is hard to imagine any intimacy between them.

When she goes back into the office, Marion announces that she'll treat them to drinks after work, happy-hour cocktails at Wally's. Let's celebrate Boetie's success, hey. Her nerves are on edge; she does not want to go home to the flat, to the silent telephone.

At four-thirty, Wally's is already heaving with people. From the speaker just above Marion's head, Michael Jackson booms out his badness. They are perched uncomfortably on bar stools, as the tables are all taken. Marion has difficulty concentrating; it is an effort listening above the loud music.

Boetie is bad, bad, bad; he gulps his brandy in a single draft. So ja, he says, now I can enjoy a drink nice and slowly, a comfortable slow screw is next on the agenda for me. He brays hysterically as he reads the lewd names of the cocktails from the blackboard.

Brenda stares at him abstractedly, sullenly; for heaven's sake, why won't Brenda lighten up? Tanya de Wet asks if it would be alright to take out her knitting – it's only three days to her Clive's birthday and she still has a whole sleeve to do.

In the noise, Marion hears nothing except the word Clive, the name of both the De Wet husband and son. She smiles, but then worries that Tanya might have said something appalling. About Clive being ill, getting divorced, being mugged? What? What was that? she asks, leaning over to hear. Bad, bad, bad, thunders Michael Jackson, so that Tanya looks chastened and shouts that she won't be staying long. No, they shouldn't stay long. It's Friday; Marion supposes they all have things to do, and on Saturdays they start early.

As soon as I finish my slow, comfortable screw – Boetie gloats at the opportunity to say it once more.

Brenda, cheered by the prospect of leaving, puts down her drink and smiles indulgently at him. What's Mrs van Graan making for dinner tonight? she asks. Marion rattles her keys. There's no accounting for that girl. They wait for Boetie to go to the caballeros.

Brenda looks in her bag and is dismayed to find that she's left her *Cape Times* in the office. She thought it was in her bag; she'd assumed so because it wasn't on the table, of that she is sure, and Tiena always brings her paper for her.

Ag, never mind, Marion hears herself saying; it's only a paper and tomorrow you'll have the weekend edition – the news will be newer. She is surprised at wanting to keep the *Times*, and at what has just issued from her lips. It is theft, she supposes, taking someone's newspaper, but she might not be able to find another so late in the day.

Boetie is on his way back to the bar. He grinds his hips and swings a jerking arm above his head. That's now a crazy guy, that Michael Jackson. Can't be so bad being white, hey, 'cause you know what he's gone through to have a white skin and straight hair and a moffie nose? Have you seen recent pictures? Looks beaten up, like one of our own mad terrorists.

Ag no man, Boetie, behave yourself, Tanya reprimands. A person can't take you anywhere. They shuffle like children off their high stools. It's time to send Boetie home.

Still no word from Geoff. Cellphones ought to have brought an end to this juvenile misery, but they have not fulfilled that promise. Marion, consumed with waiting, cannot decide whether to go home or not. It's preferable to be in your own place, where you can at least wash and dress should a call arrive. On the other hand, being home indicates your availability to the caller, whereas answering a cellphone from elsewhere … She will go to see her father instead, a far more sensible use of her time, and then, should something come up tomorrow, should Geoff call, she'll be free.

It confuses John, hearing the sound of her car at the robots in Main Road. The days do tend to roll into each other … but he was so sure, had adjusted earlier to today being Friday, sure because it is tomorrow, Saturday, that Marion will come. But then his mermaid usually comes in the afternoon, after work, and it's well after six o'clock now – he was just wondering whether he shouldn't have had some supper after all. No need to go through the whole rigmarole if you're not hungry, although that doesn't mean he has to forego the brandy he's allowed to have on Friday nights after his meal. There is a Tupperware of stew that he could have bunged in the freezer, no, he means microwave; he keeps on confusing the words. But who cares, as long as he does not actually put the thing in the blarry freezer or washing machine or whatever. He pours himself a third brandy.

It was Helen who had rationed the brandy. Although he'd complained at the time, he knew that if it hadn't been for her he would have taken to drink, for what was one to do with the troubles that lodged like stones in one's heart, that grew colder and heavier as soon as the Harley-Davidson came to a purring halt at the end of the day?

Helen had put her foot down: her husband falling about like some drunken Toiings? She wouldn't have it. If he could pull himself together, pull it off for the chaps at the depot with jokes and horseplay, she'd be blowed if she'd allow him to inflict low-down, ash-heap misery on his family. On Friday nights, yes, he could have a brandy or two, but control was what she demanded, control was the key, she said, to being respectable, acceptable people. Once, he slobbered drunkenly over Marion: he was sorry that she was an only child, a lonely child; he was a brute, with nine brothers and sisters ... but Helen spoke sharply and took the little girl away. Could he not be trusted with anything at all? she asked bitterly. Did he want her to take control of the bottle, pour out the two brandies for him?

Helen was right. A woman of strength and principle who, above all, gave him a beautiful, clever daughter. In the loneliness of Friday night, the memory of Helen takes on a different glow. Perhaps in their old age she would have been more tolerant of him, more at peace with herself as they sat together watching the modern antics on television. Perhaps in the New South Africa, with the past all done and dusted, she could have returned to the girl who astonished him with her beauty on that Sunday that explodes once again into the brandy-fumed present.

The young woman lodged at the Bateses, and that glorious evening, when he finally took his leave, still hoping for a moment with her alone, the entire family lingered on the stoep. Then, before his very eyes, a tangle of greyish foliage that he'd barely noticed before and could not then even have identified burst into shocking moonflower. A cluster of creamy trumpets, edged in delicate pink, flared open above her head like so many angels singing her praises, so that he was struck dumb and left abruptly. Only at the corner of the street did he look back to see her leaning with arms folded on the gate, still watching, as if she could not drink more deeply of him.

John had come to Cape Town only a few weeks earlier, and just as everyone had said, the city was indeed a promised land of hustle and bustle and the clink of coins. But he was also a man for gardens, and at his first port of call at Wynberg Park found work looking after the nursery, a job that would do quite nicely until he found his way about town, found something that was better paid. Ma had arranged lodgings with second cousins of hers, and that Sunday they'd invited him along to their friends the Bateses, who were christening a first baby. To think that he'd tried to wriggle out of going, for what interest could he possibly have in couples with babies? But then, how could he have known of the Bateses' lodger, who had arrived in town herself that very week? His moonflower girl, modest and timid and pretty beyond belief, with creamy skin and copper-tinted hair. There at the dinner table, he was driven to nervous chatter and the laughter of adoration, until Helen gave in and smiled her beautiful country-shy smile, and when the Cornelissen cousins left, he said with surprising courage that no, he would stay a while. Not that he got to see much more of her. Mr Bates took him to the back garden for advice on ailing cabbages while the women cleared dishes in the kitchen.

Little more than three months passed before he wrote home for permission to marry. Ma, who checked on Helen through cousin Cornelissen, said that it was about time, that although she would normally recommend a longer courtship, John had always been fussy about girls, and at thirty-two years old there was no telling whether he'd have another chance. How proud he was to take Helen home to the farm, where she rolled up her sleeves and knocked together a pan of crunchy biscuits they'd never seen before, made with oatmeal and honey, so that Ma said she was a jewel, a ruby, that a good woman was hard to find.

Marion is at the door, and pleased as he may be to see her, John wonders why she is there on the wrong day. This kind of thing will only confuse him. So that he is petulant, and treats her to an exaggerated account of the plagues of arthritis, the bad knee, his poor digestion. And no, he does not want dinner.

But Marion does not slip into wifely irritation; she listens patiently, if abstractedly; she is not Helen. She explains that she may not be able to come tomorrow after all, and then he is ashamed of himself, sorry that he has subjected her to his complaints.

They drink rooibos tea with crunchy biscuits. Before he gets up from the table, he looks ruefully at the crumbs around his plate, then swipes them onto the floor with the palm of his hand. Marion is astonished: he has been fastidious all his life. Ag no, Pappa, she says, that's not nice, wait … but intent on getting himself back to his chair by the window, he doesn't hear. It is too late: the crumbs are crushed underfoot. She stares at him anxiously. This is the beginning of the slippery slope; he is ageing fast. What will she do with him?

It is past ten o'clock when Marion takes the *Times* out of her bag. On her bed, she smooths out the paper, then folds it into a quadrant from which the face of the woman looms. She cannot bring herself to read the article; these stories are all the same. The eyes of the stranger hold hers accusingly, calling her to account: for what, for the callous fold across the face? But no; it hisses a command to remember, remember, remember … Marion feels the room shrink around her. She is trapped in endless folds of muslin; the bed grows into the room, fills it, grows large as a ship in which she, bound in metres of muslin, flounders. It is with superhuman effort that she manages to escape to the balcony, with the crumpled paper clutched to her chest.

She skims the first paragraph of the report and gathers that Williams had been imprisoned, that she had suffered regular interrogations, that her jaw and nose had been broken, that she had been dangled out of high windows, that she had been sexually abused in unspeakable ways. That was in the late eighties, yet the face retains the memory of these acts.

54

There is a hint of asymmetry, of distortion, as if the marks of a fist lie as a trace just below the healed features. The ghost of the past hovers in her gaze.

If it were not dangerous, Marion would walk down to the sea. What's the point, she thinks self-pityingly, of living by the sea and not being able to walk down to the shore at night. She believes that in any other country it would be possible for a woman to walk alone at night along a deserted shore. The sea is restless, the tide is full; a small cluster of lights on Robben Island winks drunkenly. From her balcony, she stares in horror at an enlarged face floating on the water, a disfigured face on the undulating waves, swollen with water. A smell of orange, the zest of freshly peeled orange skin, wafts up from the shore, mingling with the brine. It is not until she goes back indoors that recognition beats like a wave against the picture window: Tokkie, it is Tokkie's face on the water. Not the smiling, doting woman who holds her tightly against a breast doused in the orange-blossom cologne that Helen gives her on her birthdays; but rather the stern face that the little girl, squatting in the grass where she's made a marvellous structure of sticks, glances up at. That face, lost in reverie, starts as the child calls repeatedly, impatiently, Tokkie, Tokkie, look. The dear face that looks down and for a moment is lost, does not know her, so that the child, whose heart explodes, smashes her tepee of sticks and runs indoors to hide under her bed, where Tokkie must find her and kiss her better.

Marion telephones her father. It is late; he will certainly be asleep, but it can't be helped. Tokkie, she shouts into the mouthpiece, what was her name?

John, still bludgeoned by the ringing that drilled through his sleep, says stupidly, Who's Tokkie? What's the matter, Marientjie? And when she does not reply immediately he shouts, Don't worry, I'll be dressed now-now; I'll be right there in a minute. Is it the kaffirs? I'll bring my stick, I'll beat them to death.

No, no Pappa, don't get up; it's nothing like that. She is impatient at having to humour the old man. Everything's okay here. It's just that I need to know Tokkie's surname. You do know Tokkie – the old lady who looked after me when I was little.

Ag child, he sighs. Tokkie, ja Tokkie, let me see now – no I just can't remember her name now. Let sleeping dogs lie now, my mermaid; it's late and you need your sleep.

Does Williams ring a bell? she persists.

Man, I'm too fast asleep for bells. He yawns loudly.

Okay, she says vaguely, and puts down the receiver. She has no doubt that he is lying, pretending not to know. But why?

When the telephone rings ten minutes later Marion is appeased, thrilled that her father has come to his senses and will solve the mystery of the face. But it is Geoff. She stops herself from saying that it's too late to talk. Geoff has been away, has just returned to town; he must have left a message on a wrong answer-phone. He wants to know whether she is free tomorrow. Marion can't think of an excuse. She says that she won't manage a walk, nor the movies; and no, certainly she would not be up to a jaunt, to being a tourist in the Boland. Then, as the face floats into her vision, holding her gaze, she blurts out that something strange has happened; but no, she doesn't want him to come over … no, she may be exaggerating, imagining things. She'll call him sometime, perhaps tomorrow.

Why did she say that something strange had happened? She must go over events in a rational manner. She's seen a picture in a newspaper. It is a photograph of a damaged face that would upset anyone. For some reason, the face makes her think of Tokkie, the old coloured servant who indulged her as a child. But that was long ago, and Tokkie is dead; instead, something terrible has happened to the person whose troubles are reported in the *Times*, a coloured woman who had been an ANC terrorist. Nothing, in fact, has happened to Marion, who has never had anything to do with terrorists.

She'd said to Geoff that she would call him. Although she understands that nowadays a woman need not wait for a man to get in touch, she cannot bring herself to do the calling, cannot put herself in a vulnerable position. She is, she supposes, an old-fashioned girl. But look how, without thinking, she's left the ball in her court. She'll feel better tomorrow; perhaps she will go out. Marion puts the *Times* in the rubbish bin and takes a whole Temazepan tablet, which sends her off into a drugged sleep on rough seas.

Saturday mornings are always busy at the agency, but today Marion has a heavy head and nothing goes well. Tanya has messed up the itinerary of an important client, whom Marion has to placate with sweet talk and a special deal on the tickets to Zurich. It will cost, but such businesses are worth courting. She's even considered dropping the holiday market and the casual travellers to concentrate on corporate travel; she ought to discuss it with Geoff. Then Marion drives into the city centre herself to deliver tickets, and on the way back scrapes the side of a brand-new BMW. It is badly parked, but the accident is undoubtedly her fault. Oh, it is the last thing she needs; she cannot face an irate owner, and so hurriedly leaves her card with a scribbled Sorry before rushing back to her own car. Fumbling with the lock, Marion manages to open the door and slides into her seat. As she leans forward to adjust the side mirror, the door slams on her thumb, so that she shrieks and her eyes flood with unbearable pain. She can't look at it.

At Casualty they bandage the thumb. It is not as bad as it seems: the nail has come away, but a new one will grow, they assure her. She takes a painkiller. Marion cannot face going home; she goes to the office and sits in Boetie's chair in the kitchen with her head in her hands, hoping that the BMW owner will not call today.

She knows he'll see it as blackmail, but that's not what keeps her from the customary visit to her father. She did say that she might not be able to come, and things are busy with Boetie and Brenda both representing the agency at a regional meeting. When John calls her at work, she is businesslike, checking on his needs, so that he says contritely, I've been trying to remember about the old woman, Tokkie; you shouldn't feel bad about her funeral. That was a long time ago, things were different then and it wasn't our fault that the politics were so complicated; we couldn't help things being what they were. Tokkie had a good life, you know; she had nothing to complain about, your mother made sure of that. Your mummy only wanted the best for you, Marientjie.

And so he prattles. Marion attends carefully to his words, which hurts her head, because she is tired and agitated, but also, she thinks, because perhaps she is not used to such attention to language. She hears that he is dissembling, that he is panicking, prattling. Her father, whom she has always thought of as transparent, as the salt of the earth, speaks guardedly. She wishes she were with him, to monitor his face, for what comes out of the receiver seems to hover between sound and the looming shapes of things that cannot come into being. His characteristic diminutives echo in the office, the -ies and -tjies that float free of their lost nouns. Where she sits, with elbows planted on the desk, the swaddling endearments grow tight as bandages, so that she rises, paces around to unwind herself, and feels suspicion surge through her veins. She hears, knows with certainty that the lies are not new. Her father, no, both her parents, have always kept something from her; something they did not want her to know. That is why John has drawn her since childhood into the nonsense of myth, in order to drown his secrets, and her heart hardens against him: she'll ask nothing, not rely on him for anything. To whom will she turn? Helen is dead and there is something secret, something ugly, monstrous, at the heart of their paltry little family. The trouble and strife of an ill-matched couple – that was what she had, throughout her life, attributed the strangeness to, but now Marion knows that there is something else. A secret. Suspicion bounds through her veins, begging for recognition: it too is not new.

Perhaps you'll pop in tomorrow, Marientjie, he says. Then we can talk, my little mermaid.

She hisses back, Don't call me that; I'm not a child, nor a mermaid. Why can't you tell me now about Tokkie, whose surname you can't remember – was that her real name? Was it short for the evil tokkelos? Or can you not be expected to know the name of every old hotnosmeid?

She doesn't expect to learn anything from him, but is surprised by the charged reply: Oh no, you mustn't ever think anything like that of her. There was nothing evil about Tokkie, oh no, a very fine somebody she was – pitch black, you know, but a lady all the same. And you shouldn't be using words like that; she was no hotnosmeid.

Marion laughs harshly. And where would I have picked up such fine words? From none other than you.

Ag, my child, you'll just have to forgive your old Pappa. That was just how we spoke in the old days; it wasn't our fault.

It is the childishness, the appeal to innocence that makes her, in turn, appeal to his fatherhood. Pappa, she says in the strangled voice of a child, I had an accident yesterday, nearly lost my thumb in the car door and it's throbbing with pain, really throbbing. She has to fight back tears of self-pity.

But it is too late to reverse roles again; it is he who has become the child, who will not give up that new privilege and be the pampering Pappa. All that has remained of that role is the name, the term of endearment. Ag no shame, my girlie, you're so good with cars, he says briskly. Look, tomorrow when you come, we'll talk things over properly.

Her hand still clutches the receiver a good minute after she's put it back in its cradle. She cannot let go of its redness. It is as if the red plastic keeps the tide of panic at bay, keeps her anchored to the world of the travel agency. Tanya is back from her tea break. Her voice – Are you alright? – seems to come up from under water, dripping, and only then, recoiling from the dripping kindness, can Marion retrieve her hand, summon it to swipe up her handbag.

Yes, she says, just a little hitch. Got to go; I'll be back shortly.

Marion parks her car at the seafront at Sea Point. She does not get out; she must concentrate, not think of her throbbing thumb. Secrets, lies and discomfiture – that was what her childhood had been wrapped in. Each day individually wrapped, lived through carefully, as only those with secrets live. Before her an image arises: the past laid out in uniform trays of apples wrapped in purple tissue paper. Marion loves apples; it is irksome that something she finds delicious should now be infected, a drop of poison hidden in the core, under the wholesome, glossy skin. Then, she'd thought of the parcelled days as simply the world of grown-ups, an alien world that necessarily clashed with that of a child's. Her parents may have hated each other, but they had connived, conspired against her in the whispering that stopped when she entered a room. Addicted to secrecy, hermetic, so that even the ordinary acquired an air of conspiracy. Like Helen's feet, groomed by John behind closed doors that locked her out. Things that then seemed ordinary now reveal themselves, after all these years, to be meaningful: clues to a world whose authenticity, she realises, was always in question.

Marion remembers a summer's evening too hot to stay indoors. They were in the garden: her father crouched over seedlings, muttering to himself; her mother upright on a kitchen chair, staring into the distance. A pale moon in the royal-blue sky lay with abandon on its back, winking at the child, so that the patch of grass where she sat clutching her ankles swelled into an ocean. Marion does not remember taking off her shorts and blouse; she was a mermaid under the moon, diving and tossing her tail through the silver waves.

When Helen came to, she swallowed her scream and spoke quietly, hissing with rage and disgust. What kind of child was she? Where had she come from? How could she behave like a disgusting native, rolling half naked in the grass? Marion knew not to say that she was a mermaid; she knew not to point to the moon, not to ask why it was bad to roll in the grass. Because I say so: that was all the explanation she'd ever been given for the endless rules and restrictions and excessive fears. Instead she said, I haven't anyone to play with. I want a sister, please can I have a sister to play with.

Helen's bitter, demonic laughter echoes again in Marion's ears. Oh no, you don't want a sister, she said in a horribly quiet voice.

But I do, the child whined, I want, I want, I want a sister …

Stop it, shut up, Helen shouted brutally. I can't have any children, we don't want any children, so just shut up, and with distaste, with her shoe, she shoved the child's clothes towards her. Marion ran off, crept into bed in her vest and broekies; she had upset her mummy. She was stricken with guilt and remorse.

And once, when John must have been drunk: she remembers her father's strange behaviour as he clutched her too tightly, his breath horrible as he muttered into her ear, slobbering, so that she struggled to get away. About brothers and sisters, she remembers, his beloved brothers and sisters, and that it was a sin that his little mermaid should grow up alone. Drunk he was, but vigilant enough not to give too much away.

Those tightly wrapped days did not admit friendship. Helen was suspicious of Annie Boshoff: children should keep to their own families; why was Annie always mooching around their house? Marion knew that other people did not live in silence. Annie had a range of aunties with warm bosoms and uncles with prickly moustaches who dropped in without warning, and noisy cousins who bounded through the house. But Marion was cautioned not to hold Annie's hand; she was not to say anything about their family to Annie. That Mrs Boshoff is a nosy parker, she needs to be kept in her place, Helen said, but at the Open Day at school, her mother seemed to stiffen and cringe before Mrs Boshoff's moon-wide face. Mrs Boshoff spread her arms and squeezed both the girls into her vanilla softness, and through her mother's enamelled smile the child caught a whiff of fear that warned her against peering into the heart of things.

Helen protected the silence and secrecy with maxims about the self: It is best to keep oneself to oneself; never rely on anyone but yourself. But in that barren world, secrets engendered secrets with abandon, wantonly reproductive, so that now, looking back, the past is contained in endless dreary rows of parcelled days, wrapped in tissue paper, each with its drop of poison at the core. Marion abandons herself to self-pity: how would she know where to start, how to unwrap those parcels? She starts the car. It is time she got back. Tanya will be waiting to lock up for the weekend.

It is almost dark when Marion gets home. She goes to the bin to retrieve the newspaper, and smooths the wrinkles out of the face that stares at her unforgivingly, demanding her attention. It is of course not Tokkie's face, and she may well be imagining the resemblance – she'd been only five years old when Tokkie died. But so strong is the memory of the old woman invoked by the young face that she does not doubt a connection. And her father's caginess confirms that something is amiss.

She isn't hungry. She sits in the dark, drinking red wine straight from the bottle. The kitchen is only a few yards away, but it is now too late to fetch a glass. Never before has she drunk from a bottle – but why not? Although it isn't easy. There is already a stain on her shirt; she must be careful not to dribble onto the newspaper on her lap.

Marion doesn't know where the uncanny certainty comes from, but she knows that the mystery is about her own birth. There can be no other explanation: she is an adopted child. In their ignorance, misguided love and rivalry for her affections, her parents could not bring themselves to tell her. She does not look much like either of them, and certainly in Helen's face she often caught a look of naked resentment. Although she cannot be biologically connected to Tokkie, she believes the old lady was, in some way in which she cannot imagine, party to the adoption. It was Tokkie who understood the child's loneliness and loss and unease, and so lavished love on her. Marion does not think that Patricia Williams, who is after all a terrorist, can solve the problem of her biological parents; instead, Williams's face is simply a sign alerting her to the truth. The truth about a child deceived by adults who have flouted her inalienable right to know who her parents are, to know her origins. Her being is flooded with a feeling that is hard to name: self-pity, indignation, anger – something that connects her to another being whom she does not know, so that, inexplicably, she finds herself pressing the newspaper, the face of the terrorist, fervently to her bosom.

$\mathcal{B}$renda is dandling a small child on her knee, holding on to both its hands. He jogs to Ride a cockhorse to Banbury Cross / To see a fine lady upon a white horse ... Again, Bender, again! the child squeals. But Brenda is tired. She ruffles the tight curls and packs him off to his mother, who sits on a bed just off the sitting room, nursing an infant. Shirley and her husband Neville live in that room, which is crammed with a modern suite of double bed, two wardrobes and a dressing table, all in glossy veneer of pale and dark wood. It is the room that Brenda shared with her sister before her marriage. A delicious smell of chicken curry wafts from the kitchen, where the cooking for tomorrow's Sunday lunch is under way.

Brenda slips on tiptoe through the kitchen into the bedroom that she now shares with her mother. Otherwise she'll be roped into the preparation of food, or worse, sent to the shop for an essential ingredient that her mother has forgotten. Ag, just quickly go get me a chilli from the babbie's shop. How on earth do you forget to buy chilli when you're planning a curry? And then, just as she gets to the door: Might as well have another tin of condensed milk, hey, or will you get that another time? As if she were a five-year-old who enjoys running along to the corner shop. What does her mother know of being subjected to Mr Mahmoud's struggle poetry, which he insists on reciting, regardless of the queue of people waiting to be served?

Customers are transformed into audience as Mr Mahmoud's eyes grow misty with nostalgia for the bad old days of resistance against apartheid. Man does not live by bread alone, he likes to announce to his customer-audience. Looking at Brenda, he says, Now here we have an educated person who can appreciate poetry, and, after a clearing of the throat, he solemnly declaims the lines he once delivered at a UDF gathering at Athlone Stadium when the People's Poet failed to turn up and Mr Mahmoud, at the very front of the crowd, took opportunity by the horns and leapt boldly onto the stage with his sheaf of poems to save the day: The wind of freedom sweeps over the Cape Flats / The wind of freedom whirls around the Casspirs . . . In the shop, the audience clap and stamp their feet in appreciation. The poet bows theatrically, with his left hand pressed humbly to his paunch, and distributes to women and children the toxic-pink sweets called Stars.

Should Mr Mahmoud have a new composition, he whips from under the counter a grubby page of lines on his most recent favourite subjects: violence, the lack of community spirit, or the fecklessness of township youth. He does not think these as successful as his old struggle poems; he has heard a beautiful young woman, a poet too, explain that after the po-litical struggle the nation should celebrate sex, free their poetry of colonial Victorian values; he thinks that may well be the way forward. Or Table Mountain: nothing less than God's gift to a poet, for the steadfastness of rock and the solid flat top offer a natural example to the youth.

Mr Mahmoud will not serve Brenda until she's commented, and he will not be fobbed off with the time-worn phrases of the classroom: very good, interesting, promising, or provocative imagery. With an encourag-ing smile and continuous nodding, his right hand pumping for volume like that of a concert conductor, he demands a gloss on such comment. Brenda knows that it is a precise proportion of ninety per cent praise and ten per cent criticism that will let her off the hook. Or a request that he read it again, louder, so that the skollies on the stoep gather in the door-way and shout encouragingly, Skiet hom my bra, blow his brains! Or, Meerderer guns 'n goosies, daai's what Mr Mahmoud need! – as if, like her mummy's curry, the poem is short of a dash of chilli.

Brenda lies on her back, luxuriating in the new single bed she bought at the end of the month. Her mother thought it an extravagance: there was nothing wrong with the old double bed they've shared since Shirley's marriage, and besides, the room would be horribly crammed. But Brenda was not to be deflected. Perhaps they should get rid of the double bed, she said, get a single one for her mother, but the old girl refused to listen. I don't like it, she complained, not having my girlie to warm my old back at night.

But it was precisely this that Brenda hated: the sagging bed that, much as she tried to keep her distance, slid her to the centre, to the sponginess of the old woman's body. Brenda hates the smell and the softness of that body, is ashamed of her revulsion at the thought of having suckled at that bosom. She has stared in fascinated horror at her mother undressing: the empty pouches of breasts, the cellulite that bubbles and sags over the knees, the withered shanks, a flash of the balding grey pubis.

Shirley is piously affectionate towards their mother; she reprimands Brenda for being squeamish, for what she calls her sister's airs and graces. Is that what they learn you at university? she asks. Well, it's no big deal hugging and kissing the old girl when she's respectably clad, but Shirley does not have to suffer the forced intimacy with that body. And now that the well-worn digestive system is failing, there is the loud, unapologetic farting through the night that Brenda should, but cannot, bear.

From her bag she produces a new bedcover, collected after work from the Oriental Plaza. At least get something that matches, her mother said, but what on earth would match lemon candlewick, other than more lemon candlewick? She smooths over the madras cover of saffron, orange and terracotta stripes that bleed into each other, and steps back to admire the effect. At university, in the Contemporary South African Literature class, she'd read a poem about the vulgarity of Cape Town culture, epitomised by foam mattresses stacked outside cheap furniture shops in Woodstock, about offensive design for the masses. She'd thought nothing of it then; in fact, much of what she read at university flew over her head, but now the image returns: mournful, windswept Main Road, piled high with slabs of foam covered in polyester swirls of lurid colour. Brenda chuckles as she removes a pillow to soften the curve. She is grateful for a vulgar, affordable foam mattress of her very own. Tonight, she'll slip into the new linen from Woolworths, white with a chain of yellow-centred daisies embroidered at the edge, an extravagance that sooner or later will have to be revealed to her mother. Lying stretched out and wriggling her bare toes on the two-metre expanse that is inalienably hers, she has never felt happier. Next year, perhaps with a new job or a pay rise, she'll be able to move out, fix up her own place in her own taste. Such fastidiousness, such inordinate concern for the way things look – does that mean she is superficial? She thinks not, hopes not, but then, how does one ever know anything about oneself? Her mother and Shirley will be wounded, but no need to think of that as yet. There is no chance of getting away while the prices in Cape Town continue to soar.

Tomorrow their De la Rey cousins and all the children are coming over for lunch, which is why her mother has started cooking the night before. She should be helping.

In the kitchen, where the old girl stands with her back to the door, stirring a pot, Brenda creeps up behind her and wraps her arms around the shrunken chest. Mummy should see how nice the bedcover looks – matches Mummy's candlewick perfectly, she says, as she takes the wooden spoon out of her mother's hand to taste the curry.

It is nearly six o'clock when, above the noise of the television, Shirley cocks an ear and says that there is a knock at the door. The door is not locked and Neville shouts, Come in, but there is only what sounds like a rustling of papers before the knock is repeated. Mrs Mackay shuffles in her slippers to open the door and Brenda freezes in her chair as she hears Marion's voice asking for her. The child, who has stumbled after his grandmother, says, It's a white lady upon a fine horse, which makes everyone laugh.

Introductions take place over the noise of the television, until Neville turns it off and goes into the bedroom, from where he can listen to the conversation in comfort. He has shut the door, but the smell of cigarette smoke seeps through. Mrs Mackay says loudly, Ag no, sis man, I've told that klong to stop this smoking. Has he opened the window?

Shirley shouts, Have you opened the window?

66

Marion wonders if that means he is smoking dagga, as people are said to do in the townships; she doesn't know what dagga smells like, but she is grateful for the cacophony, the diversion. She sneaks a closer look at the room, at the old lady in slippers and a pink housecoat, whose hair is ironed into stiff porcupine quills and whose cloudy green eyes must once have been prettily set in that brown face.

Marion is saying that she was just passing and thought of dropping in, when it occurs to her that no one could possibly believe that; indeed, Brenda's face is arranged in readiness for a raised eyebrow. But the kind old lady says, with palpable sincerity, Well, that's very nice of you my dear, and now that the ice is broken you can pop in every time you're passing and have a nice cup of tea with us. Words that dissipate the embarrassment, as warm and comforting as the nice cup of promised tea.

Marion explains to the old lady: I don't think Brenda knows, but Bonteheuwel is in fact my old stamping ground. As a young girl, I taught Sunday-school classes at St John's, just down the road, in the days of Father Gilbert. I don't suppose he's still there, or even still alive.

I wouldn't know, Mrs Mackay replies. We're Moravian Mission people, not Anglicans.

It is true that when Marion was fifteen, in her fervent phase, she fell in love with Christ via Father Gilbert, the red-faced vicar with bright white hair and a mesmerising voice, as pure as the driven snow of his native England. Father Gilbert spoke with passion about the parishes in the townships, the poor coloured people who were so lacking in facilities and resources that they were vulnerable to devil's work and dagga; so a group of freshly confirmed girls were sent out to take Sunday-school classes at the new church in Bonteheuwel, kindly donated by the ladies of the southern suburbs.

It took less than a year to fall out of love with Christ, a process accelerated by the grim surroundings of the church and the unashamed gaze of the brown skollies who came leaning over the church wall to stare at the girls. The snot-nosed children could not be relied on to learn their texts, but from the very first Sunday in February when the girls arrived, they clamoured to know what their Christmas presents were going to be. Marion braved it out for a few months, for Father Gilbert's sake, before giving up on Christ and good works.

John and Helen were surprisingly understanding; in fact, she could have sworn that they were relieved. To help her overcome the disappointment, or perhaps it was a reward for seeing sense, Marion was taken on a shopping trip to Garlicks, where she chose the cutest white shoes with baby-louis heels and a silver buckle. Helen, for all her piety, no longer seemed to mind if she didn't come to church with her on Sundays, did not mind her missing Communion, which was puzzling, but it was not in Marion's interest to question this new stance towards the church. It wasn't long before she completely abandoned Anglicanism, finding it an embarrassment, and by the time she went to university at Stellenbosch she was already Dutch Reformed. No, there was no point in trying to understand her mother, and Marion sneaks another look at Mrs Mackay, whose face is kind, open and artless as only, she imagines, the faces of the poor can be.

Brenda says, Well, who would have thought of you as a do-gooder?

Her mother remonstrates that she could well take a leaf out of Miss Campbell's book, that she could do with attending to her own neglected soul. The Reverend Jakobus had asked after Brenda last week, and her mother could only try to cover up by offering to bring an extra bowl of konfyt to the church bazaar, which, by the way, she expects Brenda to make. All that pricking of melon has become too much for her arthritic hands.

There is a crashing sound and a cry from the kitchen. Brenda goes to investigate. She returns with the toddler on her hip. Aren't you a naughty boy, you delicious little doughnut, she croons, holding him aloft for them to admire.

Marion suspects that she might be expected to hold out her arms, invite the child with the funny curly hair to come to her, that is no doubt how people measure friendliness, but she cannot bring herself to do so. Instead she says, He has lovely, velvety black eyes. This seems to go down well with the child, who gurgles appreciatively. She wonders how long she'll have to wait to see Brenda on her own. In this cramped house, it is clear that there isn't space for private conversations. She asks whether Brenda would like to come out for a quick drink somewhere nearby; they need not be long.

Brenda laughs, Unless you have in mind a shebeen, there's no such place, no bars or cafés in Bonteheuwel.

Mrs Mackay is embarrassed. Just her little joke you know, she says, Brenda most certainly does not go to shebeens. Look, it's nearly supper-time and it would be nice if you stayed to have something to eat with us.

Marion protests in vain; she does not want to put them to any trouble.

But it's no trouble at all, says Mrs Mackay. The chicken curry is already cooked; I'm just about to put on the rice.

And so it happens that the bowl of arum lilies is moved to the top of the television and tomorrow's curry lands on the table in the corner of the sitting room. As does the best cream linen, with posies of blue and yellow irises embroidered by Mrs Mackay's own hand all along the crocheted edge, which she has starched for tomorrow's family lunch with the De la Reys. It would be nice if the tablecloth were to survive tonight, but that, of course, is too much to ask, what with turmeric being such a devil for staining, but ag, it doesn't matter, she'll use the clean check one tomorrow. Better than letting Brenda down, when it's so nice of her boss to drop in.

Brenda thinks of the scramble tomorrow, and the inevitable visit to Mr Mahmoud's, since her mother will not countenance a Sunday lunch party without a starter of chicken curry. Even if it hasn't had time to infuse overnight, which is what any good curry needs.

Marion has come for information. Her mother's family were originally from the Clanwilliam district, and having remembered Brenda's geleentheid to Clanwilliam, it occurred to her that Tokkie too would have come from that area. The people in the coloured location surely knew each other. Tokkie must have been something of a family retainer, a nanny to her mother, which accounted for her devotion and for Helen's quiet humility when she was around. Marion remembered that her mother was transformed when Tokkie arrived, that she grew soft and spoke kindly, quietly; as a child, Marion knew to leave all requests until Tokkie visited, or just afterwards, for it took a good hour or so for Helen's carapace to settle back in place.

Because she is preoccupied with the question of Tokkie, of how to broach the subject, she doesn't pay attention, and replies to Mrs Mackay's question about a drink with, Thank you, I wouldn't mind a beer, so that the old lady puts down the jug of orange squash and rubs her hands in bewilderment on the pockets of her housecoat, as if she hopes to conjure a can of Castle from their depths.

Sorry, says Brenda, can't help you there.

Marion blushes deeply. No, she says, it is she, Marion, who is sorry; but Mrs Mackay blusters about a bottle of Old Brown Sherry in the sideboard, given to her last Christmas, for medicinal use, you know, but if you like …

Marion can't say too many times that she wouldn't dream of it, protests her love for orange squash, notes Brenda's smile that she does not know how to interpret, and in her consternation, blurts out that she'd hoped to get some information about a coloured family from Clanwilliam called Williams. Brenda, after all, had a geleentheid to Clanwilliam.

Williams, now let me see, says Mrs Mackay. My late husband, that's now Brenda's poor father who passed away so suddenly, well his sister was engaged once to a Williams chap, very nice-mannered he was too, didn't touch the drink, but no, that man was from the Eastern Cape. None of them can think of any Williamses from the area.

There is no point in holding back now. Actually, Marion is not at all sure that they were called Williams; it's a woman called Tokkie she's trying to trace.

Tokkie, says Mrs Mackay pulling a face, that's now an old-fashioned nickname that I for one have not come across. Coloured people are given funny names by their bosses, you know, but she would have had a decent Christian name; even country people all have decent English names. Mrs Mackay is offended. Does Marion not even know the person's surname?

Neville shakes his head as if he is amazed at the exchange and excuses himself; he turns on the television before going outside for a smoke. The baby cries, so Brenda goes to the bedroom to comfort it in a funny sing-song baby voice; perhaps she is changing its nappy. The rest of them listen to the persistent crying above the sound of an American soap opera until Brenda returns with the baby, who snatches greedily at Shirley's breast. The baby sucks, its murmurs of pleasure punctuating the televisual talk. No one looks at the light-brown swell of breast at which the little fists pummel. From where she sits, Marion can see the paddling movement of stockinged feet on the edge of a bed, all that is visible of Neville, who has retreated to the bedroom.

Mrs Mackay rises stiffly from her chair to start clearing the dishes. Marion offers to wash up, but no one will hear of it. Then she will help with the drying. No, Brenda laughs, we don't allow guests to do that. You see, if I were to come to your house, I wouldn't expect to clean the dishes; it would be like singing for one's supper.

Marion feels the panic rise systematically from her feet, as if she is slowly, stiffly being lowered into icy water that any moment will wash over her head without a sound. What can Brenda mean about coming to her house? No one has ever come to her flat. She doesn't know why that should be. When she first bought it, she brought her father, who admired the rooms in turn and especially the sea view, but that of course does not count. Her parents never had friends over, and not having any family – aunts, uncles, grandparents or cousins – she cannot recall anyone ever eating at their house. Once, when she said she was tired, Geoff asked – barely knowing her – whether she'd prefer to stay in; he could prepare something simple to eat at her place. Which she declined, thinking him presumptuous, but then, given his impeccable manners, she supposes that is just what other people do: eat at each other's houses.

Recently, a magazine article she read in the dentist's waiting room declared that this was what separated the goats from the sheep – the confidence to invite people to dinner. CHAOS, they called it: the Can't Have Anyone Over Syndrome. The article offered tips to overcome the problem, with easy recipes, readymade desserts and advice on the correct flowers, music and wine – all aimed at making entertaining a stress-free, indeed a thought-free event. Just like that, without pausing to think, you could say to someone, Why don't you come over to my place for something to eat? There were testimonies from a famous interior designer who worried about her home not being grand enough, and a quotation from a professional networker who held salons in what she pretentiously called her tiny flat, although there was in fact a separate, good-sized dining room. Marion had shuddered with distaste or perhaps fear; she found none of this information reassuring or encouraging. It was true that she did not particularly like cooking, although that could scarcely be considered a problem nowadays, but she did not think her flat lacked in any respect. Thus the article turned out to have nothing to do with her situation, except she couldn't be sure what her situation was. There seemed no advantage in overcoming a so-called syndrome when in fact she simply preferred not to have other people in her house. She supposed that this amounted to an understanding of herself, which in its own way must count for something. Besides, she reassures herself, Brenda would never drop in, would not be able to do so.

Marion believes that there is no such thing as a free dinner; she will have to come again, if only to bring something. After all, these people are poor. When she leaves, the old lady reminds her to keep all the car windows shut and the doors locked. No need to take any notice of robots at night, she advises, these gangsters will get at you the moment you stop at a red light. If she, Katie Mackay, were able to drive, she'd get a gun for the robots, just to be able to whip down a window and fire a couple of warning shots into the air.

The others all laugh. Mummy's been watching too many Westerns; Mummy's been at the Old Brown Sherry again.

The following week, Marion happens to be having her lunch at the same time as Brenda, for whom she models a new pair of Italian shoes – are the straps around the ankle not too tarty for a woman of her age?

It is only then that Brenda says, Talking about shoes, I think we may have a lead on the woman you were looking for. Apparently, her sister Shirley's friend's mother still goes on about an old woman called Auntie Tokkie, now long since dead, who lived not in Clanwilliam but in nearby Wuppertal.

Marion does not want to think of the context in which such information came to light, the manner in which Shirley would have represented her quest to a friend, who in turn would have repeated the story of Marion blundering over chicken curry and beer. But she is excited. Has Brenda ever been to Wuppertal?

Brenda says no, she believes it's a dump, nothing to see; she has no time for these old mission stations steeped in the colonial past. Unless you want to buy veldskoene, she laughs. That is still what Wuppertal is known for, the shoe industry set up by German missionaries.

Marion has read the article in the *Cape Times*, in which the young woman accuses a Brigadier du Toit of orchestrating her persecution and torture. She read it because the Williams image has detached itself from the page and has taken to persecuting her. It even appears in her father's house, where it hovers, cropped as in the newspaper, on the wall against which the table sits, for all the world as if the woman were a dinner guest. Marion must keep calm, must learn to live with it; what else can she do? She has said nothing to her father, neither about the face that haunts her nor about her adoption of which she is now convinced. Although she believes that she is trying not to be different towards him, trying to see things from his point of view, her manner is distant. She is, in a sense, waiting to see how long he can endure her withdrawal; she cannot broach the subject. John has either not noticed, or he too has adopted a strategy of waiting for the chill between them to pass. That is, after all, how he learned to conduct his marriage.

Marion is now, as they say, seeing Geoff. She has stayed at his house a few times after dinner or a movie in town; she thinks she may have fallen in love with him, but has not got round to deciding. The Williams story is too distracting. Not only is Geoff's house in Tamboerskloof more convenient and more spacious than her own, but she finds the escape from Patricia Williams a relief. That is how she came to stay over at his place the first time, exhausted by the woman who haunts her without rhyme or reason. It is not as if their family, the Campbells, has ever had any connection with the Security Police – in fact, there is barely any Campbell family to speak of, but that woman has projected her face onto the muslin drapes of the four-poster, and with every waft of air the features are dragged hither and thither into grotesque distortions, as if Brigadier du Toit has been at her with renewed vigour. Marion winces, feels the constriction in her throat, and has to pull the bedcovers over her head. At least it is less frightening than being suffocated by the blank muslin, than the abstract bouts of terror that foreshadowed Williams and that Williams has come to replace.

Occasionally, on her own, she watches on television the proceedings of the TRC, in the hope of catching a glimpse of the torturer. Thus far, she has not managed: the relationship with Geoff takes up a lot of time, and then there are the visits to her father to fit in. But she hears of the unimaginable, sees other brigadiers, ordinary men with neatly parted hair and dapper moustaches, confessing in the cosy diminutives of the language to acts that wrench a dry retching from the pit of her stomach. In this world of accusations and confessions, of secrets and lies, Marion is a reluctant traveller who has landed in a foreign country without so much as a phrase book. She forces herself to step out gingerly into its strange streets, her arms clutched, hugged to her chest. She hears the voices of people saying that they did not know, that they had no idea; there is an impulse to say it aloud after them, as in a language lesson, but fastidiousness prevents her from doing so. She does not know why she ventures into a world she has never known, never wished to explore, except that somehow it is the least she can do for the demanding stranger, for Patricia Williams, whose face is that of the beloved Tokkie, and whose eyes point at the connectedness of this foreign country with her old familiar world. Marion does not speak to anyone of these sessions before the television screen. Somehow, she bears the shame of the perpetrators; somehow she, who has never had anything to do with politics, has been branded by this business; somehow, her parentlessness has bonded her with the brigadiers. And all this she must endure without any fuss.

Geoff has come to the agency on a couple of occasions and now the others tease her, except for Brenda who says nothing at all. Boetie congratulates her on catching such a fine chap, you can just tell from the man's demeanour, from his posture, that he is of decent Boer stock, and Tanya reminds her that playing hard to get is the best strategy for keeping a man. She learnt the hard way with her Clive, who is a born rondloper if ever there was one, but once she cottoned on to his ways and kept her distance, even though in her heart – God is her witness – she was burning for him, things took a turn for the better, and now he just has to flick that philanderer's eye and she gives him the cold shoulder, withholding herself. Marion should be careful.

Marion is careful. She has not adopted a strategy; it simply is the case that she has never been effusive, that she gives little away.

Geoff is enthralled by her measured, controlled manner. A woman who makes no demands, who does not keep part of herself for cloying intimacy with female friends – friends with whom a man is daily betrayed under giggles and a cloud of talcum powder. Girlishness repels him. He has a memory of his mother at her dressing table, an image in flesh-pink petticoat, with her head coyly tilted, tears brimming, and the sickly gardenia smell of talc in a fine dust on the glass surface. But Marion is not girlish; she does not trail a waft of perfume, and she certainly would not respond to displeasure or disappointment with womanly tears and tantrums. What more could he ask? In the absence of these characteristics, an absence he vigilantly monitors, he falls in love. Which undoes the vigilance, the appreciation of her distance. Geoff has begun to long for childish, whispered intimacies under the bedcovers, for playful petulance, even misty eyes. He is grateful that she does not interrogate him on past lovers, as is woman's wont, but she appears to have no interest in any aspect of his past, nor in his family. She receives stories about his childhood with well-mannered attention, but with no hunger for more information, no encouraging questions to cheer on such presentations of himself. When he asks whether she would like to come to the Free State to meet his ageing parents, Marion says politely that that would be nice, that she wouldn't mind, but then reminds him how she hates travelling. She has never had any desire to go to the Free State; she doubts whether she could insert herself into what seems like another world. Which makes him lose his temper.

What, Geoff asks, is the matter with you? Why can't you let up and be normal, drop the guard, the affectation, just for once?

Marion doesn't know what he is talking about; she has never felt more comfortable, more at ease with a man, in spite of being haunted by the Williams face. She acknowledges to herself that her bouts of panic started when she was an adolescent at the girls' high school in the city, where she knew that others whispered behind her back and called her unkind names, but she worked hard, and from the heights of the top of the class, managed not to care too much. Girls are spiteful, her mother said; they assume that an only child is spoilt and wish to put you in your place, especially if you're clever – an explanation Marion readily accepted.

Since going out with Geoff, things have been so much better. Williams's face in her flat, the sea, or on her father's kitchen wall is of course disturbing, terrifying if the truth be told, but it is a silent, personal ghost, who inhabits only her very private life, which admittedly has expanded to include an interest in the TRC proceedings. That she manages things has something to do with being in love, and thus she is puzzled by Geoff's anger. Marion thinks of Tanya's double chin, the thick ankles and the middle-aged body still burning for her Clive, and feels inadequate; she must try harder.

It is unfortunate that the argument has arisen here, at this restaurant where they look out at the palm fronds waving in the breeze and the bluest sea nibbling contentedly at the flat rocks of Camps Bay. So what is the matter with her? Marion's reply – that she was brought up by her father as a mermaid – is inspired by several things: a memory of Johan's parting words, resignation that she will lose Geoff, and the swell of water in the bewitching evening light. But it is not entirely frivolous. She is groping for something explanatory, something to appease him. Geoff is incensed by her levity; he clenches his fists; his nostrils quiver and he pushes back his chair as if, as if … oh, she couldn't bear a scene in public, couldn't bear for him to walk out on her. So that Marion stutters her secret: she has just discovered that she is an adopted child; she has been deceived by her parents.

They leave the restaurant without ordering food. In the car, Geoff folds her in his arms, ruffles her hair and is gratified by the convulsions, by the tears that course down her cheeks, tears that he kisses away. This revelation turns her into a ragged waif in need of protection. Once home, he cooks for her. A simple pasta is comforting, he says, turning it also into a lesson. First, the grating of the lemon peel, so that the juice has time to be infused with its zest, before being tossed in the pasta with olive oil, garlic and parsley.

Marion, who has after all lost a father, feels a lemony transfusion of energy from Geoff; he says that they should set about tracing her real parents. He does not understand why she has been so tardy – she has nothing to fear. Illegitimacy is an old-fashioned notion, especially in this country, where everything that once was correct, ordered and legitimate turns out to have been nothing of the kind. Out of delicacy, he does not question her evidence. Marion notes how he has never expressed any desire to meet her father, which makes her realise for the first time that biology is not everything, that John is nothing less than her father, misguided perhaps, but only in the service of his unconditional love for her.

So that when she next sees John, her manner has softened; she reads the gratitude in his eyes, in the pressure of his hand on hers. It is out of deference for a father's feelings that she does not press him for the truth. She will do this by herself; she will not tell John of the quest for her biological parents. They have lived so long with lies; it is too late for anything else.

It is not so surprising that the agencies have no records; she is convinced that the transaction was a private one in which the old woman, Tokkie, had a hand. The scenario she and Geoff favour is that of a prominent, wealthy family in Constantia, who would not countenance an illegitimate child, and for whom their housekeeper Tokkie had the perfect solution: her beloved, childless Helen. Like children, they dwell on invented details: such private arrangements were not uncommon, especially if the people were wealthy. In that case, there is only one course of action. She will have to solicit Brenda's help in finding Tokkie's family in Clanwilliam. Geoff is more than disappointed that she wishes to do so on her own.

Marion takes Brenda out to dinner; she will drive her back to Bonte-heuwel in the dark, which does not please Geoff. The townships are dangerous even in the daylight, he says, although he has never been to one. But she is adamant: she has already visited, has had dinner with Brenda's charming family, her very kind if oversensitive mother, and has driven back to Bloubergstrand without incident.

They go to the restaurant on the Camps Bay seafront, where Brenda has never been. Brenda is enchanted by the postcard view from the balcony, by the festive lights and the palm trees and the rolling waves. In the dusk, one can almost see mermaids on the rocks, she says, and Marion starts. The woman has a knack of getting inside her most secret being; why does she have the irrational feeling that Brenda knows things about her?

Her frown tells Brenda that this is someone for whom only the material exists; no doubt the adolescent flirtation with God was where her spirit bit the dust – in the dusty streets of Bonteheuwel, witnessed by skollies and snot-nosed children who nevertheless looked upon her with envy. What would the boss of MCTravel know of the siren song of mermaids?

Brenda says that there are so many parts of this city that she does not know at all.

Is there resentment lurking in the sing-song syllables? If there is, it is lost on Marion, who has no patience with such dwelling on the past, with guilt-tripping; it is lost when the food arrives: delicate white fish in a wonderful sauce that Brenda is unable to identify.

The wine, which Brenda seldom has, puts her in an expansive mood. Oh yes, she'd be delighted to drive to Clanwilliam with Marion and visit the old mission station at Wuppertal. As it happens, there is something that she too would like to do: on the road to Wuppertal, in the Cederberg, are some San rock paintings that are meant to be worth seeing.

Marion thinks that would be interesting; she is uncomfortable about accepting a favour – far better if she believes the venture to be reciprocal. Brenda will, in the meantime, see what she can glean from Shirley's friend about the family in Wuppertal that they think is connected to Tokkie. She does not ask why Marion wishes to trace Tokkie, and Marion relies on the explanation of sentimental attachment to an old family servant.

It is surprisingly pleasant to be dining with a woman, prattling about this and that, and Marion is drawn into the young woman's volubility. Marion finds herself confiding that she has no desire to have children. Brenda is quaint: she speaks – only lightly glossed with irony – of the heart's desire; but hard as she tries, Marion is stumped by the phrase, the heart's desire, which she tosses about fruitlessly in her thoughts. Brenda says she hopes one day to be a writer, a poet perhaps, but she laughs, Fat chance. Then they talk about the trip.

As she drives back from Bonteheuwel, Marion thinks of how well the evening went, of how she has made a friend.

Geoff has arranged to go sailing with a group of friends at the weekend. He'd assumed that Marion would be going to Wuppertal, otherwise, of course, he would have preferred to spend the time with her. He wants to know why she has postponed. Oh, she says vaguely, too much to do, which puzzles him. He cannot understand procrastination: he plunges headlong into projects that may well turn out to be wild goose chases, but surely progress is also about eliminating possibilities. If there is a past that has to be uncovered, well, one ought to get on with the excavations; confront it.

Marion suspects Geoff of trying to inveigle his way into her trip to Wuppertal. His impatience makes her see the situation in a new light: she is no longer so sorry for herself. It's not as if she doesn't have a childhood, a past. A biological mother, who didn't want her or couldn't keep her, whatever the case may have been, is, strictly speaking, of no consequence. She was raised by two perfectly ordinary parents who loved her in their own ways – even the memory of Helen has softened since her discovery – and while uncovering the past may well be interesting, it cannot alter her personal history, the facts of her upbringing, the stories on her father's knee about mermaids, her mother's rare flashes of tenderness, which kept the child ablaze and lightfooted for days. There is something distasteful about the physicality of a strange woman from whose womb you have issued, even if you are anxious to know her. Equally worrying is the fact that Marion has to travel miles to find her. But Geoff is right; she should get on with it, lay the ghost.

The project may sound exciting to Geoff, but frankly it fills her with horror. Setting off on any trip is a nuisance for Marion, a wrenching from the familiar that raises only unreasonable expectations. Something is meant to happen when you travel: you are supposed to traverse the terrain, when in fact a ravenous vehicle has consumed it. As for the meaningfulness that people claim to find in making a trip, well, it makes her feel inadequate. Travel, she mocks, is what beauty queens cite as their favourite hobby – travel and its first cousin, driving. I like to tootle along farm roads or zip down the highway in my little Citi Golf, she simpers in quotation marks.

Marion is not one for landscape, does not appreciate the subtle differences in topography as her car speeds over the land, does not always register the change in flora; and when she does, there is the business of how she is meant to react to, or, even more arcane, how to interact with the landscape. This, presumably, is what the celebrated experience of travel is all about, but she is not convinced of the notion of *experiencing* the land, of waking up, so to speak, with earth at the corner of her mouth. She suspects the whole business of being bogus: does it not boil down to how the so-called experience is relayed to others? For Marion, the truth is that she is passing over the land, her only contact being through the cushioned rubber tyres of her moving vehicle.

Of course, in another era, when you walked with a knapsack on your back through the countryside and encountered adventures, meeting with lions by day and ghosts by night, stumbling upon a bearded lunatic in a cave whose words became clear some years later, well, in those days perhaps it may have been meaningful to travel. Nowadays, surely, experience is what happens over a period of time in a familiar place, when you live for years in, say, Observatory, traversing the same vacant lot on the way to the corner shop, catching the same bus to school, negotiating the same cracks in the pavements, finding days later a trace of the rectangles and squares of the hopscotch that you won, while your hand involuntarily finds on your knee the scar left from a previous game. But to report that the land is no longer green and lush, that grass has been replaced by short dry shrubs, means nothing. I have been to such and such a place, Marion could say, but no more; she will not buy into the transformative value of travel. And as for taking something away with one from a strange place, making it your own – well, what could that possibly mean?

Brenda has been wondering when they will make the trip. She has done some research on the rock paintings in the area, and shows Marion reproductions in a book borrowed from the library. Ooh, she says, raising her shoulders with pleasure, aren't you excited? I can't wait to go on this journey.

Marion feels compelled to say that they'll go next week. She is struck by Brenda's use of the word journey, an old-fashioned word, she thinks. Even if a discovery does await her in Wuppertal, it is clear to her that it will not be the act of undertaking a journey that produces it. If the people she hopes to meet could be coaxed to come to Cape Town, the discovery would be made all the same.

Brenda persists. The soul of a journey is liberty, perfect liberty: to think, feel, do just as one pleases – to leave ourselves behind, she intones with fashionable irony.

Marion snorts her contempt. Already she wonders if the whole thing is not a mistake.

The Clanwilliam Hotel is a charming old German place, redolent of colonial times. There are elegant nineteenth-century pieces of furniture in the public spaces, starched, embroidered linen, and sepia photographs of buttoned-up bourgeois families: handsome ladies and bearded explorers line the generous staircase. Brenda waits for her on the landing, unmoved by the sumptuous past. Does the girl think only of Bushman paintings? Marion will not be intimidated by Brenda's indifference; she is the one paying for their lodging.

Brenda cheers up somewhat over dinner and they spend a tolerable evening together, although it is by no means easy. The onus is on Marion to make conversation. She is also irritated by the black man who sits by himself in the dining room and stares at them, but at him at least she can lob a dirty look. Has she offended Brenda, or does the girl just regret being with her? So she says that that is another aspect of journeys: the famous experience dangled before you, but just out of reach, ruined because of having chosen the wrong travelling companion.

Or, some say, for having made the mistake of going on a journey with a companion at all, Brenda adds. But there seems to be no sarcasm in her tone; she is after all an employee rather than a companion.

And what if Marion too were to give up on the evening, refuse to make small talk – where would that get them? Marion orders another bottle of wine. Thank God for the bounty of the Cape vineyards, which comes to the rescue also as topic of conversation.

What would we do, Marion says, without all this, the wine and the weather? She would not consider living in another country. Has Brenda heard the clients who rave about Europe, the English South Africans who yearn to live their lives under grey skies? Surely they are kidding themselves, surely the wonderment would subside and leave them howling for home. How could one survive without the light, the heat, the fruit and the wine? How do you breathe in those tiny, cramped countries stuffed with people? That was why Europeans came to Africa in the first place – empty cellars, empty larders, not enough room, and rickets.

Brenda gulps down some wine and relents. There's also America, California, she says. One of her lecturers at university had suggested she apply for a scholarship to do postgraduate studies in the United States, but she couldn't face it; she found herself using her mother as an excuse. Besides, it is an interesting time to be in South Africa. She asks if Marion has watched any of the TRC proceedings, and notes the agitation in her uncertain response. Brenda wouldn't be surprised if one of those monstrous organisers of death squads were a kindly uncle of Marion's, a lover of children, fondly remembered for jolly japes on the farm ...

The topic of travel must once more come to the rescue. It's not doing the tourist industry any harm, Brenda says. The Cape is overrun with foreigners – only a couple of years ago, this hotel would have been empty.

And now the conversation runs more or less smoothly, for a while at least, but the unspoken trots alongside like a faithful dog, in the shadow, with only the faintest of footfalls.

Brenda wouldn't mind a short holiday in Europe, just to see the sights. She asks if Marion has a holiday house in France or Italy.

So that is what Brenda thinks, that she has a bottomless supply of money. She ought not to be surprised; that is what they all think of whites. No wonder she hasn't even offered to contribute to the cost of the weekend – not that Marion would have heard of it, but still, the gesture is surely lacking. It is convenient for them to believe that white people's work brings unprecedented wealth, that they have all inherited pots of money. No doubt it excuses the behaviour of the lazy and the layabouts.

No, Marion says wearily, I come from a poor family. My grandparents were dirt poor, my parents hardly better off, and they didn't have much education either. Dirt poor, she repeats.

Brenda finds this offensive. She does not like the construction that binds poverty to dirt, but more importantly, for someone like Marion, who lives in Cape Town, who drives regularly past the informal housing of Khayelitsha, where whole families cram into what amounts to no more than a giant carrier bag, it is surely not possible to speak of the poverty of one's grandparents. Marion must know that this is why they are so resented: the descendants of these dirt poor who nevertheless had servants and needed no more than a decade or two to make themselves more than comfortable, while ... Ag, she takes a swill of wine, what difference would her protest make? Besides, she must mind her manners; she is Marion's guest. She ought to know that it is impossible to have conversations that do not slide into awkwardness with people like this.

The next morning, when they wake up to birdsong and citrus blossom, the world seems whole as an orange, and vast; bougainvillea and pale-blue plumbago are in full flower and the women are in jubilant spirits, last night's tension quite forgotten. Brenda is in charge of the map. They drive out of Clanwilliam on the tarred road to Calvinia that soon turns into gravel.

One of the first Rhenish missionaries who came to South Africa to establish a Protestant station at Wuppertal was the grandfather of the famous Afrikaans poet, C. Louis Leipoldt, says Brenda. Eighteen-twenty-nine it was.

Funny, isn't it, Marion replies, that people come all this way to get away from that darkness, only to name the new after the old? What do you think that says about their expectations of travel?

Brenda has done her homework. No, although there is a Wupper river, a tributary of the Rhine, the German city of Wuppertal, an amalgamation of small towns on the river, was not established until the twentieth century. Nice to think of it as a reversal, a European city being named after our humble settlement ... But back to our Wuppertal. Not only were the Germans concerned with the souls of the savages, but one look at the poor unshod people hopping across the red-hot stones brought another resolve, this time about their scorched soles: they would teach the people to make shoes out of local hides, keeping them out of mischief and so killing two birds with one stone. Actually three, since the missionaries could not rely forever on the mother country for revenue; the shoes also brought self-sufficiency. And that's how the Wuppertal veldskoen was born, not just for the black people at Wuppertal, who could barely afford them, but for the footsore all over the country, those who trudged for miles through rough terrain, taming the land and rearing animals that in turn would be slaughtered for their hides.

Brenda continues to deliver a potted history of the mission station. Of the shoe factory – which unfortunately they won't be able to visit because it's Sunday, damn, they should've thought of that – and the picturesque thatched roofs, another skill brought by the Germans.

There'll be brochures, Marion says, photographs of people at work with their old-fashioned awls and leather aprons; that will do for me. Lederhosen! she exclaims. Now there's something we can be grateful for: at least the missionaries didn't set up factories for the making of lederhosen, or insist that local people wear them.

They are driving into the Cederberg mountains, approaching the Pakhuis Pass. Would Marion like to pay her respects to the poet, whose grave is in a natural rock crypt at the very crest of the pass?

Marion sniffs, sniffs at the aromatic air. I thought you people weren't interested in Afrikaans, she says.

Ah, but if you're a poet, want to be a poet, Brenda corrects herself, you don't care about things like that. Leipoldt was a fine poet; he also inherited his grandpa's love of coloured people, especially little boys. She giggles. At school we called him the moffie poet; what else could all that stuff about krulkop-klonkie and Mali the slave be about? Then the biographical note in the Verseboek said that he was unmarried and raised a number of boys, and unlike the other poets, his picture showed him to be good looking too. Obvious, isn't it, that he was gay? Listen to this, and Brenda intones in a flirtatious voice:

Krulkop-klonkie
Wat wil jy
Op die wêreld
Hier by my
Nou kom haal of lewer, klonkie? Wat is hier te gee of kry?

Krulkop-klonkie
Slaap gerus,
Van die drome
Onbewus:
Vroeg genoeg kry jy nagmerrie; wie sal jou dan, klonkie, sus?

You see, she mocks, it's the contrast between those short, clipped lines and the breathless, lengthy last lines, the flirtatious questions, that's the giveaway. And see how the boy is responsible for coming on to the innocent man – good God, I haven't thought about this before; what on earth is this wicked stuff doing in the Afrikaans canon?

Marion says, Look, forget it, we're not going to this poet guy's grave. It's thyme, she says, and sniffs appreciatively. Wild thyme warmed by the sun.

And dagga, Brenda adds, that's why we're high.

They descend onto a plain and drive in silence, until in the distance a vehicle appears, coming towards them, a donkey cart perhaps. Except there is a shimmer and a sparkle as light bounces off the contraption. Marion slows down, and just below the purr of the Mercedes they hear the curious echo of a rattling sound.

Hooly-ha, Brenda shrieks. They brake to a halt. Coming towards them, galloping dangerously along the road's incline, is a man in harness, dragging behind him a ramshackle cart decorated with outlandish shiny things and streamers of coloured cloth, piled high with objects made of beaten, painted and pierced tin, including what look like toy windmills, whirring in the movement of the cart. He waves with both hands, laughing; his teeth are very white in the dark face creased with laughter lines, and his tall, lean frame bends with the burden he draws. He is a bundle of bric-a-brac that will surely crash headlong into the Mercedes. But no, he swerves expertly into the scrub and comes to a halt, slips off his tinselled harness and, ignoring the women, leaps deftly onto the wagon.

Hooly-ha, Brenda says again – in the face of this apparition, it is her mother's oath that comes to mind – and he's no spring chicken either, must be at least seventy.

The women sit speechless, watching the man, who seems to be searching for something or checking his wares: shiny tins, decorated bottles, shards of coloured glass that wink in the sun, motley streamers of cloth, plumes of dyed ostrich feathers. His trousers have grey flannel clues to their origin; now they are patched all over with coloured cloth, and brightly patterned scarves flap gaily around his waist. When he finally turns to them, tugging at the feathers sewn on each side of his wide-brimmed hat, he bows gallantly. A lovely morning ladies, he says in rural Afrikaans, rolling his r's, and a lovely place for a picnic too.

The instinct to lock the car door comes and goes in a flash; instead, the women get out, mesmerised by the man. By his extraordinary eyes – for they are different, one green and one black, set in an ageless, mahogany face, and bright as the bits of coloured glass and tin that flash from the cart. He is a peacock man, a brightly coloured creature from mythology, a messenger from the gods; his teeth are as brilliant white as a young man's. Brenda stutters a Morning Mister, er, Oom.

He grabs her hand, pumping it jovially. Outa Blinkoog, he says, that's now me. He capers over to greet Marion, his lithe body buckling like that of a boerjong with a tin guitar.

Ag no, Oom, Brenda says, no need to call yourself Outa. That's not nice at all. She restrains herself from adding – for such a beautiful man.

But he laughs heartily. No, my child, that's always been my name and it's a good name too. Ou Ta, he says, snapping the word into two. Yes, Ou Ta, and I do have lots of children – he waves his hand vaguely across the veld – all out there in the wide world, so you too can call me Outa Blinkoog.

It is as if the man has waited all his life to tell his story: a flood of words bursts unsolicited from his curved, girlish lips. He is unstoppable, barely comprehensible, as he launches into a narrative that has no end, each fragment leading to another. With his foot he clears away pebbles to smooth a patch of red earth, where he draws stick figures to represent his father and himself as a child, and some blobs for sheep. This is wiped away with the same foot to make way for a new frame, a new story. Of children in a schoolroom, an inspector towering over them; of two women he loves sitting side by side; of the pepper tree in which he lives in summer, but with the confetti of jacaranda, for he has seen such heavenly blueness in the town and has carried the picture with him ever since. But such a shower of blue can't be told, can't be drawn in the sand, and can't be made into tin treasures. That is why he would rather have his stories embroidered on white cloth.

You see, ever since I was so big, and he holds out his hand to indicate the height of a small child, they said I was an outa; I've never been a child. In those days I was Baas Pieter van Schalkwyk's shepherd, started when I was at school – I know the veld like the back of my hand – and it was Baas Pieter who called me Outa Blinkoog. Magtig, he says, this talking makes a person hungry, hey. The school inspector says, read from the English storybook, and then you must learn to read: Joe doesn't know; Joe can't read. And then the constable pulls your ears: Come on, get a move on Joe, move on. So you see, I do the travel; I go where I please, all over the show, and no constable can move me on.

Brenda manages to get a word in: And what about the plants? Does Outa know all the plants, the ones you can eat or the ones that can cure diseases?

Oh yes, he says, and waves dismissively across the veld, but there's no time to dig about for veldkos; you tell me, who eats veldkos these days? I for one am too busy; I've got my things, all these treasures to make. The world is so ugly, so dry and grey that one's got to make the Pragtige Goeters. Let me show you, he says, and they watch as he unpacks.

Some of his Beautiful Things are scraps of coloured cloth bunched into little mops that he holds up and twirls. It works much better in the wind, he explains. Others are objects made of shiny tin: commercial cans of all kinds, flattened out, beaten, punctured all over for texture and reshaped with settings of coloured glass.

Light, he says, that is what we take too much for granted; coloured glass helps us to remember the miracle of light. You should see my cart, a palace at night, when all these lanterns are alight. People are kind, they collect things; the women save pretty things for me, all the scraps and broken bits that are wasted and thrown away.

Then he hauls out his prize possession, an unbleached linen cloth covered in roughly written text and embroidered line drawings. He doesn't want them to examine it too closely. One of my chapters, he says; I write out my stories with a pen and then the women must embroider the chappies for me with coloured thread.

Marion asks if he sells his things in town. He shakes his head decisively. No, they wouldn't want the Beautiful Things there. No, he wouldn't want to sell any of it anyway; he has quite enough money for his needs, and his treasures are all from found things that others throw away. It's just a pity that they want to keep him off the roads. Not that he ever goes into the village with his wagon, no point in doing that, but they say he has to keep off all the small roads in the veld as well. He doesn't like being in the same place all the time, has always kept on the move, but nowadays he is forced to keep moving. Move on Joe, move on, for people complain about him and his cart. A hazard, they say. Eventually they will find the courage to drive him off the road for good. They say he is too old to pull the wagon, but anyone can see that he's as fit as an ox, and he has cut down to a single cart. They should have seen him in his youth, when he had the wagon of carts hitched to each other – what a grand affair that was. But the truth is that people are dazzled by the Beautiful Things, struck dumb and given headaches, so he can't altogether blame them.

Outa Blinkoog draws himself up to his full height and, with his head thrown back, his extraordinary eyes lifted to the heavens, says how nothing can stop him; that he has learned long ago, when he first gave up being a shepherd, that a person must do as he pleases, go where and when he likes. It is God's veld and God doesn't say when, where or what, and that means you do what must be done. Then, switching abruptly from the sombre talk, he crows with laughter, does an elegant caper and, announcing that this is now a good place for a picnic, gets from his wagon a lump of bread wrapped in a filthy patchwork cloth sewn together with a man's rough stitching. Look, he shows them, my sewing is coming on nicely. There's a lo-ovely woman – he tilts his head and winks – who comes to see me, she knows where to find me in the veld, and teaches me to sew; her body is soft as a featherbed. The chapters on cloth, they must be embroidered in different colours for the different little stories that grow inside the big story, but that can only be done by a woman with the small fingers.

Although they only an hour ago tucked into a huge cooked breakfast, Marion fetches from the boot of the car a small bag of oranges, a bottle of water, a bar of chocolate and yesterday's stale muffin. It's a feast, he crows; he finds a branch of thornbush with which to sweep clear a space of red earth, outlines a square table with a stick, and arranges the food in the centre. The chocolate he hands back to her – no good for the stomach. He takes the oranges out of their bag, bunches up the green nylon mesh and arranges the fruit in the nest of concentrated emerald green. Ooh, he shrieks with pleasure, just look at that! If the miesies doesn't mind, he'd like to keep the green stuff.

Marion laughs. No, the miesies doesn't mind. With this man, one can say anything: outa, miesies; here language is not the fraught business she has come to fear. Words are fresh, newborn, untainted by history; all is bathed in laughter clean as water.

The women are transported to another world; they eat and talk and laugh and pass the time of day with the man out of a storybook. Marion asks Outa Blinkoog about the Bushman paintings and he says yes, he has seen them many years ago, and very nice they are too. But the pictures are faded, they are the things from a long, long time ago, and now people must make new Beautiful Things.

He is self-centred, like a child, relating all things to himself, and he talks continuously, excitedly, telling and repeating as if he were spellbound and would expire if his story were not spoken. He shows little interest in them, except when Brenda manages to say that they arrange for people to travel overseas. So everyone is now flying like birds across the water! He claps his hands. It is too wonderful; he's glad that they are helping people to keep on the move. He has been to the edge of the water once, to Cape Town, but then he frowns, his eyes cloud over; he can't remember anything about that time. He thinks he may have been locked up, his cart confiscated, so there really is no point in remembering the details – except there was the jacaranda, the whole of town strewn with blue jacaranda flowers, at which he brightens up and eats yet another orange, for the beautiful women have brought a feast.

What a pity that they have a date with a Mrs Murray in Wuppertal. Does Outa Blinkoog know the Murrays? No, he doesn't really know the people of that place, there is no room for him in a place devoted to the making of shoes. He supposes there is a time and place for a good pair of veldskoen, especially on the tar roads, but here he really would recommend getting to know one's terrain through the soles of one's own feet. He pats his own appreciatively, hard as leather; he thinks they have covered a million miles. A stubborn pair of travellers they are, he says affectionately. If they decide to get going, there's just no stopping them.

Outa Blinkoog will not let them go without a present. He digs around in the back of his cart; he knows exactly what they should have – an exquisite thing of scrunched-up tin with something of a rim in which disks of red and green glass are embedded. He holds it up admiringly to the light so that the colours shine like jewels. It's a lantern, he explains, but especially for when the candle grows short. Then the last hour of candlelight is sweetened with bright colour, so there's no place for sadness.

For a moment, Marion wonders if she should give him money, but she looks at Brenda and simultaneously they shake their heads.

Outa Blinkoog gets into his harness, carefully positions the bunched green mesh of the orange bag to stick out from a tin container, doffs his wide-brimmed hat with ostrich plumes on either side, and shakes their hands. It was a fine picnic, refreshing to have a good chat – he puts away the remaining food in his cart; he could not have hoped for a better day, and with such beautiful women too. But he would not dream of leaving before them. It is a fine motorcar and he would like to see them take off, would like to watch the red dust fly from its wheels. They wave, and he strikes a dancer's pose and capers an enthusiastic, theatrical goodbye.

Brenda keeps the lantern on her lap, holds it up to the light so that green and red flicker on the dashboard. The lantern that is for both of them, that neither one nor the other will own.

As the road unwinds down to a valley between the Cederberg and Tra-Tra mountains, where the village of Wuppertal lies spick and span in the sunlight, Marion is sick with apprehension. Now she wishes they'd taken longer over the rock paintings or delayed at the poet's grave. They park under a clump of eucalyptus trees near the Moravian church. In the bright light, the whitewashed buildings gleam as in a film set, the original vision of its nineteenth-century German founders immanent in its crisp orderliness: the immaculately thatched roofs, the picturesque old-worldly row of terraced cottages, steepled church and the long building in which shoes are made – so beautiful that the word factory cannot be used. Brenda is ecstatic.

The house that Shirley's contact has arranged for them to visit is not one of the lovely old whitewashed places with thatched roofs. The Murrays' residence, as the young man whom they asked for directions called it, is a newly built house with a small verandahed stoep and asbestos roof. Pots of flowering rosemary flank the front door, where they wait for an inordinately long time before it is opened; they carry in with them the medicinal aroma of the herb, against which their clothes have brushed.

The wiry little woman in best wear introduces herself as Mrs Murray. She looks sixtyish but could be older, and is not at all what Marion expected;

for although it is unreasonable, although she knew in advance that the woman was not in fact related to Tokkie, Marion had in mind someone very different, someone motherly, perhaps. Thus she is disappointed; she does not hold out any hope that Mrs Murray, who is relentlessly formal and who keeps her thin lips fastidiously pursed, will have anything to reveal. A tray prepared for tea awaits them in a dining-cum-sitting room; they negotiate their way around heavy dark furniture.

They chat about the history of the mission station. Brenda has many questions to ask, also about the shoe factory; she is sorry that they won't be able to visit, that they had to come on a Sunday. Oh yes, Mrs Murray says, we are quite up to date here; we've branched out some years ago from veldskoen to those comfortable buckled shoes that young city folks started wearing, also sandals for both men and women, in fact a variety of new styles.

Then they move on to the rock paintings that lately have become quite a tourist attraction. The municipality is going to develop the site, put in some decent amenities, a nice bakkie to drive people from cave to cave, and of course make a good bit of money, because, says Mrs Murray sipping her tea delicately, these old Bushman paintings have also become very fashionable. Even foreigners come all the way specially to see what she understands to be quite unremarkable things, quite lacking in artistry and what's more, hardly visible any more. She imagines that with all the improvements, the municipality will touch them up a little; sounds like they're in need of renovation. One of these fine days she may even be persuaded to go and have a look, see what all the fuss is about, except it's quite a trek.

In spite of the pursed lips that suggest reticence, Mrs Murray turns out to be something of a talker; it is hard to get in a word edgeways, and there is a strange dissonance between the chatter and her formal manner. Marion wonders how she will find an opportunity to ask about Tokkie, especially since the woman announces that her sister, who is the village juffrou, will be coming over to meet them. Perhaps they got it wrong, perhaps it is the sister who is the contact. She finds it oppressively hot in the house, even though the curtains are drawn against the afternoon sun; it is hard to concentrate on the conversation. A blanket of anxiety enfolds her: sweat pours down her armpits, pools between her breasts, beads on her forehead, and her head throbs as if the image of Williams's face is struggling to come into being. She needs to find a lavatory, and stumbles down the dark passageway to splash her face.

The lavatory is much like Mrs Murray. It too is dressed formally in deep pink with ruffles, as is the toilet roll, and behind the door a curious hanging of pink broderie anglaise from which elaborate posies of ribbon peep saucily, and which on investigation proves to be a successful device for hiding extra toilet rolls. Marion sits on the lavatory seat. Everything hurts, from her head to her feet; indeed, her right foot when she looks down seems swollen. But she must brace herself for returning to the sitting room; she alights on the strategy of starting to speak before entering the room.

So, she says loudly from the doorway, as if resuming a conversation, the old lady, Tokkie, who died about thirty years ago – I'm sorry, I don't know her real name – I imagine you are too young to remember her?

Mrs Karelse? No, I knew her well when she was still a youngish woman. I used to do little jobs for her, and very generous she was too. Often had a tickey for me and a sweetie as well, although in those days children helped grown-ups without expecting payment. Once, she couldn't find a tickey after I carried a huge pile of wood to her outdoor oven, so she pierced a hole in one of those very small tins of condensed milk, sixpence they cost, and gave it to me to suck – no, you need two holes – and I swear that was my undoing, that little miniature tin was the beginning of my sweet tooth, and Mrs Murray reaches for another slice of cake with granadilla icing. No, a very, very nice lady she was. I don't know if it's the same family you're thinking of, but her husband died when she was quite young. She had only two children, a son and a daughter, but she never married again. Turning to Brenda, she says, Quite a dark-skinned woman, you know, although with good features and wavy kind of hair, but nice and smooth.

Marion explains that Tokkie had worked for her mother's family in

Clanwilliam and later for wealthy people in Constantia, that she is interested in tracing Mrs Karelse's family, and would like to find her son or daughter.

Mrs Murray looks puzzled for a moment. Yes, I know she went to Cape Town to work for posh people, but not as a servant, never, rather as a housekeeper, a kind of manager. Her daughter, whom I don't remember – but they say she was now a real beauty, fair with long hair – well, she is said to have disappeared in town. The last we heard was of a hurried marriage, although to quite a presentable chap they said, then after that not a word, clean off the face of the earth she slipped. Perhaps Mrs Karelse went in search of the girl, but all I know is that she found a respectable position with English people.

Marion frowns. But I don't think Tokkie had any children; I don't remember my mother ever mentioning…

Oh yes, there was a son as well, says Mrs Murray; but as for working for a family in Clanwilliam, no, that can't be right. The Karelses were decent people, not the sort who went into service for Boers. You see, she and her husband both worked here with the shoes, which wasn't at all like working in a city factory; no, it was a respectable kind of work, making things just as the missionaries set it up all those years ago, and all to the glory of God. Mr Karelse's people had been in Wuppertal ever since the beginning, although there are now none of them left here. I don't know what happened to their son. Wuppertal was thought to be quite dull in those days before television, and not everyone likes to work with shoes, so many young people just went to the city. But I remember Mrs Karelse telling me how the factory used to be in the olden days, prayers in the mornings and all that. Her own family, the Plaatjies, were originally from the Boland, and again there's none of them left here now.

So, a false lead. Not their Tokkie, who Mrs Murray would think disreputable for being a servant. Marion blushes at the thought.

Brenda too is embarrassed. Looking away from Marion's crestfallen face and shoulders hunched with disappointment, she exclaims, Heavens, what's the matter with your foot?

Marion's foot is swollen, taut as dough risen in the confines of its pan, the strap of her sandal parting it into two unequal loaves. Although she wore trainers on the hike to the caves, she must have twisted something on the way back. Now that her attention is drawn to it, the foot is excruciatingly painful. She rises to test it and shrieks with pain, Jesus Christ, I can't walk!

Mrs Murray's lips are tightly pursed. They barely open for the reprimand: she would rather not have the Lord's name taken in vain in her house. Marion is panic-stricken; she has a vision of being stuck in this pious Moravian house, unable to drive herself home. She finds herself saying how sorry she is, how inexcusable blasphemy is, but such is the unexpected pain that she could not help it. She hopes that a good woman like Mrs Murray will forgive her.

The good woman takes pity on her. There is nothing to be done except soak the foot in mustard water. She disappears into the kitchen for water and returns with an old-fashioned pink enamel basin and its matching jug with sprays of blue cornflowers. Her antique set, she calls it. But look, she boasts, as good as new, not so much as a chip out of the enamel. What a funny coincidence, she explains – even though her Mrs Karelse is not Marion's Tokkie, this antique set was given to her by the old lady when she left. Then Mrs Murray was already engaged to the schoolmaster, and Mrs Karelse said she could have the set as an advance wedding present.

She stirs mustard powder into the water and helps Marion to remove the sandal, roll up the trouser leg and lower her foot into the basin. Ag, Mrs Murray says, it will be easier to have both feet in the water. After that long walk to the old Bushman stuff, the other foot won't mind a soak.

Brenda, who has registered the dead end of the enquiry, is bored and asks about the elections. How did the ANC fare in Wuppertal? Their hostess does not want to talk about politics, had quite enough of that through the terrible apartheid years. But Brenda persists until Mrs Murray says that the decent coloured people of Wuppertal voted for the Nationalists, that they don't want to have anything to do with violence.

Brenda folds her arms ostentatiously; she cannot bring herself to drink any more of the woman's coffee or eat her cake. It is up to Marion to keep up a desultory conversation.

After half an hour, Mrs Murray sinks with remarkable agility to her knees to check the foot. She is quite the nurse with a first-aid box, a packet of frozen peas and a white towel on her lap, and will hear nothing of Marion's protests. Marion is embarrassed, but what can she do? The woman is determined to administer to her. She wishes that she could think less ill of the woman.

Mrs Murray lifts the swollen foot out of the hot water, places the packet of frozen peas on it and looks up at Marion to check her face for reaction. Then she gasps loudly and drops the foot as if it's on fire, so that water splashes on her dress and onto the floor. Her eyes are wide with recognition.

O gits, it's like seeing a spook, because from down here with your face tilted like that you look the spitting image of Mrs Karelse my dear! Funny that I didn't notice before. Imagine, Mrs Karelse spooking here by me today; must be because I'm using her antiques for a change, come to think of it, I've never actually used these before. She chatters nervously. Are you superstitious at all? she asks Marion. I suppose a good Christian shouldn't be, but you know I can't help it, sometimes funny things just happen, sometimes the dead speak to us in this way. But who would have thought old Mrs Karelse would want to come and spook me, of all people? Now that really is something, that her shadow should fall over your face like this. Look, the swelling has gone down a bit, don't you think? she asks after removing the compress of frozen peas.

Marion tries to nod, but has a feeling that her head hasn't moved, that she has no control over it, that in fact it is not her own. Marion is drained; she wants to protest but can't when the woman dries both her feet with a new guest towel.

Mrs Murray rubs Zambuk ointment into the swollen foot before bandaging it expertly. Yes, she explains, she trained at Somerset Hospital, although that was a long time ago and she hasn't nursed for a number of years now. Mrs Murray is careful not to look at Marion, perhaps out of superstitious fear, or more likely, embarrassment.

Brenda comes to the rescue. While the woman struggles to her feet, she whips away the bowl, mops up the water and starts clearing away things. It is time for them to go, she says briskly – they must not outstay their welcome. She, Brenda, will drive; she does not say that she doesn't have a driving licence. She tells herself that it will be alright, that there won't be much traffic on the road to town, not on a Sunday. If she is somewhat nervous about driving through the city she says nothing, must hope for the best. What choice does she have?

Mrs Murray protests that they ought to wait until her sister, the juffrou, arrives; she'd so been looking forward to the visitors from town. But no, Brenda is firm; they should get that injured foot home.

With Mrs Murray's help, Marion hobbles to the passenger seat, but the woman avoids meeting her eye, even when she explains how to nurse the foot. Instead, the instructions are addressed to Brenda – as if that one will be lifting a finger.

Brenda gets off to a shaky start, stalling and juddering, which takes a huge bite out of her confidence, but Marion appears not to think it strange. You'll soon get used to the Merc, she's pretty powerful, she says listlessly, if not without pride.

Brenda is silent, concentrating, her eyes fixed on the road, which fills Marion with unexpected bitterness. Is she really going to behave as if nothing has happened? It's not Brenda's fault that she's been drawn into this situation, but now that she has, now that knowledge, however unwelcome, has been foisted on her, does she not have an obligation to engage with it, with Marion?

Marion's head hurts, but at least she knows herself not to be a coward. She must pull herself together; she must speak. The authoritative mode is the one that habitually asserts itself in moments of difficulty, and so, under cover of stating, she demands in a strained, bossy voice: I would have expected you to say what you think, what you make of all that.

Brenda says nothing. She mouths a silent Fuck you. Not only does the woman come with some pathetic, bogus enquiry; she also expects Brenda to smooth things over, to participate in her fictions. Frankly, she wants nothing to do with Marion's stories.

Is it not enough that I'm driving the car? she finally asks, without taking her eyes off the road.

Yes, Marion replies, chastened. Yes, of course it is. She hangs the head that hurts and yet does not belong to her, fixes her eyes on the black fabric of her trousers; she does not recognise her voice, does not recognise the linen-clad legs on which her eyes have come to rest. But she will not break down in the presence of the unsympathetic person who is driving her car. No, she says to herself, over and over; she will not break down.

Marion's left hand moves up and down her left leg, up and down, so that Brenda has to take deep breaths to prevent herself from asking her to stop.

Thus they drive in miasmal silence to Cape Town, along the dreary coastal road of ugly housing to Bloubergstrand. Brenda helps her into the flat, then returns for their bags. Marion says Brenda should take the car home and pick her up the next morning for work. Brenda laughs. If she were to do that, there may well not *be* a car in the morning. They do not have a garage in which to keep it hidden.

There is nothing to be done. Neither of them relishes the thought, but it is late and Brenda will have to stay the night.

It's funny seeing Brenda there in her flat, on her sofa. Marion thinks about the magazine article, about the preparations one is supposed to make for a visit; she can no longer remember why it was of interest. She rings for a pizza, which they eat listlessly. There are fortunately things to be said about where cutlery, plates, linen can be found. Then they both retire.

Brenda is restless. The leather sofa is not a comfortable bed. She watches the red flashing light of a digital clock; she would like to go out onto the balcony, but is wary of making a noise. It is just after two, when she's finally dozed off, that she is woken by Marion's eerie cries. She lies stock-still, but the woman thrashes, moans and weeps so pitifully in the clutches of her nightmare that Brenda goes to her, finds her way through the muslin to soothe her, to try to wake her up. Marion clutches at the hand that strokes her hair, clings for dear life and shudders with sobs. It would seem that she can't be woken out of her dream. She sits upright, stares wildly, and screams something that Brenda can make no sense of. Her terror is distressing, infectious; Brenda can do nothing but lie down on the bed and coax Marion into doing the same, hold her tightly in her arms, stroke the shaking shoulders, rest her cheek on Marion's face to keep her from rising. She whispers that everything's alright. Marion clings to her, until the taut, arched body finally stops shaking and the breathing subsides. Helpless as a baby, her arms are tightly wrapped around Brenda; her head rests on Brenda's breast.

Like lovers, they wake together. Still entwined, they are disturbed at dawn by the crashing noise of the garbage truck. For seconds they lie stock-still, then Marion disentangles herself limb by limb and rolls to the other side. With her back turned, she asks tersely, What are you doing here?

Brenda explains about the nightmare, of which Marion has no memory. In the light of day it all sounds very odd, Brenda realises, as if she has made it up. Well, I'm exhausted. Worse than sleeping with my mother, Brenda says. She feels guilty; she has lain close to this stranger without feeling a trace of the revulsion she feels for her mother's body. Briskly she gets out of bed. She'll make the coffee.

In the kitchen there is a bowl of peaches, which she prods for ripeness. Dare I eat a peach? Brenda calls theatrically, but doesn't listen to the muffled reply from the bedroom. I never understood it, she says, the idea of being challenged by a peach, but it's simple, isn't it? Refined people struggle with the possibility because of the juice that will dribble down their chins. So the answer to Prufrock is to eat the fruit before it's ripe, or to tackle it with a knife and fork.

Marion hobbles into the kitchen. Nonsense, she says, it's about eating fruit when it looks perfect, before it's over the hill – firm, perfect shape, perfect colour.

Brenda snorts. The gospel according to Saint Woolworths: packed in polystyrene and labelled ripe, when the rest of us know that ripeness doesn't go with looking perfect. She dips a couple of peaches briefly into boiling water and slips off the skins. In the glass bowl, in the light that slants into the kitchen, fur from the skin drifts on the water. I love the way it comes off, she says, holding the slippery, naked fruit between two fingertips before biting into it. She wipes the dribbling juice with the back of her hand.

My father never thought of that, Marion says. He hates the fur, but he thinks it's too wasteful to peel a peach; he will only eat nectarines. And my mother hated him for taking such pleasure in calling them kaalgat peaches.

Marion scrapes together the skins into a sorry pile. She stares at her peach; she cannot bring herself to eat it. Naked, slippery – that's me, that's who I am, she thinks. Hurled into the world fully grown, without a skin. But she cannot say this to a virtual stranger, a woman in pink Mickey Mouse pyjamas who sits at her kitchen table eyeing her coolly, who may or may not care for her, who waits for her to eat a peach. How much longer can they go on talking about peaches? Or the skin of peaches? What is she meant to say? She chants: Skin and bone, by the skin of one's teeth, skinflint, skin deep like beauty, thick skinned, thin skinned – can't think of any more skins.

You sound like Outa Blinkoog, Brenda says, and prods the lantern on the table.

What shall we do with it? Marion asks. Do you want to take it home? She holds it up to the light.

No, I've nowhere to put it; my mother won't want it in her lounge. It wouldn't go with her furniture and stuff. Brenda looks at Marion's foot. Hey look, the swelling's gone right down. That Mrs Murray is a witch if you ask me. Bet it doesn't hurt any more. With that she swipes the second peach, biting into it hurriedly.

Marion presses down onto her left foot, testing for pain. It does still hurt, but not a fraction as much; she's sure she could drive. Then Marion asks, Do you really think Mrs Murray's a witch? Was she having me on, making fun of me? Perhaps she was just trying to frighten me, or put me in my place? There is nothing she can do about the pleading tone that slips into her voice.

It's not for me to say. Only you know whether she was telling the truth or not.

Marion understands. You think I knew about Tokkie, about who she was. That I went there to get information about my family, and got caught out.

Well, why make up a ridiculous story about an old family servant? I feel a right fool. If you couldn't tell me the truth, you shouldn't have involved me at all.

So you think I'm a play-white; that I'm a fraud, that I lied to you – to the world?

Brenda pushes a cup of coffee towards her. Since you ask, yes, that's exactly it. What else could I possibly think? I mean, what's going on, what's your story?

And so she tries to tell all: the theft of the newspaper; the ghost of Patricia Williams; her father's lies; Tokkie's death and the oppressive silence, weeks of silence in that house where she crept under the bed to snuggle into the old woman's apron; the dry, white childhood; her recent belief that she was adopted; and now this terrible emptiness.

So it turns out you're coloured, from a play-white family, Brenda says. So what? Haven't you heard how many white people, or rather Afrikaners of the more-indigenous-than-thou brigade, are claiming mixed blood these days? It's not such a tragedy being black, you know, at least you're authentic. And just think of the other benefits: you need no longer speak in hushed tones – you're free to be noisy, free to eat a peach, a juicy ripe one, and free of the burdens of nation and tradition.

So that is how Brenda understands her emptiness: through race. Is that the only way to examine the human condition? But then, Brenda would say there is no such thing as the human condition, that there are only men and women with different backgrounds, and who therefore behave differently, according to their means. Is that really all Brenda is capable of, or is this all that she will or can allow? Perhaps she's being ironic, but Christ, how is Marion supposed to tell? What she does know is that she's being let down by a person she has begun to think of as a friend, as someone she could talk to, someone who would understand. So she says, perversely, That Mrs Murray, why should I trust her or believe what she says? And even if I do, this might not be the correct conclusion, she didn't exactly say ...

Marion will not say aloud: How am I to bear the fact that my Tokkie, my own grandmother, sat in the backyard drinking coffee from a servant's mug, and that my mother, her own daughter, put that mug in her hands? And she will not cry, even if these words are being swallowed like shards of glass.

Ag, Brenda scoffs, one shouldn't expect the messenger from beyond to spell things out, but then neither does one expect her to be a pink-frilled Murray. But that's the modern world for you. Not even poets can catch a glimpse of the winged feet of the god of secrets, which doesn't mean the old hag hasn't brought a message from your Tokkie; in fact, there's no need to think about Mrs Murray at all, as long as the story works. By the way, what happened to Annie Boshoff?

Any diversion in order not to engage with her plight, Marion thinks. She says that she doesn't know, can't remember, that they should get to work. They have exactly ten minutes in which to get ready.

When they get to the city, Brenda says that she'll get croissants for everyone, that Marion should drop her off. Thus they do not arrive together, and so avoid any questions.

$\mathcal{G}$eoff is terse, irritable. He doesn't believe that the trip came to nothing. Why did she switch off her cellphone, when she knew how anxious he was? Really, he'd thought of contacting the police.

All this on the telephone in the office, with Tanya making no attempt to disguise her interest, especially in Marion's irritable parting shot: So why didn't you contact the police?

The police, Tanya says over lunch, a no-good bunch, you just can't rely on them at all. Her sister-in-law had a break-in only last week and of course they called the police, although she would have advised them not to waste their time, and true enough, the cops turned up two days later or perhaps it was the next day, but anyway, a pair of them in such scruffy clothes one could swear they'd spent the night breaking into people's houses themselves. Not so long ago, you knew that you could rely on the police: the neatness that is so like godliness, pressed pants, nicely parted hair and always a comb kept in the sock. But nowadays smartness is the last thing you'd expect from that lot: the country is going to the dogs.

Tiena, who has to leave early today, is clearing away the dishes. She takes up the chant, quietly, ruefully: To the dogs, to the dogs, the country is going to the dogs.

Boetie adds that his dogs are driving him mad, they bark all night long at the skelms. The country is going to the dogs, he says.

So, have we all now got echolalia? Woof, woof, Brenda barks, so that Tiena jumps and giggles hysterically and Boetie says, Look who's swallowed a dictionary for breakfast, no wonder you've got indigestion. Brenda woof-woofs at him.

Marion, staring ahead, says nothing. Why, she wonders, are they all in the kitchen? But when she tries to speak, not a word issues from her lips. She slips into Boetie's chair, light and empty as a ghost.

You need a holiday, Tanya says sympathetically, a break from this place where everyone has gone crazy, acting like schoolkids.

Brenda has to be taken home that evening. Mrs Mackay insists that Marion stay for dinner, although it's nothing fancy, only pickled fish, but Marion has to be back. She's promised to have dinner with Geoff who, not knowing that she cannot tell him everything on the telephone, is hurt and bad tempered.

Geoff has, as they say, got the wrong end of the stick. They are at Alibi, where Marion has explained as plainly as she can about Mrs Murray's revelation. He says that it doesn't matter, that he along with the entire country has got beyond all that old stuff about race, and that she too should put it behind her. They've just had the first democratic elections. It's the New South Africa, almost a new century, a new groove, so what is she fretting about?

What was that, she asks, a new groove? He is a perfectly sensible person, so why the new vocabulary?

Geoff draws up his hands, fingers at the ready, and, with an absurd see-sawing of his shoulders, clicks his fingers by way of demonstration: grooving.

Groove? she says again, Groove? Then laughs for being stuck on the word, stuck in his groove.

It's simple, he says – and, thank God, drops his hands. You just go into that office tomorrow and make an announcement to everyone. It will do Boetie good to come to terms with it, he smirks. Actually, there we have a brilliant scenario for a training session ...

Okay, she interrupts. Can we talk about something else? She'd like to ask him to gloss the *it*. What precisely does he mean by the *it* that Boetie has to deal with? Instead she says, It's just – I think – you've got the wrong end of the stick.

She starts telling him about Outa Blinkoog, but it is surprising how little there is to tell. Have she and Brenda imagined the man? It is a mistake: her account of him is silly, a betrayal. Try as she may, she makes him sound clownish. Well, she says lamely, it was amazing, coming across him in the veld, like some kind of creature from another world. I can't explain.

Geoff says that with all this unemployment, especially in rural districts where farmers have had to cut down their workforces, there are many turned vagrant, dwaaling around the countryside and peddling their trinkets. But you should be careful, he warns; these people won't stand for being called outas and aias any more; you'll get yourself into trouble. Probably next time you see your man he'll be on stage at the Baxter, performing his tricks, telling his story – terribly in demand, these vagrants, now they've been discovered by fashionable artistic people.

She wonders if the barb is directed at her, but then she is neither a fashionable nor an artistic person.

The terrible feeling of emptiness persists, and Geoff too does not seem to be himself. She is, after all, not the person she thought she was, let alone the person he thought she was. It may be true that being white, black or coloured means nothing, but it is also true that things are no longer the same; there must be a difference between what things are and what they mean. These categories may have slimmed down, may no longer be tagged with identity cards, but once they were pot-bellied with meaning. The difference – that is what Marion cannot get her head around. How can things be the same, and yet be different? Is the emptiness about being drained of the old, about making room for the new? Perhaps it's a question of time, the arrival of a moment when you cross a boundary and say: Once I was white, now I am coloured. If everything from now on will be different (which is also to say the same), will the past be different too? Is that why she cannot tell about the meeting with Outa Blinkoog? This is how she tries to explain to Geoff.

Geoff laughs. Quite the cod philosopher you've become, that's the difference. But there must be thousands of play-whites who nowadays ...

Look, she interrupts vehemently, let's be accurate about this. My parents were the play-whites; *they* crossed over. I was white, now I will have to cross over; but if those places are no longer the same, have lost their meaning, there can be no question of returning to a place where my parents once were. Perhaps I can now keep crossing to and fro, to different places, perhaps that is what the new is all about – an era of unremitting crossings.

Geoff thinks that is too exhausting; it's a piece of nonsense, he says, perhaps utopian nonsense. You should be so lucky, he laughs, but without conviction. Is she theorising the rainbow nation?

They leave the restaurant and he loops his arm through hers. Under the deserted lamplight he spins her round; she twirls lightly, mechanically to an imaginary jig. At least, he says, things are cleared up. At least you know who Tokkie is.

Yes, Tokkie. Marion finds herself wincing at the name. Yes, she will spend the night with Geoff, for she is not yet ready to be left on her own. In her own apartment, a reading and writing lesson awaits her, but later, she promises herself, tomorrow, another day. Then she will spell out the word, whatever it may be: Grandmother, Grandma, Granny, Ouma, Mamma – a new word, naked and slippery with shame.

A man comes into the office just before they are about to close and asks Boetie if he is Mr Campbell. Tiena, peering from where she stands pressed against the kitchen wall, lets out something between a snort and a giggle, so that Marion looks up. Boetie blinks; he has been struck dumb by the thought of being Mr Campbell. Marion rises and, holding out her hand, introduces herself.

Vumile Mkhize, the man says, holding her card in his left hand. His is the black BMW she drove into some days ago. In town, in Long Street, he reminds her.

Yes, I know, she says, it was at the bottom of Long Street. The other car I drove into was in Scott Street, in Observatory – a Ford Cortina it was, and that was my first driving lesson. It was on my eighteenth birthday.

Not so long ago then, he says; and the man, who is tall and handsome and expensively dressed, laughs a deep, roaring belly-laugh that makes her start. It happens, he says, shit happens. The dent in my car was just the first of a number of terrible things that happened last week. That's why I didn't get in touch earlier.

The others are packing up, ready to go home. Marion, fearing that he might tell her of the terrible things that had happened and by way of making amends for her sarcasm, says she'll make some coffee. But the phone rings.

It is Geoff. She explains that Mr Mkhize is there about the car, the accident. Geoff says he'll be over right away, that he'll sort Mkhize out for her. No need, she protests; there's no problem. But no, he says, of course he'll be over. Does she think he'd leave her there alone with a stranger? Really, she ought to have called him.

Marion flushes. She hopes that Mkhize has not heard any of it, but when Geoff arrives she knows that the man cannot fail to infer that he has come to protect her. They have already agreed that she will simply pay the panelbeater's bill, the damage is nothing much. There is nothing for Geoff to negotiate, and thankfully he does not interfere. But Marion is embarrassed, she must make amends, or perhaps she is touting for business. She hopes that Mr Mkhize will pop in, should he be in the vicinity. Perhaps she could help out with air tickets, perhaps they could go for lunch, she says nervously. She gives him her card. He appears not to notice that he already has one in his left hand, and leaves clutching both the old crumpled card and the crisp new one.

$\mathcal{I}$t was still dark, still night, with the dense blackness that you did not get in town, where streetlight turned the night sky to a murky brown. John turned on the lumpy horsehair mattress to check the time, and the iron bedstead creaked; he looked anxiously across the room to where the child slept. She swallowed and muttered. In the dark he thought he could see the glow of her pale face, her golden hair: Marion, his darling mermaid. In the kitchen he heard the shuffling of his mother's feet on the linoleum, the sound of pots and pans. It was five o'clock. He crept out of bed, took the bundle of clothes and shoes, and dressed in the narrow passage.

The stove was already lit, logs glowing red in the lamplight, and the coffee beans in the pan were just beginning to discolour, releasing the aroma of his own childhood, so that when Ma came out of the pantry to give the pan a shake, he would have liked to bury his head in her aproned bosom. Instead, he said that it was early, that it was still darkest night outside.

Ag no my child, listen to the finches out in the willows – they've been busy for hours, their families already fed, and here I am still roasting the coffee.

In town, he said, the sky is brownish, never fully black.

Well, that's a pity. You won't be able to see the stars properly then.

No, he said, not much of a show of stars.

The truth was that he hadn't really thought about stars. What kind of boer was he, he chided himself, who didn't care about the night sky, who slipped so effortlessly into city life? Of course he belonged to this land, to the farm, and the next morning he would be out there with Pa, milking the cows, setting the cabbage seedlings. Now that they'd all left to make their livings elsewhere, his father had hired a boy from Bergplaas, but John should have remembered how much there was to do, should already have been out there on the land like a proper farmer.

One of these days I must come to town, said Ma, come and see how you people live there without stars. It's a disgrace that I've had to wait so long to see my own grandchild, and who knows when I'll see her next. That Helen of yours will think of some excuse why she can't come on the train with you. I don't know what's come over Helen, such a nice girl, shy and modest she was when you first brought her, but now so full of airs and graces, as if we're not good enough.

Ma-aa, he remonstrated feebly. There was nothing to say in defence of Helen.

Perhaps in the autumn, the old woman said, after the harvest, I'll come to town. But I don't like the train, you know; I'm too spoilt by the horses that do as they're told.

She was sitting with her legs astride, the coffee grinder on her lap, an old woman with painterly wrinkles, her right hand grinding with effort and her slanted eyes following the hand abstractedly, as if she'd forgotten that he was there.

Through the whirr of the grinder he said, Ma, you must come. You'd love a little holiday in town and have coffee brought to you in bed for a change.

John spoke from the heart. He meant every word, although he knew that she could not come to stay with him. But then, his mother would not really have been able to leave the farm, would in any case have found an excuse not to come. He would get another bed put into Marion's room, where Ma could have a lie-in. Early in the morning, at five, be-cause she was sure to be awake at that time, before Helen woke, he'd bring her coffee; he'd shut the door, and the three of them would sip cof-fee and dunk their rusks in that room sealed from the city and its devilish complications. For that was now city life, full of complications, but he had no trouble envisioning the impossible, substituting the cosy image of familial harmony. His heart lightened at the promise of such a visit.

So that Ma's next question pierced his heart. He did not even recognise that clipped dark voice, the angry eyes lifted from the grinder. Yes, Johnnie, so many of my children now in town, but what about you, hey? You are the eldest, their ouboeta; you should be keeping an eye on them. They are your blood brothers, your only sussie; your house should be the family home away from home.

He squirmed. Ag no Ma, don't spoil things now; Ma knows what a business it is there in town. Of course I see them all. Elsie will tell you how I drop in for Sunday lunch; she phones to say when the others are coming. Sussie Els is such a good cook, it's just like being here at Ma's table, and then we sit lekker together talking about the old days here on the farm. And she sometimes drops in at our house of an evening, she used to; she gets on quite well with Helen. You should see our Els, she is now a bliksem of a driver, just scoots all over town in that black Ford of theirs.

The old woman smiled briefly at his account of Elsie, who had married so well. If she'd ever had reservations about Fourie, they were quite dispelled by the image of her girl being so comfortable, so modern. But she shook her head as she put the cups of coffee and the plate of butter biscuits on the tray and said, My boy, I understand. These things may be necessary and God is good to his children and stepchildren alike, but it's a sin, the whole business is a sin. She looked at him anxiously. It is not enough to have money clinking in your pockets. You must go to church every Sunday, ask God's forgiveness, that's all we can do. So far God has been good to you, giving you this lovely little girl with golden hair, but you must be careful Johnnie, careful to keep an eye on your own flesh and blood.

He wanted to put his arms around her, to reassure her that things were not like that at all, that the world was changing, that life in the city made no such impossible demands of blood relatives. That bettering yourself, taking opportunity by the horns in a country where rules and regulations whizzed like so many darts about your head, could not be such a sinful thing. That the God of the city was not the demanding God of the farm. But she would not understand that, would not want to be hugged, had saved the softness of bodily contact for her grandchildren; she would not accept that human relations, or the demands of blood, could be different in the city.

When Pa came in for breakfast, he tossed the little girl on his knee. Marion squealed with delight, Again Pappa, more horsie-horsie! The old man fondled her golden hair, called her a demanding kleinnooi, and promised her a ride on a real horse the next day. Later, John took her up the ladder to the loft, where he turned the drying apricots and checked the biltong. Marion turned up her nose. It smells like the babbie's shop, she said. She did not want to touch the strips of drying meat. These things were nothing; the dangerous trip up the ladder was no longer so exciting. Who cared about a loft with a black door high on the side of the house, when tomorrow she and Pappa would fly through the land on horseback, on a real horse? She no longer wanted to be a mermaid; she wanted to be a horse. Could she not be a sea horse?

In the doorway of the loft they sat with their feet on the first rung of the ladder and surveyed the world. They could see the river lined with willows trailing their fingertips in the shallow water, and the proud weaverbirds darting in and out of their show homes. Which Marion, starting fearlessly down the ladder, had to visit right away. Now she was a bird darting hither and thither in a world without boundaries; she would fly off to the river. Ouma marvelled at her energy, at her belief that she could do as she pleased, be anything at all she fancied.

So that, said the old woman, forgetting her own indulgence of the child, that is what it's like being brought up as a kleinnooi.

John no longer minded that Helen could not take her holiday with them. He'd wanted to present Ma with a family, but now, suspecting that Helen did not want to come home to the farm, he was glad that they were on their own. It wasn't loyal, but without her he felt a loosening of his shoulders; here he could be himself, as they said, although he was not entirely sure what that meant. At least he was not responsible for the city traffic; he had a fond idea that the city would snarl up without his guidance, an image that developed into stationary motorists and pedestrians, all promiscuously tangled.

The child lay on her stomach, muttering to herself and trailing her right hand in the water. She'd found a clump of maidenhair fern with leaves of palest green, its partially exposed roots on the very edge of the riverbank, rooted in both earth and water. She held her dripping fingers aloft. Tears dripped from her fingers onto the leaves, so that the fern trembled from its watery roots, and with her left hand she gathered the leaves together like a bunch of garden carrots. Hush little baby, she crooned, don't you cry. Poor, poor little fern, hush for mummy; everything will be alright.

Had she heard them talking last night? Pa's tired, defeated voice: The Boere want the farm, John. It's the river – they want the water.

Ag no Pa, he'd said, everything will be alright; they won't, they just can't. You've been here so long, you've turned this piece of veld into land, into a farm; no, you mustn't worry.

His throat had tightened, stricken with panic, as he uttered the *they* who couldn't, who wouldn't. The Campbells were the ones who farmed this land, small as it was. They too were farmers, boere.

His father had looked at him with incredulity. No? Well, I'm just waiting for the papers. It will be no more than a year before the area is reclassified. You forget, the land belongs to old Serfontein, and he may not be happy about this business, but what can he do? The law is the law. We'll have to try for an erf in the Bergplaas area.

Bergplaas, John repeated in a thin voice. Bergplaas was just not a possibility, not amongst those raggedy hotnos. It was a stunning thought. His little golden girl could not be exposed to that. What on earth would he do?

God will guide us, his mother had said, resignedly. Bergplaas is not such a terrible place.

John had no quibble with God; he was as obedient, as fearful of God as the next man. But no, much as being home suffused him with guilt, he knew then with certainty that he'd taken the right course. Bergplaas, all higgledy-piggledy smallholdings, was really no more than allotments farmed by defeated coloureds – not on your nelly. He, John Campbell, would never be bullied like that by the law; and as for his child, his little mermaid, she would hold the world in the palm of her pretty hand.

Can I take it home, Pappie? she asked.

He started. No, no – what, the fern? Whatever will you do with it? It would rather be living here in the shade, sipping at the water.

But look, she said, worrying it like a loose milk tooth, it's crying, it doesn't want to go to Bergplaas, and I want to look after it. Then it will grow into the long hair of a mermaid.

So she tugged, and indeed the roots had lost heart and came up with an easy sound of suction. Back at the house, he helped her plant the maidenhair fern in a pot, an old milk pail painted red, that they found on the stoep and from which he shook the dusty corpse of another plant in order to make way for the new one. Ouma will look after it, Marion said.

Patting the child's head abstractedly, the old woman sighed, thinking how her chores seemed to multiply each day, how the smallest task had become such a burden. Already she saw in the fresh greenness of the fern the dried brown skeleton of each frond.

On the train home, John unpacked Ma's basket of fried chicken, ostrich biltong studded with coriander and heavy wheat bread for the overnight train journey.

I've written to Paul. He's at the police station in Mossel Bay, so smart in his uniform, Ma had said proudly. The train arrives at about eleven at night and stops for half an hour, so Paul will be there to see you. She packed a separate bag of biltong and biscuits for John to deliver to her fourth son.

He hadn't seen Paul for a couple of years; he chuckled fondly. Marion, tired of exploring once again the scaled-down, counterfeit world of the coupé – the wooden panelling that concealed a bed of green leather upholstery, the table unmasked to reveal a shiny little stainless-steel sink and a mirror in which to admire herself – was asleep. Which was a pity, since

Paul would so love to see her, would be charmed by her pretty kleinnooi speech. Paul would sit with them in their coupé, sipping Ma's coffee from the flask. They were so lucky to have a compartment to themselves. A coupé is nice and private, Helen had said, having made the reservation herself. Although he felt that it took the joy out of travelling if you didn't meet people, share in their outsiders' delight at the sweetness of the child. He liked a good old chat, and people would tell you all kinds of wonderful things about the world, about themselves – especially the new kind of people he met nowadays. Oh, it would be wonderful to see Paul, tall, dark and so handsome, full of jokes and rough talk, but with a heart of gold, oh yes, and John's eyes pricked at the thought of seeing his boetie.

It was not until the train puffed its way over the mountain and through George, and the lights across the bay winked feebly, that panic set in. How would Paul find him in that section of the train? John thought of Ma's pride in the khaki constable's uniform – but for all he knew Paul might even be a railway constable, patrolling the coloured platform, in which case he just didn't know how they would manage. Would he have to lean out of the window and somehow hail Paul down at the far end?

The squeal of the rails as the train puffed into the station tore through his heart; the acrid smell of coal and hissing steam were rough, squeezing hands around his throat. John pulled down the blind and switched off the light.

In the morning he gave the sullen bedding boy a bag of biltong and home-made biscuits.

$\mathcal{M}$arion sits cross-legged on the floor, leaning against her mother's dressing table, from which she has taken the Black Magic box. There is nothing among the meagre remains of Helen's possessions that gives anything away. Only a few photographs of Marion: as a baby, as a toddler, school photos, one in the garden with another child, but the photograph has been damaged, the other child's face scored. Only when she holds it closer, to the light, does she see that it is her old schoolfriend, Annie. There is one of Helen taken with Marion in an academic gown at her graduation at Stellenbosch. There is a single wedding photograph taken by a street photographer, the poverty of Helen and John's dress disguised by time, by the vagaries of taste and the charm of the old-fashioned – in fact, they look quite stylish. A registry office marriage without any guests, with no family. There is Helen's green identity card marked WHITE, with a photograph that does not do justice to her beauty. A marcasite necklace with a broken clasp, some of Marion's school reports, a couple of pink shells, a trashy earring. There is a scattering of dust-dry, crumbled leaves that once must have been a herbal sprig – of wild thyme, Marion would like to think, a bunch picked in the veld, in the fading light when the herb still warm with sun releases its fragrance. Surely picked in the Wuppertal of her childhood. Marion sniffs hungrily, but there is of course not the faintest trace of smell – the plant will tell no story of the past.

None of these things, much as she studies them, turns them this way and that, yields any meaning, any insight into the past or into the mind of the woman of whom she knows so little. She had hoped for a photograph of Tokkie, perhaps in her wicker chair in the backyard, but there is no such thing. Anger and shame rise like heartburn in her throat. Marion bites her lip. She is rifling through the rubbish of a calculating woman with no conscience, no heart, no shame: Helen Karelse, alias Helen Charles, her mother.

She rises stiffly from the floor; she has taken only a faded Sunday-school card with a picture of two bearded men in biblical garb poring over a book while a lamb lies at their feet. It is the only thing that puzzles her, especially since the image does not illuminate the text. Pious trash: she can't believe that it was meant to be attractive to children. She shouldn't expect it to make sense, but believing that everything about Helen is imbued with hidden meanings, she takes it to her father all the same to see if he knows why Helen had kept it, if it meant anything special. But John doesn't know.

Since she confronted him earlier that evening, his throat has given in; his voice is rough, almost a whisper, and it is an effort to hear him. Marion pulls her chair up so that they sit close together. Through the lace curtain, it would seem that she leans tenderly towards him.

Her cold anger frightens him. It is not easy to summon that past that they had so long ago suppressed, indeed for a while he simply did not know what she was talking about. So thoroughly had their lives moulded into the fiction, there was barely anything to recall. What they had done had slowly lost its meaning, as a table might weather with time and use and eventually be relegated to the garden shed. But Marion is stern; she spreads his story like a broadsheet before him – he who has no time for newspapers, who does not find such things easy to read. But it is not his story; rather, it is her constructed version, so that he must correct the details. They were not the monsters she seems to think they were; that was just how the world was.

When John first met Helen, she had a collection of such Sunday-school cards kept in a chocolate box, but he does not think it the same box. It may have been red; it was smaller and contained other girlish trifles. Later, when they were married, with new identity cards, he thinks she burnt the box of treasures. He knew of her childish attachment to the collection; probably to do with calf love, with a boy at Sunday school – that's what he thought at the time, but she would not admit to it. Helen was meticulous: the cards bore the stamp of the Moravian Mission Church. See, he says, pointing to a faded, barely perceptible smudge on the back below the text. He has no idea why she kept this one, unless the stamp was illegibly smudged from the start, so the card held no risk at all.

Marion reads the text aloud:

'As a sheep led to his slaughter or a lamb before his shearer is dumb, so he opens not his mouth. In his humiliation justice was denied him. Who can describe his generation? For his life is taken up from the earth.'

— Acts 8 verse 22

No, John shakes his head. He feels dizzy with the attempt to concentrate, but no, he doesn't understand it, doesn't understand what it means or could have meant to her.

Marion laughs bitterly. Imagine giving children such nonsense to learn by heart, with pictures of bearded men who look like terrorists, except they're white. And surely there is a difference between a sheep being shorn and being slaughtered. Why are they conflated here? No wonder the two of you, led by stupidity, lost the plot, she says cruelly.

John is tempted to say that it was not his fault, that he'd never meant things to go so far, but it would be cowardly to blame Helen. Ag my liefie, he begs, it's late. He is worried by her irreverence, her godlessness, which, he supposes, must be his fault. Can't you let it be now? There was so very little to this business of identity cards. It was so long ago and there was nothing to it really. I'm sorry you're so upset, but can't you see it wouldn't have worked, it wouldn't have been right to tell you, to get you all worried about things. We just did what we thought best for you.

Marion knows that. What precisely she is enraged about is not clear, but rage is preferable to emptiness. She has to remind herself: *He is your father.* These words that echo in her ears issue from something obsolete, a prelapsarian world of kitsch Sunday-school cards that no longer have any value. An impulse to hurt him throbs deep inside like a heartbeat; she would like to place him under a searing electric light and fire questions – like the death-squad commandant with Patricia Williams.

He is your father. The words may not mean what they meant before. Yet they do have a blind force. She pours him a glass of brandy and bends to kiss him on the head. Yes, she says, you should go to bed. We'll talk another time.

He wants to ask when she'll come again, but he does not have the courage. All is topsy-turvy; he is the child at her mercy, hungry for her forgiveness.

Marion does not have a Bible. The next day she spends her lunch hour in the National Library. She is irritated afresh by the Sunday-school card: they didn't even get it right. The text is indeed from Acts 8, from the wonders and signs and miracles of the Apostles, but the verses are 32 – 34 and they refer to an Ethiopian eunuch being converted by someone called Philip. Were all the texts printed on the cards in quotation marks? Did her mother know that the eunuch is in fact quoting from Isaiah? That the repetition is about the fulfilment of a prophecy? Her guess is that Helen learned her texts by heart without questioning – which, after all, was the point of Sunday-school cards: that memorising texts would displace impious thoughts and so cleanse the soul. Helen would not have known what it meant, would not have looked it up; would not, in fact, have known what a eunuch was. Most likely it was a case of being drawn to the sentimental image of men from bygone days in their long white frocks, and the conventional connotation of the white lamb of God. The card leads nowhere. There are no leads. Marion is struck by the paucity of her parents' lives.

She is not comfortable in libraries. She knows them to be silent, inhospitable places, defended by the custodians of knowledge from the noisy ignorance of the public. As children, she and Annie Boshoff spent much time in Observatory library. There were no books in their homes. But once, for a whole month, they were banned for giggling at an instructive passage about kissing in a book Annie had found. They would practise the kissing later at home, Annie said, but, chastened by the stern librarian, they never did; they pretended to have forgotten. Even as an adult at university, where in any case she could never find anything in the library, anxiety gripped her chest like asthma. But here, the woman in navy blue who has noted her look of defeat and disappointment asks so soothingly, so kindly whether she can be of any help, that without hesitation Marion says yes, she would like to find out about play-whites.

The librarian shows her how to use the old-fashioned index cards, but there are no entries for play-whites. Hang on lovey, the woman says; she is puzzled, and does the search herself, but none of the possibilities leads anywhere. Play-white, they imagine, must be a condition of whiteness; but whiteness itself, according to the library's classification system, is not a category for investigation.

We will have to look up coloureds, the woman in navy blue says sheepishly. Which doesn't make sense, but what else can they do? There are indeed hundreds of entries on coloureds, but, not surprisingly, they do not address the condition of play-whites. Like Helen's chocolate box, the National Library search produces a blank.

The librarian is intrigued; she urges Marion to stay, to persevere. At least they can look up the classification law itself. The kind woman, who has curly grey hair, plump cheeks and sensible shoes, is nothing short of motherly, and Marion has to admonish herself for having become such a sissy, for wanting to bury her head in the strange woman's bosom and sob over that motherliness.

Together they pore over the laws and confusing racial definitions. The 1946 franchise laws allowed mixed blood in one parent or grandparent, but the new bill of 1950, designed to formalise and fix the categories of coloured and white, conflicted with the earlier one. Coloureds could now elect European representatives to the House of Assembly, but many whites who until then had thought of themselves as European were in the fifties transferred to the newly established separate coloured voters' roll. On the other hand, Act No. 30 of 1950 defined a 'white person' as:

> one who in appearance obviously is, or who is generally accepted as a white person, but does not include a person who, although in appearance obviously a white person, is generally accepted as a coloured person.

Marion cannot make sense of the Population Registration Amendment Act of 1962. The librarian reads aloud the amended definition:

> A 'white person' is a person who (a) in appearance obviously is a white person and who is not generally accepted as a coloured person; or (b) is generally accepted as a white person and is not in appearance obviously not a white person, but does not include any person who for the purposes of classification under this Act, freely and voluntarily admits that he is by descent a native or a coloured person unless it is proved that the admission is not based on fact.

But is that any different, Marion asks, from the 1950 Act? She reads it again, more slowly; she looks at the woman's puzzled expression, and then she hears shocking laughter pealing from her own throat. The librarian lifts an admonishing palm, purses her lips to silence Marion, but it is not long before she too succumbs to laughter. In vain they try to stifle the sound; they stagger drunkenly between the aisles before sliding with the heavy tomes onto the carpeted floor, where they rock with quiet laughter. Tears stream down their faces. There are decades worth of folly trapped in these pages.

Must have been a hell of a confusing time, between the fifties and sixties, when whiteness was not yet properly defined, the librarian says. This amendment suggests fear that whiteness might be undermined if people go about speaking of their black blood.

Marion notes that the amendment, unlike the original, defines whiteness in terms of what it is not. How very odd. Should one infer that some people who had been classified white were subsequently, and bizarrely, either insisting on their native heritage or falsely claiming black blood? And how extraordinary that the state should want to investigate, and insist on people's whiteness where such claims were proven to be false.

What they cannot understand, what does not make sense, is why those who had or who achieved the desired status of white identity, with all its privileges, would then repudiate that identity. Surely the scramble for whiteness made such a clause unnecessary, and surely such claims could only have been private utterances? They cannot imagine circumstances under which people would freely and voluntarily admit to being coloured – or, for that matter, circumstances that would require such an admission, in which case it would hardly be free or voluntary. There must have been a conscientious race squad, dedicated to rooting out flaws in the classificatory system.

It could be, says the woman – whose name Marion wishes she knew, but it is far too late now to ask – that the state was concerned about losing people who were white, or European as we called ourselves in those days. Even in the seventies and eighties, there were Nationalist campaigns to boost the white population, she explains, and that while Depo-Provera was being given free of charge to rural blacks. Yes, there were slogans like Babies for Botha, if I remember correctly – chivvying the tannies to reproduce themselves for the nation. Anyway, lovey, thank God it's all over, all ancient history, and we needn't bother our heads about that nonsense any more. I must be getting on. Only a couple of months left now before I retire, she whispers confidentially.

In the corridor, Marion takes the wedding photograph out of her handbag to look again at the country-shy couple who betrayed their families, who obliterated their histories, who stripped themselves of colour to be play-whites. According to the National Library, they did not exist. Did they think of themselves as dissidents, daring to play in the light? Or as people who could mess up the system, who could not be looked up in libraries, who had escaped the documentation of identity? She thinks not. They thought only of their own advancement.

Play-whites: a misnomer if ever there was one. There was nothing playful about their condition. Not only were they deadly serious, but the business of playing white, of bluffing it out, took courage, determination, perseverance, commitment – the list of qualities from which schoolteachers draw up end-of-year reports for star pupils like Helen. Not even in the privacy of their home, between their own four walls, could they let up, act the fool, laugh at those who'd been duped, or mimic their public selves. In the blinding light of whiteness, they walked exposed: pale, vulnerable geckos whose very skeletal systems showed through transparent flesh. With a child to raise, a public-private distinction was a luxury they could not contemplate; the public selves required all their energies. Playing – as others would call it – in the light left no space, no time for interiority, for reflecting on what they had done. Under the glaring spotlight of whiteness, they played diligently, assiduously; the past, and with it conscience, shrunk to a black dot in the distance.

Play? Play-whites? Helen repeated with puzzlement, years later to John who had been drinking, and who'd dared to say the word. What on earth was the man talking about?

In the beginning, when John spoke to his sister Elsie about his fears, she said that there would be no problem. He just had to be himself – there need be no difference, it was only a matter of stupid laws. But Elsie was wrong. He supposed he might have been himself when he visited her, which is to say his old self, but even then, how could he be sure? By then, the self was already a mended structure; it was a matter of mixing as best you could your own mortar with which to fill in the cracks that kept on appearing.

Helen thought that he had the wrong model. Yes, being newly white was a deadly serious business, but it was a pity that he thought about himself in such old-fashioned terms. There was bound to be some stumbling and swaying until they found their feet, fixed the lineaments of the new roles; fluidity was precisely what they needed. Keeping alert, checking which way the wind blew, seeing how the land lay – all needed for shaping themselves to their own advantage. Vigilance was the key; it would take time and steadfastness to stand their ground. There was indeed nothing playful about that, nothing of the levity of the Rembrandt Van Rijn Variety Show, written up in the *Times*, which they were now qualified to see.

They did not exchange anecdotes about close shaves. If there were cold shivers when colleagues talked about hotnos or uppity coloureds, they did not tell each other, did not giggle about it in their bedroom, for that space had lost its privacy too; instead, they learned to use the vocabulary of the master race, were the first to note with distaste the traces of native origins in others. Ja nee, hottie se kind, the child would hear them say to each other in rare conspiratorial moments, but then it meant nothing, just grown-ups' talk which found its way into her own understanding of a world shaped by colour and the mystery of roots.

Playing in the light? Perhaps not, Marion thinks. More like hiding – hiding in the light. For without education, which brings not only knowledge and understanding of mores and manners, but above all confidence, that timid pair in the surrounding glare of whiteness must surely have been recognised as play-whites. For the first time, Marion feels a flash of sympathy for her parents, scuttling anxiously in the light, for Helen, who never got to see a single Variety Show.

Campbell, that is what Helen came to call him. Clean forgot his first name. And issuing from her lips, by now a Cutex vermilion, he heard his name as no more than a fibre caught between her teeth, stripped of its status. The syllables summoned the past: the smell of an ash heap, the longdrop lavatory, the Sunlight soap that lingered in shirts short of another rinse in summer, when the river was a mere trickle. She brought back the horror of schooldays, of the barefoot boy in khaki shorts stuttering over the r's of the English verse he could not recite: I re-remember, I re-remember / The house where I was born / The little window in the er er brow ...

It was the pregnancy that Helen held against him. Having avoided it for twelve years, the pregnancy unleashed a hatred she found impossible to hide. It was all his fault; he was an animal who had ruined their lives. John thought that it would pass. All would be well once the child was born; he could not see why there should be any problem with the child's looks. Which was typical of his thoughtlessness, his irresponsibility, she said; and by the time the child arrived with pale skin and smooth hair she was too addicted to anxiety to be relieved. Helen foresaw further problems: the child's hair would grow into a mass of frizzy curls; she would be slow to learn, mentally retarded; she would become a kaffirboetie – until she decided that such ironies need not be taken lying down, that she would fight back. The child at least would not be racked by fear and insecurity. She would grow up in ignorance, a perfectly ordinary child who would take her whiteness, her privileges, for granted. Far from being punished, Helen would see her project completed in the child. Of Campbell she could expect nothing, but Helen at least would never let up. If fear gnawed at her viscera, it was her duty to appear confident. Polished and self-assured, her Afrikaans vowels grew rounder and drawn out as a lady's, while her English came on very nicely thanks to the SABC. And with pinkish pancake make-up applied even on Sundays, she held her poise throughout the long, anxious days of watching over the child's progress.

As the manager of an exclusive linen shop in the city – the best, actually, in the country – Helen's knowledge of napery, of linen and fine embroidery was sought after; her advice on trousseaus was what posh young women embarking on marriage came to depend on. So who could blame her for finding her own bedroom, so devoid of lace and broderie anglaise, distasteful? Under the thin cotton sheets she turned gingerly, careful to avoid Campbell, who in his sleep tried to trap her feet between his own. There was no spare bedroom into which she could move – that was occupied by the baby, with whom he was besotted. He wanted to call the child Marina, seeing as they were in Cape Town surrounded by the sea, and seeing that he could not very well call her Mermaid.

Marina, she scoffed, that's not a name. Only hotnos give their children stupid names like that. Don't you know what a marina is? It's a place where rich people keep their pleasure boats, a place that is not meant for traffic cops. So they settled for Marion, and only in private did he call the lovely little girl Marina, Marientjie, his darling mermaid.

John stopped going to church, even as Helen was establishing herself as the model parishioner on whom Father Gilbert could always count.

He would rather worship on his own, he announced, rather listen to the Dutch Reformed Church on the radio. It was no fun sitting there among the snooty parishioners of the Anglican Church, the Scots and Irish who called themselves English – so confusing – and who grinned awkwardly at his jokes before turning away. No sense of humour, plain rudeness; what his Ma, who may be a plain old tannie, would call vulgar. Do these people not know who they are, calling themselves English? At least the Boere know that they're Afrikaners, South African.

Helen flew at him. Fun? No fun? What makes you think that fun has anything to do with it, anything to do with this new life, this life of luxury that I've carved out for us? You've just fallen with your bum into fresh butter and you dare talk about fun?

John started at her outburst. She was not one for using rough language, so he'd better not say anything, although he had his doubts about the butteriness of their lives. Never mind, all he knew was that he was never again going to set foot in the blarry snobbish English church with its incense and silly chanting. He couldn't be accused of not trying. With Helen he had studied the Anglican Book of Common Prayer, familiarised himself with the rituals, the restless bobbing up and down from kneeling to sitting positions. Surely prayers should be either spoken or sung; the inbetweenness of chanting made them sound half-hearted. No, enough was enough; there was just no beating the plain old khaki-clad God of his childhood, whom he was sure would have no truck with the pretences of the parish church of St Luke's.

John simply did not pay enough attention. He fell short of her vision; he did not take the task of reinvention seriously. Innocent of the nuances of whiteness, he settled into ignorant complacency. I *am* mos a Boer, he said with conviction, and while there may not have been, in cultural terms, much to choose between coloureds and rural Afrikaners, the affinities blinded him to the finer points of advancement in the city. He was content to be mistaken for a Boer. Indeed that was what had sparked the idea of becoming white – not an act of imagination on his part, no, merely a happy case of mistaken identity. And so he would not attend to his language, believed that there was no reason to clean up the scatological that peppered his speech, for that, he said, is precisely what proved he was Boer, that was how they all spoke at the Traffic Department. But why, she pleaded at first, why settle for being Boer when you could be anything at all? By which she meant English.

It was in ignorance, not knowing that the job of traffic cop was reserved for whites, that he had gone to the Traffic Department in Green Point; and the superintendent, a plattelander himself, heard with nostalgia the sunburnt young man's rough, rolling r's as the language of a white farmer. With his shoulders held back, and drawn to his full height, for that was how a traffic cop should hold himself, it finally dawned on John, when the man spoke passionately about job reservation for whites, that he was being mistaken for one of them. It was important to keep up standards, the superintendent explained. A city can't function without good traffic control, it is its very heartbeat, and once you slacken on discipline, let coloureds into the system, things can only go downhill. It was a practised speech, newly debated in the Traffic Department where the orthodox position prevailed: it would be an affront, it simply did not make sense for a coloured cop to reprimand his betters; and motorists were, after all, predominantly white.

John, who had been caught on the hop, settled for a feeble test: Ja-nee Oubaas, he said to the kindly superintendent – although the Campbells would never, not in a million years, have called a white man baas – we can't have any messing about with the heartbeat of the city, can't have any clotting in the donderse arteries. I'm your man for keeping the blood flowing, he said, running with the metaphor. The boss did not flinch at the Oubaas, read it as an affectionate mark of respect rather than a sign of racial deference, and shook the enthusiastic young man's hand. And that was that. Try-for-white? A piece of nonsense. There was no question of needing to try on his part. Caught accidentally in a beam of light, he watched whiteness fall fabulously, like an expensive woman, into his lap.

Or so he thought. What Campbell failed to understand was that that was not enough. To be like a bywoner in the city, a poor white in a safari suit who betrayed his humble farming origins every time he spoke – well, what was the point of settling for that? Helen wanted to know. She'd read his triumph at the Traffic Department as an epiphany. It was a gift, a sign from above that they should set about the task of building new selves, start from scratch and not be content with what happened accidentally. The fine linen shop had alerted her to the many shades of whiteness, and there was no need to settle for anything other than the brightest. Which made him shudder, but so enchanted was he by the lovely young woman he had chosen, that he did not object to her bothersome plans.

Helen Karelse was indeed lovely. She was fair skinned and rosy cheeked, with copper-coloured hair and a cuprous flexibility to match. And she was clever, adapting easily to city ways. She realised within days that to anglicise her name would rid it of the nasty possessive. Could it be that these Afrikaans names that ended with -se spoke of an unspeakable past, of being the slave of someone called Karel? Becoming Helen Charles was as easy as she thought it would be. It was simply a way of claiming her liberty, especially since nice coloured people, those with at least good hair, would have nothing to do with Afrikaans. No, Campbell's success at the traffic depot was more than a revelation; it was also a reward for her own forward thinking, a helping hand on the path she had in a sense already chosen.

Helen Charles had been in the city for three months only, a lodger in the Bates's respectable coloured home, where she puzzled over the bed's second sheet – indeed, went to sleep lying on top of it, feeling the customary, comforting roughness of blankets, before the explanation dawned upon her: another sheet to protect against that roughness. For Helen, that midnight moment of staggering out of sleep, out of the bed, to perform for the first time what is known as slipping between the sheets, was a decisive one. Then, wide awake, she knew that there was no need for half measures, for sending John off daily into a white world of lies and evasions only to return to darkness in the evenings. She would secure new identities for both of them. But first they had to marry. There was no point in being known in the coloured neighbourhood when, frankly, there was no future in attachments to such people, when the new lives she envisaged demanded a clean slate. As for the poor-white estate across the railway line, from where barefooted children threw stones at the coloured houses, shouting Swartgat, swartgat, that too was an object lesson. That raggedness was not what she had in mind at all.

And so it came about: the hasty marriage without family or friends; the embarrassing coloured photographer in Bree Street who danced about them, sensing the occasion and drawing their images in light; the bold application for a job as white saleslady in the city; and the retreat to Observatory without giving her address to anyone. Not even to Mrs Bates. They were going to live in a couple of rooms where she could not possibly entertain anyone; besides, they would only be there temporarily.

Helen, leaning against Mrs Bates's glass-fronted sideboard, heard the clink of ornaments as she said goodbye, promising to come and see them soon. And when they moved to their own place – it wouldn't be long – she hoped that the Bateses too would come to visit. It was not too hard to utter these words: she genuinely would not have minded seeing the light-skinned, respectable Mrs Bates again; it was just that circumstances would not allow, that her destiny pointed in an altogether different direction. The expensive ticket to the tennis club dance at the Majestic Hotel, which the Bateses had kindly bought for her, she slipped under a doily on the sideboard. She had indeed looked forward to it, her first dance. John was not interested, but Mrs Bates had said that Helen, with her lovely cop-per hair, belonged in that set of socialites, the coloured elite, and that the Bateses would be happy to take her along. Mr Bates would teach her the steps and a graceful girl like herself would soon get the hang of it, would have no lack of partners. It would have been a terrible waste not to use the ticket. Helen banked on God's understanding and forgiveness, which after all she needed only to see them through, like a bank loan, until they were established in their new lives.

In the early days of their marriage they lay in bed on Sundays, drinking ready-ground coffee with chicory at five in the morning: country folk who woke with the first lick of pink in the sky, who did not know how to sleep in, how to stay in bed after sunrise. John winced at the Koffiehuis coffee; soon he would take her to the farm, where his mother roasted and ground the coffee herself each morning. In the rented rooms – no more than refurbished servant's quarters, but in a decent white area – she hatched detailed plans for their new lives: they would buy their own house, move up the slope of the mountain where they could see the curve of the bay, and speak English.

He said that it was too hard, that he simply could not get his tongue around the hand and tand of a language that required you to part your jaws so unnaturally wide.

In those days, Helen laughed. There's no such word as tand, she said, it's tooth, and there is no such thing as can't.

Besides, Campbell was a respectable English name, or possibly Scottish, as his father seemed to think; they would just be taking their rightful place in the world. It was all very well being a Boer, but in this business flexibility was important. This was not the platteland; to advance in the city you must also be able to pass as English, or at least try to keep a foot in both camps. They would have a big garden and a coloured boy called Hans to mow the lawn. Only, they would not be able to afford any children. Reproduction was too risky a business and besides, there was nothing so special about doing what any sheep or donkey could do.

John laughed appreciatively at her cleverness, but he treated these details as idle talk, like the game they played as children – looking at a magazine and scrambling for the desirable goods with every turn of the page, pointing at the cars and tractors and lorries. I pick this one, was the utterance by which you laid your claim, while at the same moment being the first to place your finger on the picture, and for the duration of the game, those representations were as real as silver coins. When a couple of years later he asked about children, she looked at him with pity and distaste: Campbell, she said, you just have no idea. And indeed, he had no idea how she had so cleverly managed their new identity cards.

Helen's heart sank at the paucity of his ambition. He was wedded to a boy's vision of a smart uniform and a powerful motorbike, vroom-vroom on his Harley-Davidson as he set off to control the chaos at the cross-roads, waving a white-gloved hand for all the world like the English queen. It was not that he did not cut a handsome figure, and in the early years of her marriage she was proud of him, but he was not interested in changing his rough ways. People would have to put up with him, voet-stoots as the property agents said, and he spread his thighs comfortably. She could not forgive Campbell for taking things so easy, for appearing to relax into whiteness as if it were nothing. He had a decent name which he ought to live up to, and she shuddered at the memory of an adolescent crush on a boy called Willemse, with the giveaway possessive.

If history was on their side, reinvention was nevertheless a slow proc-ess of vigilance and continual assessment. Helen would settle for no less than respectable whiteness, certainly not for a destiny determined by the vagaries of their distant European ancestors. If that lot could sink so low as to consort with hotnos and slaves, as to fuck with hotnos – as she took to saying in a lowered voice after the business with the identity cards – she would redeem them, and naturally in such a crusade there would be suffer-ing involved, sacrifices to be made. Years later, as she looked at Campbell with distaste, at his bent shoulders, the flap of hair that at her insistence he plastered with Brylcreem across his pate, she felt no more than a rush of self-pity.

History was on their side. It was the Population Registration Act that allowed them brand new lives. Before long, they had their own little ter-raced house in Observatory, nothing as swish as she had hoped for, but there was time enough for a detached house with a broekielaced veran-dah and a view of the sea, and Helen was proud of it – until she suspected the neighbours of being coloured. There was nothing to be done but to hold her head high and refuse to socialise with people who could not keep their bargain with history.

In their home, all the loose ends were tied, the rules established. Campbell had won the battle of Afrikaans schooling for the child. So that he ought to have known better than to badger her about his sister Elsie.

Once the child arrived, well, it was obvious that it was in her interest not to be burdened with such relations or be taken to strange neighbourhoods. Such knowledge would only make the child insecure, and indeed, it was wonderful to see her grow up so confident in her whiteness.

John had to confess that his little mermaid was as self-assured as any Boeremeisie. The posh school brought the miracle of new knowledge, the lovely drawn-out vowels and Boere songs: Daar kom die wa, die vier perdewa, hy het nie naam nie, sy naam gaan hy nog kry. Talientjie swaai, stadig draai ... and she twirled cutely in her fully gathered dirndl, and curtsied. Swinging her on his knee, John told his Marientjie of the farm and the horse-drawn wagon that he steered over the barren wastes of the Groot Swartberge. But he couldn't help wondering if the anonymous wagon of her song represented their kind, waiting for a name. Why did the promise of a name to be given later sound so much like a threat?

Helen's mother doted on her pale-skinned, skinny child with rosy cheeks and tints of copper in her hair. She held the little girl on her knee to tilt her head so that Helen hung upside down like a ragdoll – to show others how, when the sunlight caught her hair at a certain angle, it glinted with reddish-golden lights, and how the roots held no telltale frizz. Those distant genes from Europe will out, and that child was the chosen one. So Helen knew that Mamma, who was forward-looking herself, would be delighted with the new identity cards, would see that they were the only way out.

It was Mamma's idea to wear the funny wrap-around apron when she came to visit at the new terraced house, to use the back gate; that way, in the role of servant, she could visit every week and at the same time provide a history of an old family retainer, which the types who were working their way up in that part of Observatory could not boast of. Helen did not think it was necessary, but Mamma insisted that one could not be too careful with neighbours. Older than her fifty-five years, Mamma sat on the wooden bench in the backyard with her feet apart and elbows planted comfortably on her knees. Wednesday was her day off as a housekeeper for the grand Macdonalds in Constantia. Helen would rather she gave up the job, would rather provide – although of course she could not afford the full wages, as the Macdonalds were fabulously rich – but Mamma wouldn't hear of it. Mamma was also supporting her dead sister's son, putting him through college, and besides, her quarters in Constantia were nothing short of lovely. In the Observatory backyard she sipped coffee from an enamel mug, which embarrassed Helen. But no, Mamma said, it was her favourite mug; she'd had it for years, and there was after all so little to this walk-on role as servant to lesser whites that she enjoyed playing the part.

How often in that Constantia drawing room did she imagine her own darling Helen, sitting on the sofa with her long legs elegantly crossed, having tea with dumpy Mrs Macdonald? She was able to advise Helen on matters of décor and taste. The Constantia garden could easily be repli-cated in Observatory – in miniature, of course, since the Macdonalds had acres of land. So she brought cuttings, took pride in rooting bits of stem. Helen was mad about a velvet corsage of flowering pelargonium that she wore on her lapel, and Mamma not only gave it to her, but brought a cutting of the exact shade of velvet maroon for the garden. Also fran-gipani that Mamma had nursed on her windowsill. Campbell, who was in charge of the garden, uncommonly large for such a small house, pro-tested; he wanted the space at the end for vegetables. Frangipani grows into a blarry tree, he said, but Helen sulked. She did not want pumpkins or beans. In the city, one simply had to have a flower garden.

When Helen fell pregnant, her mother brought cuttings of lavender and wilde als. It was important to keep her nerve, Mamma said, patting the wood of the bench, just keep calm and steady and all will be well, all will come right, she soothed. They sipped the lavender infusion at the kitchen table. The wilde als was for nausea. Mamma had had such a time of it with carrying her other child; without als tea she didn't think she would've survived. Which quite undid the benefit of the lavender, as Helen thought anxiously of her brother's dark skin. She had not seen him for a number of years, although she always sent a modest gift at Christmas, just a small token, because they barely knew each other by now. It was only years later that her mother said there was no point, that Thomas, speaking about this or that, always tossed the prettily wrapped gift into the rubbish bin without opening it, without even interrupting his sentence. Why did Mamma choose to tell after all these years? Helen was angry; she would have preferred to go on sending the little Christmas presents.

What will the child call you, Helen whispered, as the first contractions came, and Mamma said without hesitation, Tokkie, just plain old Tokkie, that's what your father called me, and she smiled fondly. Your father was a real gentleman. Helen remembered very little of that father, who had died when she was eight years old. She thought his hair had been good, his eyes green and his skin of ruddy complexion, but could she be sure? It did not seem right to ask Mamma, whose complexion was so very dark. So she abandoned herself to the pain, in terror and fury, for it was Campbell's fault that the baby was on its way. Campbell, who laughed his carefree belly laugh, said there was nothing to worry about, his people had good European blood, which was of course nonsense. She thought of the baby as an uninvited guest, arriving with an extraordinarily large, cheap suitcase that bumped along through the birth canal.

*T*homasina, she had been christened, but from the very first he called her Tokkie. That was Flip Karelse, a handsome, light-skinned man with dreamy hazel eyes. She had no choice but to act haughty, hold her head high and look right through him, coldly, since such people as the Karelses would not think her good enough. So he called her Tokkie, to take her down a peg or two, to teach her humility, and to force her to look at him. She told him of her own blood, her mother's sister who was white as driven snow with good red hair, but he laughed. He was no butcher; what did he care about blood or skin?

Flip, who was smart, was already the foreman when she left school and came to work at the shoe factory. She would've liked to have gone away to high school, but there simply wasn't the money: too many young ones left in the family to get through primary school. Flip liked her for her cleverness, for her way with words; he said he could listen to her all day, that for one so young she was astonishingly cheeky, and skilful with the leather to boot. She was astonished to find how much better that was than being thought beautiful, although he claimed to be smitten by her looks, but that came much as an afterthought, one she took, at first, with a pinch of salt. How could he possibly value what he called her long slender limbs, her delicate facial bones, her almond eyes, all black as the night? But it turned out that he did; that, watching her handling the sheets of hide as he checked her work, his eyes lingered over the nimble movements, the expressive hands that continued working effortlessly as she modulated her careful speech. Yes, she expected to finish the batch by lunchtime, that was if someone did not keep her from doing so with idle talk.

And so she stopped dreaming of high school, of the proper navy-blue school tunic with a girdle knotted like a man's tie that she once saw in a magazine, and instead came to love being at the factory.

The veldskoen may be a rough-looking artefact scorned by city dwellers accustomed to the finish of fancy shoes, the fashion of this year's ankle strap or tapered toe, but for Tokkie it had the beauty of the functional, of having been fashioned by her own hands. She loved to feel under her fingertips the texture of tanned leather, its warm peppery smell, red-brown as the sunny earth. The animal shape of the hides, of bluntly severed head and legs, came to life under her touch, so that she winced as she wielded the knife around the template. They learned it all, the entire process from hide to shoe. Tokkie breathed the smell of leather deep into her lungs; she thrilled with pride at her first shoe, at the transformation marked by its different smell, somehow redolent of her own body's toil. Before leaving in the evening, she checked the rows of finished shoes, lingered over the size fives – her own, she guessed. In such a shoe, as if by X-ray, she saw the human foot, imagined a slender black ankle that turned, broadened to a foot that flattened then tapered towards five perfect toes. The curved sole, tough and yet tenderly arched, would rest on smooth, cool leather.

They started the day in a semi-circle, as if grouped for a photograph, each finding a place in God's sight. They would bow their heads and be led in prayer by Flip Karelse: to thank the Lord for his bounty and infinite mercy, to beg him to guide their hands and to bless the skills required to fashion the shoes. For the rest of the day, their heads were bowed over the cutting bench, the awls and sewing machines, as if the praying never stopped. At the end of the long shed-like room in which they worked, the finished veldskoen of various sizes were stacked. There was little variation, apart from the high, boot-like style that supported the ankle and the lower, more comfortable cut for everyday wear. After a month of pay packets, she would have such a pair for Sundays – for now, her father said, she was a working young lady who could no longer go to church unshod.

It was on Sunday afternoons that she stepped out with Flip Karelse in her clean cotton frock and new shoes, which were a hymn of comfort. On the hills where they roamed, where they knew every outcrop of rock, every curve of the earth, the smell of leather was quite displaced by wild thyme opening up to the sun, releasing its dizzy aroma. When one day his caresses went too far, when they feasted feverishly on each other's lips, helpless under a red and gold sky, her father forbade her from stepping out with him again. No girl should be brought home after sunset; that was the rule, and it was because the Karelses thought of themselves as white, and therefore superior, that he dared to disobey. The next evening, Flip arrived in his Sunday clothes to ask for her hand in marriage. Marriage, he whispered, was the only way to keep them on the straight and narrow path, not that he kept his hands to himself after their betrothal, but by then Tokkie was mad for him, would have done anything he wanted.

Oh, she was the envy of the village girls, who said that she, being so black, must have used witchcraft, for no husband could have been more devoted than Flip Karelse. He adored every inch of her, took delight in the mysterious darkness of her skin, and on Friday evenings after work and after their weekly treat of vetkoek and eggs, he tended to his Tokkie's tired feet. She was a talker, which he loved, but she shut her eyes and was silent as he rubbed away the weariness. Then he massaged cooking oil into her feet until they were a lustrous black, were two live black starlings throbbing in his lap.

All was topsy-turvy. Only the previous day it had been wintry with steady rain, an icy wind, and the mountain invisible under low-slung cloud. But that day it was unmistakably midsummer, even though it was only September, barely the beginning of spring. Councillor Carter was dressed in a grey suit of worsted wool, and a tie of darker grey was responsible for a moat of sweat around his neck. Not long before the moisture seeped down to his chest, turning his crisp shirt into something like the suspicious-looking grey-white favoured by the lower classes. That, he knew, was how the criminal and the lower classes betrayed themselves, how they could be distinguished from the decent citizen – through the colour of their shirts. Try as they might, that was where improbity would out. Mrs Carter was meticulous in this respect: the amount of Reckitts Blue had to be carefully judged. She supervised the final rinse of his white shirts, since such things could not be left to servants.

He was on his way back from the office of the supervisor, a man newly arrived from Surrey who had a knack of making him feel inferior, inadequate, even stupid. When the man deemed their consultation to be over, he simply planted his elbows on the desk and flicked his right hand in a stiff gesture, as if to wave him out. Carter knew that he had been dismissed; he knew that an imprint of defeat was stamped on his retreating back. Which was unreasonable, for who was to know whether this authoritative-sounding man was not in fact a cockney, or whatever they called them over there, come here to lord it over hapless colonials? All types had been known to come over, including toffs who had disgraced themselves back home, so there was no need for him to be deferential. Next time he would be on guard, nip in the bud any attempt at asserting English superiority. It was not as if his own people were not of good English stock.

As he approached his office, his hand went to his throat in anticipation of loosening the collar, but a woman was waiting at the door, and the gesture had to be turned into one of straightening the tie, which tightened like a noose around his neck. Helen Campbell sat down according to the instructions of her well-thumbed etiquette book, with her legs at an angle and crossed at the ankles. (She also knew that one did not eat a banana from its half-peeled skin; that was what primitives and primates did, although she had not as yet tried tackling it with a knife and fork.) Carter believed that you could not inspire respect without looking people straight in the eye, drilling your eyes into theirs, which was precisely how he would be fixing the new man from Surrey, but the young woman sitting across the desk from him, cool in a lemon shirt, had breasts that, if he was not mistaken, throbbed gently like frightened doves, so that his eyes drilled instead through the buttoned shirt and found, beneath the layers of petticoat, vest and bust-bodice, the nipples: first the right one – her chair being at an angle, her body was twisted just slightly towards the door – and then the left. Blushing brown nipples set in dark aureoles, for in spite of the reddish-auburn hair she was dark; he could swear they stiffened to attention under his direct address. When he looked up fleetingly, to command her eyes, he saw that the rosiness of the nipples had spread to her cheekbones. If he was not mistaken, there was a certain prominence about those cheekbones. Her right hand plucked nervously at her throat, then at the plain gold wedding ring, the cheap engagement ring, as she stated her business. Which indicated to Carter that she was not immune to his admiration.

Something urgent has come up since you made the appointment, Mrs Campbell, and I wouldn't like to rush this matter.

Helen nodded. Yes, she was able to come back just after five; yes, she understood that this delicate business was best tackled after hours, without disturbances, without involving his secretary. He got up to escort her to the door. A fine pair of legs, the seams of her nylons immaculately centred, although she had far too little of her calves showing – a prude. In these post-war days, the hemlines had shot up dramatically; fashionable women were only barely covering their knees. After shaking her hand he retrieved his own slowly, in stages, allowing his fingers to linger on the cushion of flesh below her thumb, while saying a slow goodbye to each breast in turn.

Helen, biting her lip, counted her measured steps until she was out of sight. A block of blinding pain severed her head from the rest of her body, so that it was an enormous effort to put one foot before another, but she had to hold herself together, hold her head high, since that was the only defence against obliteration. She would have liked nothing more than her very own bed, nothing more than to hide under the rough grey blanket of childhood and to sob into the pillow that the child herself had helped her mother stuff with chicken down; the child wanted to see just once more the outline of Mamma, stooping to say night-night. But the image of that bed, the narrow canvas fold-up that precisely fitted a stretched adolescent body with arms held close to her sides, was sobering. There was no room for weakness. Which was exactly why, although she still had fifteen minutes left of her lunch hour, she returned to her place behind the counter and smiled her knowledgeable smile at starry-eyed young women in search of linen for their bottom drawers, young women so absorbed in the relative merits of broderie anglaise and appliqué that they had not the slightest interest in the saleslady's flaming cheeks.

Helen, who had thought through every step meticulously, had not imagined that the plan would include humiliation of this kind. She admonished the sad face in the mirror of her powder compact, coaxed it into smiling, for sacrifices had to be made and she had no one to rely on but herself. But her master plan was galloping ahead of her and she did not know where or how to find God in it. She knew God to be just, knew that he would not, for instance, have taken offence at her change of denomination. Not only was the Moravian Mission Church unacceptable, it was a giveaway; it had to be abandoned in favour of the Anglican

Church. Then there'd been the research on Councillor Carter, so that St Luke's, where he worshipped, became her chosen parish. Which was a blessing indeed, for Father Gilbert was a liberal young Englishman: plump, rosy-cheeked, modern, and happily uninterested in her past. She understood that the prim piety of the Moravian Sunday-school teacher would count for nothing with him, that there was plenty of room for inventing a new self.

Father Gilbert spoke enthusiastically about the future and the infinite human capacity for renewal, which Helen read as a good sign. He hopped eagerly from one foot to another and flung his arms wide apart as he spoke, quite unlike an Englishman she thought, although she hadn't met one before. But she spoke sharply when Campbell called him a bit of a clown. That is not how one speaks of a man of God, she said, and if you don't want to pull yourself up by your own bootstraps then you'd better keep out of the Church of England.

John worried about all that talk of keeping out. At the depot, the chaps spoke of new laws that would keep certain types out of the gardens and parks. He thought of the Company Gardens, where he sometimes wandered with his sister Elsie through the flowerbeds and watched the birds twitter sadly in the big constructions that were cages all the same. But Helen stared at him sternly, so he said he was sorry, that he'd had a drink too many, although he continued to joke about there being plenty to drink in an English church, where they had to cheer themselves up by celebrating Communion so very often, every week, in fact.

Helen did not show any agitation as time passed, as it marched inexorably towards five o'clock – one of Father Gilbert's charming phrases. She also liked his idea of opportunity as a window through which, with minimum effort, you could manoeuvre the body. That was exactly what her first visit to St Luke's had offered: the jewel colours of the stained-glass window aslant on the stone floor, leading her like a star directly to the pew opposite the Carters. The man's smile had been warm, welcoming; with her head held high, Helen had failed to note the defeated eyes of Mrs Carter. Lately, however, in the urgency of having to act, she favoured the image of a door: opportunity as a threshold over which you stepped lightly, without fuss, without so much as an old-fashioned lifting of the hem of your skirt, although she had of course not bargained on the degradation that Carter seemed intent on meting out.

Helen took refuge in the idea of obliteration. She now understood that this was the nature of the bargain: in order for her to forge new identities for Campbell and herself, the old had to be obliterated. She could not rely on Campbell to lift a finger; it was left to her to make the sacrifice. She found a ready example in Christ, who died on the cross before rising as the Saviour, whose love washed away the past, the old misdemeanours, and who would not object to renewal. It was a matter of endurance, of being strong and keeping her weary head high at all costs, like the bright face of the sunflower following the radiance of the sun, even if it drooped by the end of the day. That was what Mamma called her, her bright sunflower.

If only she knew precisely what Carter required of her, she could pre-pare herself, talk herself into the necessity of whatever had to be done. Helen knew that virtue was the special responsibility of woman; it was she who had to protect the man against himself. Thus she looked in the mirror to buck herself up, but not to refresh her lipstick, nor to rearrange her hair, nor to dab on seductive perfume for the return to his office. Such innocence was her only defence.

Carter pulled up a chair next to hers. She was alarmed to see him without his jacket and tie. He was surprised at how much more beautiful she was than he had thought, and was drawn to the chest that heaved with apprehension. He took both her hands in his and said how a pro-gressive man like himself was appalled, simply appalled by the devasta-tion that the new Population Registration Act had brought to so many families. Helen drew back her shoulders and lifted her chin for the deliv-ery of her story. She foresaw no problems for her family – they had always been white, on the right side so to speak; it was just that she could not bear the business of having to fill in forms and have humiliating inter-views with low-class bureaucrats, and who knows, stand in queues with all sorts of undesirable chance-taking types. And all because Campbell had lost his birth certificate. An affidavit from Councillor Carter that the Campbells were known members of the white community, that they belonged in his ward and worshipped at the parish of St Luke's, would save them so much trouble. Helen hoped that the reference to the house of God would temper the man's lewdness. Her lips were dry but she dared not lick them.

Carter felt her distress as if it were his own. He took her hand once more, examined the palm as if to ascertain her future, then slid a finger under the cuff of her shirt, resting it on her pulse – which made her leap out of her chair. Carter too rose. His left hand, by way of steadying her, slid down to her waist; he patted her back in an avuncular fashion before drawing her closer.

So very distressing, too distressing, these new laws, he murmured, for he had seen the liquid gathering in her eyes. The lovely breasts throbbed against his chest, and with his right hand on her left buttock he pressed his hardness against her. Helen would not cry. In a thin voice, focusing hard on her vowels, she begged: Please Mr Carter, this is not right. I'm a married woman; the body is the temple of the Lord.

It is just, he explained gently, that he was overcome by her loveliness, her lovely breasts. For a moment it seemed that she would get away with having them pressed and squeezed, but sensing her haughty distaste, he added, as if he had already seen them, Such luscious blackberry nipples, before he fumbled with the buttons of her shirt. Thus Helen was reminded of her obligation. Trembling in her petticoat, she understood that she would not get away with being simply the object of his attentions, that the price was to show willing, that she would have to cooperate. So she placed her hand on the head of the man whose face was rooting in her cleavage, noting the patch of thinning hair and deftly avoiding it as she massaged upward from the nape of his neck, a gesture that no doubt saved her for that day. Carter raised his head gratefully, returned to his desk and said in a strained, stern voice that she would have to come back another time, the following evening, to collect the affidavit, that as a liberal he would do anything in his power to help against those infernal laws, that he hoped with their common political principles they would be friends.

On the fourth visit – by then she had taken to wearing her lipstick, a woman could not expect to retain her courage without and besides, the touch of red made her skin look paler – Carter slipped off the straps of her petticoat and asked her to undo her bust-bodice. Which she did without flinching. She stood tall as a sunflower with her hands at her sides and thought of the fold-up canvas bed while he licked and pummelled and muttered about blackberries. Then he placed her hand on his flies, took hold of her index finger to trail the line of concealed buttons. Where it remained, frozen on the last button, but she knew to not withdraw, to endure, until he ruffled her hair affectionately and turned to his desk to hand over the affidavit.

I trust, Mrs Campbell, that this will do the trick, he said in business-like fashion.

Helen smiled warmly and thanked him for the trouble. Her gratitude was heartfelt. It would do the trick alright. She knew by heart the definition of whiteness according to Act No. 30:

'white person' means a person who in appearance obviously is, or is generally accepted as a white person, but does not include a person who, although in appearance obviously a white person, is generally accepted as a coloured person.

Like the signs and wonders of the Acts of the Apostles, the miracles where men and women rose and made their beds and started their lives anew speaking in fresh tongues, so Helen was remade. The Sunday-school texts of her girlhood, learnt by heart and seldom understood, grew clear with the music of meaning, of revelation. She may have been defiled, but she'd also been obliterated, and believing in the miracle of rebirth, her own thoughts had remained pure. Not once did Helen doubt her actions. Necessity – not unlike her mother destroying an old frock the child had outgrown in order to lengthen another, inventing the new contrasting border – could not be offensive to a God who exalted the poor.

And so it was accomplished. Only once, while waiting for the identity card to come through, did Helen consider changing pews at St Luke's so that she would neither have to see nor be looked at by the Carters. But Carter kept his eyes decently averted, and once the papers were in order, the image of the man slobbering over flesh-pink satin was quite erased. Helen, artless as a sunflower, smiled warmly; her former self – the woman in the lemon blouse, the one obligated to Carter – was obliterated, was no more. Thus there was no need to avoid him. Indeed, she spoke with such civility, such ease, that he could not but bury the memory, which is to say that he never again allowed his eyes to stray below her chin.

Campbell would never know what she had sacrificed for him, for their new life. Could never have imagined her visits to the municipal office. Did not even ask what had happened to the lemon blouse he so liked to see her in. She allowed herself the single indulgence of cutting it up with a pair of sharp scissors before putting it in the dustbin, where it bonded with greasy scraps of stew and stale coffee and chicory grounds.

*W*ith a husband like Campbell, what could Helen do but stay indoors, spend weekends at home, shut in with only a radio in the stuffy bedroom? There was no gaiety in this new, silent world. Sometimes she thought dreamily of dancing at the Majestic Hotel – Mrs Bates had had no doubt that she would be a hit, the belle of the ball. From Mrs Macdonald's cast-off water-silk gown in shimmering aquamarine, Helen's mother had cut and sewn a frock with a sweetheart neckline and frilled hem. Helen would run her fingers over the smooth fabric, listen to its rustling promises – until she heard the laughter of jolly coloured people. They were always jolly, noisy; that is what made them impossible. She could not be sure that this frock she'd never worn was not vulgar, unsuitable, although unsuitable for what, she could not say. Nevertheless, her hands were on occasion drawn to it; she'd pull a bunch of skirt out of the wardrobe, hold aloft the fabric and watch the play of evening light on the ambiguous blue that shimmered and darkened, then faded with the light. But then she shut the door decisively: the aquamarine silk was of the past, which might be a shame for Mamma, who would've liked to have seen her step out in the frock, but there was no place for it in this new life.

Helen would reward herself with the new shoes advertised in the *Cape Times*. She was drawn to the slogan: Forward looking – the Venus pump created by Panther with the cunningly cut-away silhouette. The advertisement claimed it had taken the country by storm, and Helen just knew that the subtle forward slope of the heel was precisely what would whisk her off into another world. A Venus pump in white, to match her new crepe costume in navy blue with white trimming.

At first, on Sunday afternoons, she went for walks in the Gardens with Miss Fisher from work, but there was no question of inviting her to the house. How could one rely on Campbell to behave properly, and Miss Fisher a spinster too? But Miss Fisher for some reason gave up on her, said that things had changed, new commitments or something or other that did not bear talking about. Miss Fisher lowered her eyelids; she ran her middle fingers over her eyebrows, over and over, smoothing the arches as she spoke volubly about the impossibility of saying certain things. She would not come walking in the Gardens again. And when Helen became the manageress, Miss Fisher pursed her lips and left.

Occasionally, Helen insisted that they go out as a family, promenade the seafront, eat an ice cream together in public. Then she would dress the little girl in long white crocheted socks, patent leather shoes and a frilled nylon frock with smocking. Her mother had ironed a dotted transfer onto old-fashioned primrose georgette but her eyes were too poor to do the smocking, for which Helen was relieved. There was nothing to beat the modern, ready-made frocks. How beautiful Marion looked, her hair golden in the sunlight, but Campbell would spoil it all by rattling on about mermaids, filling the child's head with stuff and nonsense, and saying yes, of course she could take off her shoes. As if he hadn't heard her saying that the child shouldn't, as if he wanted to turn the little girl against her own mother.

Come now, Lenie, I'll do your feet, Campbell would soothe, trying to compensate for the demands he made in the marital bed. She tossed her head haughtily – she would not answer to the country name of Lenie; but he brought the enamel basin of warm water with a splash of 4711 eau de cologne and coaxed her into removing the stockings she always wore, even in the summer heat. She turned her back to undo the suspenders and felt for a moment the childhood freedom of going barefoot. A fleeting moment, for only low-class tannies went about with bare legs, and more importantly, her treacherous feet, her bête noir, had at all costs to be covered. Years of going barefoot in the village had conditioned those wayward feet into growing a tough hide capable of withstanding the buffeting of stones and the penetration of thorns, a hide that cracked around the unsightly heels and the edges of her toes. And when she was shod for high school, the discomfort of shoes prevented her from realising that the stiff new things were too small, too tight, so that the bones elbowed their way out into unsightly bunions.

Campbell was suprisingly adept; he used his pocketknife to shave off dead skin softened in the water. The newly exposed layer he left in turn to soak, for there was no end to what was removable; besides, he loved to prolong the process. Disgusted as she was by her horny feet, Helen had a suspicion that the roughness of her soles was what saw her through the trials and tribulations of life in the city. Something hard of her own between the pale, soft body and the asphalt of the world was perhaps necessary, so that she always left it too long, let things slide, until the skin had grown once more into tough leather. The astonishing memory of skin: there was patently no longer any need for this hide. Surely the body, she thought, could forget its past, could allow her to forget the un-shod coloured child. But no, it wouldn't; nature would assert itself. To her shame, the skin, like any weed, grew more vigorously in spring, bubbling here and there, moulting as a tough new layer pushed its way through. If Helen was affronted by the continuous production of redundant, leathery skin, by the obstinate reproduction of cells, by the body's refusal to ac-knowledge the new woman, she found herself inexplicably moved, hum-bled, by the pile of yellowish-grey shavings.

After the second shaving, the feet soaked once more before John buffed the soles with a fine wire brush, so that tiny particles of skin turned the water into a milky suspension from which the feet emerged smooth and soft as newborn babes. John, the proud midwife, was pleased to see Helen moved, even if her tender feelings were reserved for her own hide and hue. The feet he massaged with Rexall's olive oil were brand new; the beast was tamed, if only for a couple of weeks or so.

John loved the ritual, loved those wayward feet that gave him access to her. Beyond her control, and boldly asserting their past, they kept alive the memory of the pretty young girl from Wuppertal. It is these feet, he joked, that keep us together. He was not sure what he meant by that. Massaging the soft white feet, he would feel a stir of desire that had to be suppressed.

Once, concentrating hard on a fine black Pontiac he would one day have, his hand slipped so that the knife plunged to the quick, and bright red fairytale blood trickled from the white skin. Helen cried out loud and the child came rushing into the room.

John sat on the floor with Helen's right foot wrapped in a dark blue towel, through which blood oozed, black as bile. Marion threw her arms around her mother's waist. On the floor were sheets of newspaper under a basin of water with the whiff of cologne that the child hated. Beside it was a vicious-looking knife and a hideous heap of skin. It was no sight for a mermaid: her face contorted with disgust as she let go of that unyielding waist and fled the room.

Years later, when Marion left for university and the silence grew so heavy that even ghosts spurned that house of choked history, Helen started muttering to herself, going over her achievements, the decisions, processes, petitions to various offices in town, but she did not remember the visits to Councillor Carter. She had a friend who asked helpful questions, a confidante whose role was to prompt, a real lady, not unlike Miss Fisher, whose questions she answered without uttering a sound. Helen was not going mad; she was not one of those sad, mad people who talk to themselves. She knew what she was doing, and thus the lady friend remained nameless. Oh no, she contradicted her friend, it wasn't Campbell's doing; it was she, Helen, who hatched and executed the whole plan, from A to Z. Admittedly Campbell, being a man, was the one who had to do some signing on the dotted line, but the entire white life was shaped by her.

Occasionally, distracted from her story, she would practise a new word heard on the English programme and weave it into the conversation. Execrable, she intoned in the broadcaster's voice. My dear, she said to her lady friend, all my life I have waited for this word. And indeed, looking back she could see the gaps, the holes in her story that could be plugged by such and such a word. Her friend said that it was the little things in life that should be appreciated, the new words that fit so perfectly, that make the world whole and stave off disappointment.

They had not prospered in the ways she'd imagined, but Helen's achievement was her legacy to Marion, a new generation unburdened by the past. Of course, they had Campbell's execrable backsliding to thank for not having moved out of that part of Observatory, for not crossing Main Road to the mountain slopes. For years he'd disappeared on Sundays, at lunchtimes, and there was no need to ask: he went to his sister's, crept right back into the nest of jolly hotnos. For the sake of the child, she said nothing at all.

*W*hat is whiteness?

What is this chimerical thing that they strive after?

Is it not enough that they have come to the City, that they have stepped off a train with sleeves rolled up, ready for the hard work of forging a new life?

Can they not rejoice in being lucky, in having escaped from the mission station, the farm, from rural lives of toil?

No, there is no question of letting up. Just look how the world around them is being ordered, shaped according to colour, restricted: coloureds on a new voters' roll, job reservation, Group Areas Act – legislation upon legislation that proves how right they were.

Whiteness is without restrictions. It has the fluidity of milk; its glow is far-reaching. It's up to them to make it work.

Which means that they sweep and scrub and brush, maintain a home of unforgiving hygiene, with floors that you can eat off, and a garden with soil freshly dug over, raked smooth in readiness for planting, for the labour of cultivation. Just as their parents had taught them.

Then it is not so different, John says, resorting to the buffoonery Helen so hates. He has returned from his sister Elsie in an argumentative mood, dissatisfied. We are ourselves Boere; we too live according to the maxim, 'n Boer maak 'n plan.

But it is not as simple as that. It is not a matter of donning whiteness as you trip daintily out of the house, and then on your return, as you lock the doors, slumping back into your old ways – hotnos ways, as they have taken to saying, the parodic usage of the farm having lost its humour.

Vigilance is everything; to achieve whiteness is to keep on your toes. Which, John reasons, indicates that they cannot achieve it after all; being white in the world is surely about being at ease, since the world belongs to you. But they, it would seem, cannot progress beyond vigilance, in other words, beyond being play-whites, which as far as he can see has bugger-all to do with playing. Only once, with a gleeful, spiteful vision of her destruction – the demise of her pancake make-up like the cracking of mud into geometric patterns in the sun, the buckling of knees, the crumpled heap – does he think of saying this. But for the sake of sparing the child, of giving her the ease of whiteness, he keeps the peace. They must raise the child without the burden of history.

The pursuit of whiteness is in competition with history. Building a new life means doing so from scratch, keeping a pristine house, without clutter, without objects that clamour to tell of a past, without the eloquence – no, the garrulousness – of history.

If the whiteness they pursue is cool and haughty and blank, history is uncool, reaches out gawkily for affinities, asserts itself boldly, threatens to mark, to break through and stain the primed white canvas that is their life. For, having primed it, they do not know where to start, how to make a mark. They are alone in the world, a small new island of whiteness. (Or so they think; they do not know, or perhaps they do not want to know, that the neighbourhood is full of people like them.) Thus they are steeped in its silence.

Tokkie's visits are a relief. Tokkie brings colour and sound. Sitting in her old wicker chair in the backyard, she offers an invented past for the family, a history for the neighbours (other play-whites, as it happens, who are envious), a history for her granddaughter: that is her gift. Tokkie can shout and crow all she wishes; that is what coloured people, servants, do. It is the Campbells who have to be still, who have to mind their p's and q's. Which is not such an effort. Little happens in the house; they have little to say to each other. John's noisiness, his boisterousness, is buffed at the edges by the single gesture of a silent index finger that Helen puts across her mouth. They have slipped noiselessly, imperceptibly, from youth to middle age, leeched by vigilance, white and loveless. The child plays as children do. The parents like to hear the tinkle of her toddler's chatter running like fresh water through the house, but as she grows older, the silence draws her in. Except when Tokkie is there. Then the laughter is heartbreaking. When she goes to school she makes a friend, Annie Boshoff, whom they watch anxiously. The child has also spoken across the fence to the child next door, a boy she understands, but her mother says one friend is enough for anyone to bear.

*H*elen had not known of the oath he had to take. John thought it unmanly to burden her with such details, believed that he should shield her from unnecessary distress. Now he is equally determined to shield Marion. These are not things with which to burden women. He is her father; he is there to protect her. Only, Marion wants to know everything, and when he is vague, when he prevaricates, she returns with direct questions that cannot be avoided. Yesterday he could take no more. She may be a determined somebody, but he could do no more delving into that past. A tight band settled around his head and his bowels felt dangerously slack. Like a child he had to plead, please could they talk another time. Yes, she said, I'll come tomorrow. She has no intention of letting him off the hook. He is shocked at her lack of compassion, her cool conviction that he owes her a full explanation. Has she forgotten that he is her father? Mercifully, he drops off; his head lolls and then he starts, shudders on that threshold of sleep and wakefulness: he has never given her the belt, but damn it, he is her father.

John has, as usual, heard her car idling at the robots, accelerating up the street. He must remember to ask her about the carburettor; if he's not mistaken, it doesn't sound so good. When she gets to the door, John is there at the ready with his stick. He is a man of his word and besides, there is nowhere to hide from this girl who pounces like a hawk. He remembers the terrible guilt of childhood when it was his job, his responsibility, to mind the new chickens, freshly hatched and infinitesimal under the wide Karoo sky. How often he would turn to dreaming, turn momentarily to pick up a stone or examine a rally of ants, only to see the streak of a hawk swooping out of nowhere, carrying off the very bundle of yellow fluff he had held just now in a hand that still throbs with the memory of its heartbeat.

John has decided that this house where he and Helen lived their silent, disappointed lives is not the place in which their story could be told. They will drive somewhere; he does not get out much. To Wynberg Park – that he remembers as being a grand place, nice and quiet, with grand sweeping lawns and cool trees. There is a grove of early-flowering jacarandas that may already be in bloom.

Marion puts her hand to her mouth to suppress a gasp. Her father stands in the doorway like a ghost from the past. With the help of the doorposts and a newfound courage, he is fiercely erect, all but salutes her. He is dressed from head to toe in his old airforce-blue traffic-cop's uniform. The buttons strain around his expanded belly, but he stands smartly to attention, his braided hat fallen deep over the shrunken head. The gloves, yellow with age, are slack around the withered hands. In this get-up, his skin waxy like a corpse and enveloped in the mustiness of dust and mothballs, he is an emblem of the phantasmagoric past.

John barely recognises his own courageous voice: Come child, we'll go to Wynberg Park and I'll buy you an ice cream. There we can talk nicely in the shade, clear up this whole business and forget about the past.

Oh Pappa, Marion says in a strangled voice, and feels the tears pricking, but there is something about his demeanour, his determination, that demands courage. It is he who comforts her.

My Marientjie, my mermaid, everything will be alright, Pappa promises, and he takes her elbow. Together they stumble to the car.

He has no idea, she thinks, none at all of the terrible injury he has done to her, to his family, to himself. His belief in the might of whiteness surpasses everything else; he does not know that the world around him has changed, that it has lost its pristine, Reckitts Blue whiteness. He is a child, selfish in his drive to escape, selfish in his belief that he has done the right thing. He is about to open the passenger door for her when she pulls herself together. It's alright Pappa, she says, I'll drive. Why don't you sit here right next to me.

It is like a jolly jaunt of her childhood; there is a reckless, carnivalesque air to the trip which buoys them along as they bomb down the highway, down to Claremont. She would not be surprised if a mermaid appeared on the bonnet of the car. At the first set of lights, John salutes smartly; indeed, whenever he remembers, he turns to fellow drivers and salutes. He advises her to stop at the robots even when the lights are green: one can't be too careful, my little one, and it looks like there's trouble ahead anyway. At the traffic island he exclaims at how things have changed. My word! he shrieks with delight, these roads are now like a bundle of intestines; we certainly have got the best here in South Africa, hey. But ahead all is chaos: the robots are not working. Just as well he is there to help out; his gloved hand is at the ready, held smartly out the window. Marion must stop immediately.

No Pappa, she placates, you've given your whole life to the traffic of this city, now it's your turn to sit back and enjoy the drive. See, it's not such a problem with the slip road on the left; things are moving already.

He agrees reluctantly, but keeps turning in his seat to salute all and sundry, the white glove flapping around the emaciated arm. Marion swallows hard; she will not cry.

It is eleven o'clock and she does not want an ice cream, but it is his treat and so they settle on a bench under the blue haze of jacaranda blossom. John launches into his story immediately, repeating with pride that the Traffic Superintendent mistook him for a Boer. He is unexpectedly lucid. He should never have told her mother, he says, the whole thing just set her alight with ambition to turn white. Then he revises the account. No, he must be fair; he too was taken with the idea. Things were not easy. Although the first coloured speed-cop was appointed in 1953, a year after he joined the Traffic Department, things soon clamped down again. Job reservation forced the City Council to stop taking on coloured traffic-police, because how could you expect white drivers to take any notice of the coloured cops? But what caused the big mix-up in the early fifties was when coloureds lost the vote. Many of the well-to-do families emigrated to Britain, but the Campbells didn't have that kind of money.

With coloureds being put on a separate voters' roll, there was a helluva mix-up with identities. Many white people who didn't even realise that they were coloured were now reclassified; some coloureds became white and some were reclassified as native. That is his explanation – it was a time of uncertainty, of general upheaval as people were shuffled about like so many packs of cards, waiting to find their lawful places, or just any place at all that could then be made lawful. A matter of opportunity. Marion does not understand. It doesn't make sense, but he is adamant that there was enforced crossing to and fro in order to get the coloured voters' roll off the ground.

With the affidavit proving that they were known to be white, which Helen had secured from a councillor, it was just left to John to sign a form at the Barrack Street offices. Now he slumps, shrunken and wizened in his moth-eaten uniform. His head drops into his hands; he winces. It was like turning a knife in his own flesh, his very heart. He'd told himself that it didn't matter. The week before, his brother Roelf was in town visiting and Elsie made a very nice dinner of sheep's head and beans and trotters, plaaskos just like Ma's, and they had all laughed at their ouboet's adventures with the law. Paul, Roelf and Pieter joked and poked fun at the oath because they knew, of course, that it would make no difference. Blood is thicker than water, Elsie said. The signature would be nothing, a piece of bureaucratic nonsense, just a case of signing on the dotted line that he would relinquish all contact he might have with coloureds. Of course something like that could not possibly be monitored, and besides, with a close family like theirs there was no question of being kept apart by a flimsy law. If Helen was difficult, a bit stand-offish, and wouldn't have his people in the house, she was after all not a blood relation. And he even thought that his siblings were a little proud of his achievement, although things didn't turn out quite right in the end.

Marion wonders why she has never noted what in others she calls coloured theatricality, as John warbles his voice to show the solemnity of the occasion. He shows with trembling upturned hands the weight of the Bible on which he had to swear. And swearing before God that according to the laws of the land he no longer had brothers and sisters had been the very worst thing, a shooting pain through his heart and nothing short of a sin. He had to swallow hard, several times, and barely made it to the lavatory to throw up, the turn-ups of his brown pin-stripe suit splattered with vomit. He never wore that suit again; he had in any case decided that he would no longer go to the English church, so what reason would he have had to wear a suit? Although her mother tried to get him to wear it when they promenaded at Sea Point on a Sunday afternoon, he would not give in.

Marion puts a hand on his trembling shoulders. He wanted to ask their forgiveness, Elsie's and his brothers', but to do so would have meant acknowledging the force of the oath. He only asked them not to tell Ma, for it would have killed her. Now he is racked with dry sobbing. Things became so complicated in the country, so political, he croaks, that they agreed to stop seeing him; he was excluded from Elsie's dinners. Marion cradles his head in her arms. His crumpled uniform is smeared with ice cream.

On the way home, John takes off the hat and the gloves. At traffic lights he still waves at other drivers, but the gesture has lost its precision. The hand moves apologetically, like a faulty windscreen wiper, and in tandem with his slack jaw that opens and closes involuntarily. By the time they reach home he is asleep, dribbling onto his uniform.

Father Gilbert's time at St Luke's was not without controversy. Having allowed himself a few years to settle in and acclimatise to the rigours of excessive heat and the Cape fruit and wine, he now felt the time had come to act. Being English and therefore a radical, he had to demonstrate the parish's abhorrence of apartheid, especially after the example set by Trevor Huddleston, the young firebrand priest of the north, who for all Father Gilbert could see spent rather more time messing about with young jazz-playing tsotsis than serving God.

Helen was unhappy: it would not do to mix religion and politics, although it soon became clear that the eloquent statements issued by the parish were innocuous and quite inconsequential. But Father Gilbert's project of getting young people to collect from the *Cape Times* and the *Argus* all reference to race was both worrying and puzzling. Reports on traffic offences, good works, civic achievements, court cases, any type of ephemera that mentioned the race of people involved had to be collected. To what purpose? Helen asked outright.

Oh, Father explained, scratching his head, to make young people aware of the iniquities of racialism and apartheid. He had developed a system of classification by which the articles could usefully be collated, as an invaluable archive for the future. Also, one should not underestimate the importance of projects that keep young people out of mischief. It encourages them to read the broadsheets and keeps them away from the scandalous new coloured tabloids.

Which put Helen at ease; being neither a young person nor being drawn to mischief, she need not worry too much about the unsavoury task. Father Gilbert was somewhat miffed that she saw no sense in his race-naming project. The church must make a stand, he said, or so Trevor Huddlestone preached, and history, he was sure, would prove him right in his endeavours to fight the iniquitous system. However, he conceded that Helen had a point: one should not spread oneself too thinly, and the proposed Sunday school in the townships was perhaps a more valuable endeavour.

Father Gilbert opted for another way of making his mark at St Luke's. He would institute the Maundy Thursday midnight ceremony of humbly washing the feet of his parishioners, as Christ himself had washed those of his disciples. Moreover, his chosen twelve would include a woman. The Bible, he explained, was not immutable; the Church must move with the times. Many members of the parish council felt this to be an outrage. Besides, they argued, to return to an obsolete High Church practice was hardly helping the priest's reputation as a radical. But at the council meeting they were defeated by one of Father Gilbert's supporters, who shut them up neatly with the retort that it was just a question of semantics, a word used by broadcasters which was only just coming into fashion and against which they could not argue.

Helen was the woman chosen for the washing of the feet. An abashed Father Gilbert told her himself, after evensong. She felt a glow of success, of vindication, flood her being. It was a triumph, nothing short of a triumph. Then she meekly dropped her eyes. She was an ordinary person, not without sin, not worthy of such an honour. But no, Father insisted, it was precisely her humility, her modesty and dependability that made her an obvious candidate. It would be through washing the feet of the good and humble of St Luke's that he too would be humbled and cleansed. Helen knew that he was the mouthpiece of God and thus that God had forgiven her. The last trace of her sins would be washed away, and she would finally be white as driven snow.

Only, there was the memory of skin, but that too was surely conquerable; nothing could stop her from putting her best foot forward. Campbell's pedicure was supplemented with daily scrubbing and grating, so that his efforts were no longer so visible and thus no longer rewarding. So meagre were the scrapings now from that indefatigable hide that he gave up.

The Good Friday ceremony was indeed a triumph. The glow of candlelight, the incense, the modest white basin, the organ music – all these contributed to a rush of holiness that converted the most hardened sceptics. Father Gilbert, sloshing pure water over the representative feminine feet, had no reason to think that they were anything but the extremities of a pampered white woman. If another of the chosen, Councillor Carter, thought that sitting next to Helen would in any way dent her confidence, he was mistaken. Cleansed and bathed in holiness, her very feet tamed and certificated by God, the woman gave him a beatific smile that wiped out the last memory he may have retained of blackberry nipples.

$\mathcal{W}$hat happened to Annie Boshoff?

Marion has no idea; she can't remember, hasn't really thought about Annie since – well, since she was a child. But you must, says Brenda. That's the kind of thing Brenda would say. She has a friend, Tiki or Riki, whom she's known since kindergarten, and although their lives have taken very different paths, they still see each other regularly. People have personal histories that they share with others, you know, she admonishes; it's normal, healthy.

Brenda's normality makes Marion sick; it's what people proudly parade like Sunday hats, when all the while flakes of dandruff have settled on their shoulders. Some people, she retorts, grow out of their childish attachments. Marion supposes that it is because people live so closely together in the townships, bodies packed into cramped rooms – Like sardines? Brenda interjects mockingly – that they get so involved with the lives of others. It's a defence mechanism, Marion says, presented as virtue. Material comfort would relieve people from such forced intimacy, such unhealthy attachments.

Brenda is outraged. Why do I bother with you, she asks, but Marion assumes the question to be rhetorical. And so they spar.

Brenda harangues her about reading. Her failure to understand human relations can apparently be traced to the fact that she doesn't read good novels or poetry. Marion, who does not accept that she has such a problem, is not always amused by Brenda's impertinence.

And how does one know whether a novel is good or not? Why spend time on something that may turn out to be no good? Marion asks. To get oneself into a stew about fabricated lives sounds distinctly unhealthy to her.

Nonsense, you know a novel is worth reading because the reviewers and critics say so – or rather, they argue about it, and then when you try it you either agree that it's good or disagree. And so you get to know the authors you like.

Marion shakes her head, astonished. It sounds all too arbitrary, not her cup of tea. If the experts can't agree …

You may even enjoy novels, says Brenda, looking at her with tilted head and slightly narrowed eyes, for all the world like a hairdresser considering a new look for a client. She adds, To live vicariously through other people's words, in other people's worlds, is better than not living at all.

That's how irritating Brenda can be. That's the strange way in which, out of working hours, they speak to each other, yet Marion has come to rely on her, not least for her tactfulness at work, where there is no hint of their out-of-office sparring.

Is Marion jealous of Riki or Tiki? She is not prepared to consider that, although there is sometimes the worry that Brenda might blab to the friend who has prior claims, discuss Marion's story, shouting to make herself heard above the noise of the television and the children and the others flitting in and out of the room. Which is why she ought to be more circumspect, but she finds it difficult not to consult with the girl, who has been in on things from the start. If Brenda knows of this dependence she does not let on; she keeps her distance in the office and never asks for information. It would seem that she doesn't care whether Marion tells her about the latest developments, and Marion, who doesn't know the ways of friends, is puzzled. What is she supposed to make of that? Is Brenda her friend? And why has she never been introduced to Riki?

So she does not tell Brenda about the quest to find her father's sister Elsie, decides not to ask for help. John is confused; he has lost touch so long ago – when Elsie, by then married to Fourie, was still living in the old house in Claremont, before that was declared a white area. No, he remembers that Fourie was full of bravado, refusing to move – resisting, he called it, so that in the old end the house was expropriated and they got next to nothing for it.

He drops his head with the effort of remembering, and Marion fears that he has once again taken refuge in sleep, but then he slaps his thigh and declares triumphantly, Yes, they went to Wynberg for a while, Liverpool Street if he's not mistaken, a respectable coloured area even if it was called a street; they had rooms in someone's backyard. That was before the Fouries moved to a brand-new estate. John frowns with the effort of summoning the past. He visited there once or twice but no, he just can't remember where it was. He'd promised Ma on her deathbed that he would always keep an eye on sussie Els, but things became too difficult. Fourie's nonsense, he says vaguely, came between them.

Marion has him sitting squarely in his chair; she urges him to concentrate. She has become kinder, less judgmental, but he blinks with the effort and has nothing more to offer except the threat of tears and a pleading tone that interrogates in turn: Why is she bullying him? Has he not done his best, mediating between Elsie and Helen? Is Marion no longer his child?

In spite of her resolve to be kind, Marion is disgusted. There is nothing to be gained from speaking to her father. She pats his hand mechanically, and notes that the cuticles have grown halfway down his nails, themselves long, yellow and filthy. She says they will have to get someone in to spruce him up, do his nails and things, upon which he straightens up smartly and in a firm voice declares that he'll have none of it, that it is his house, that he's been a traffic cop all his life, that he will decide on who crosses that threshold, and he gropes for his stick to point at the door.

Right, Marion snaps, next time I come we'll get those nails done.

But she doesn't manage. There are no nail scissors to be found in the house, and, preoccupied with her quest, she forgets to bring any along.

It is not hard to find Elsie. The street in Wynberg is short, and it is clear that only one house has separate back quarters. No one answers the door, but on the stoep across the road old Mrs Titus happens to be sitting in the winter sun.

Of course she knows Elsie; it was she who found her the place to stay when the Fouries were destitute, and Elsie just pregnant with her first child too. They ought to go to Fairways right away and give her a double whammy of a surprise. A lovely neighbourhood Fairways is, and her old friend Elsie has a very beautiful house – too big, of course, with all the children gone; and Mrs Titus, her oldest friend, who's known her since they were both young, blushing brides, does not always get a chance to visit.

Ye-es, young people have no idea, you think the world is your invention, to have and to hold; but me and Elsie too were once young, proper beauties in our white veils. A double wedding it was, and if it weren't for the apartheid business our photos would have been in the *Cape Times*, that's what everyone said. The Saturday paper always had a lovely double page of brides, in that old-fashioned brownish print you know, so much more realistic it looked; but nowadays it's mos just pictures of houses and more houses for sale at ridiculous prices. What exactly is Marion's business with Elsie again? She hopes it has nothing to do with trouble, because that poor woman has now had her double share of trouble.

How can Marion extract Elsie's address from this woman, for whom everything is double, without promising to take her along? But she stands her ground and says firmly that it is private, that she has to see Elsie on her own. Mrs Titus rises, straightens up, and with both hands tugs decisively at the hem of her jersey. She buttons up over her bosom. She for sure has no desire to interfere in other people's affairs, and anyway her daughters, both of them doubly good drivers, would take her any time she wished. She spits out the address in Fairways, and she wishes Miss Campbell, it is Miss isn't it – her eyes flick contemptuously over the ring finger – a very good day. Marion is swiftly ushered off the stoep.

Elsie is a giggler, as they say of women who laugh a lot. Every utterance is preceded by laughter, so that there is no possibility of her words taking on a grave aspect. She is a wiry old girl, conspicuously flat-chested, as if bosoms were an obstacle to her policy of taking things on the chin.

That's now one thing about me, she says, I take things as they come; nothing surprises me. And it is true that she receives Marion as if it were nothing out of the ordinary, as if she'd been expecting her. Well, actually she had, since the day John came to say that he was no longer allowed to bring the little girl, and she'd said, That's quite alright, she'll come by herself. What's thirty-odd years if you're as old as I am? Elsie says, and allows herself a complacent nod before another shower of laughter and a tugging of her jersey, as if her midriff is in danger of showing.

Is that what coloured women do when they grow old, tug at the hems of their jerseys? Even before the thought is fully formed she can hear Brenda's sigh of exasperation, and Marion finds her own hand fluttering awkwardly to the hem of her shirt. But she does not plan to be old like the woman sitting across the table, although laughter must be an antidote to wrinkles and sagging, since Elsie looks so much younger than John. Her English is not as shaky as John's, although guttural r's do escape between chortles, and her syntax totters in moments of passion. She is, however, firm about not speaking Afrikaans. Your father turning himself into a Boer ... the shooting of the Soweto children in '76, and then my William shot dead by Boers, she explains tersely, shaking her head. I know you've been brought up Afrikaans, but you must excuse me. Speaking the language, that's where I put my foot down, and she stares for a while at her shoes, lost in thought.

We've always been a close-knit family, so it was a hullabaloo of a business with Boetie John, but of course as far as your mother was concerned it was all about a fancy tablecloth, and then she laughs uproariously.

At first Helen was delighted to meet Elsie, the fair-skinned sister dressed respectably enough to visit, and it was important for the neighbours to see that they had family. She suspected, though, that the young woman was lacking in ambition, and when Elsie showed the photograph of the man she'd fallen in love with, Helen was appalled by her folly. She had made an error of judgment: Elsie was not the person she thought she was, and over tea one Sunday afternoon it pained Helen to see that Elsie's manners were not up to scratch either. She stared transfixed as Elsie slurped tea with the cake still held in her mouth, literally savouring the event of tea-and-cake as combination. And all that slosh and mush did not restrain her from giggling and carrying on with her story, so that bits flew from her mouth and landed on the best tablecloth, where she swiped at the offensive gobbets. Particularly galling was the fact that she made no attempt to do it surreptitiously; instead, openly, unapologetically, she pushed her hand across the cloth to remove the fugitive bits of mush. It was beyond the pale. Campbell could not expect Helen to put up with his sister's vulgarity. He would have to tell Elsie that visits were barred. What if someone had been there to witness the display?

There's nothing wrong with Elsie, John pleaded; she's my only sussie, we've always been just like this – and he held together his middle and index fingers to demonstrate their closeness, like twins. Besides, who are these people who would mind her enthusiastic manners? They had no friends, no visitors, could not have anyone come to the house until they acquired decent things, from decent furniture to decent teaspoons, although, no sooner would they get a coveted object than it would be superseded by something even more desirable, more decent. Decency, it transpired, was an endlessly deferred, unachievable goal.

It was an example, Helen said, an object lesson in slipping up. Had he not seen the photograph of the fiancé? With manners like that, Elsie was clearly going to be nothing but trouble, just look how, for all her respectful Boetie-this and Boetie-that, she refused to follow his example. Was Campbell incapable of thinking ahead? They were only beginning to transform themselves, and already he was settling into complacency – her eyes flicked to his expanding belly – while it was left to her to keep on her toes. There was something indecent about his casualness, and to wear so pained an expression about his sister was itself an instance of slipping up.

Elsie was his favourite, his only sister. It was she who kept the family together here in town; he could not possibly cast her off. And she was not making too bad a marriage. Fourie may have been dark skinned, but he was a teacher, a man of means who would give her a good modern home with a telephone. She was, he said proudly, going to have driving lessons in Fourie's smart black Ford.

Helen was outraged. Well, then it's her choice; Elsie knew how things stood and she deliberately chose to make an impossible marriage. Helen would under no circumstances appear at such a wedding. If you're so close, she taunted, Elsie will understand that we're just being law abiding; besides, she would not want to visit us without her educated, prosperous husband.

John held both Elsie's hands as he explained. It was something to do, he mumbled, with tea and cake and spitting on an Irish-linen cloth, obviously some kind of misunderstanding. The cloth was an elaborately embroidered affair, done by Helen's mother who sat in the backyard with her mug of coffee and her needlework, in case the neighbours saw, though what could the neighbours possibly see, with every window in the house dressed in Sunday-best lace? As for him, he cared nothing about these things; he had nothing against eating and drinking from a good wooden table that could be wiped clean. Actually, he could not abide that cloth with its funny flowers embroidered all around the edges, salmon-pink gladioli, Helen said they were. Her favourite flowers, he gabbled; couldn't understand how anyone could like salmon-pink gladioli. Helen could cajole for all she was worth, but he would not stick things like that in the garden. Now dahlias and Christmas roses, he knew how Elsie loved those. And he had nothing against Fourie. He would help her with the garden when she married.

And again, when they went to Fairways, although things were already strained after the Fouries' resistance to being moved. The new house was at the edge of the development and the garden was nothing but builders' rubble. Already Port Jackson bushes pressed at the fence, elbowing their way back, but a Boer, he laughed, always makes a plan. John cleared away the rubble and prepared the soil. Gardening was not for ladies, and

Fourie, an educated chap, was no good at that kind of thing. Red dahlias, Christmas roses, pink and blue, and seedlings of petunias – his arms were full. He'd picked them up cheaply at the Parade for her, and together they planned the planting, just like in the old days on the farm. Sussie Els was quite the madam, pointing here and there with her stick, telling the outa to get a move on, and they laughed and laughed at the piquancy of the scene. And when the garden was done, he cleared the Port Jackson and planted a row of prickly pears on the other side of the fence to serve as a buffer zone. Fourie said that it was not only ugly, those multi-limbed cacti policing the fence, but also presumptuous, as that land did not belong to them. But John said that the land belonged to God, and that Fourie, a city chap, knew nothing of such matters. John feared the man was turning against him.

Come, Elsie says, and leads Marion to the kitchen window, where the prickly pear all but blocks out the view. As the housing expanded, the new neighbours were more than happy to keep the cacti, although they never helped themselves to the fruit, despite Elsie's urging. Too grand, she supposes, but she would pick some prickly pears for Marion, it makes such a wonderful konfyt.

Marion eyes woefully the ugly prickly disks that parade their fruit, perched on the edges – like so many township children. Where the fruit has been picked, the wounds of childbirth, of motherhood, are proudly displayed.

Ag ja, Elsie sighs as they return to the table, your mother must have been fed up with him for spending so much time here, but that was Boetie John's life – gardening. You know, he refused to grow the gladioli for her in that small garden, just said the soil was too acidic. That, I'm afraid, was his idea of protest, of standing his ground.

Then Elsie laughs again her running-water laugh. She could not even recall the tea, cake and spittle incident, let alone the embroidered cloth in fine Irish linen that John so painstakingly tried to describe. Ag,

I suppose we didn't have stain-removing detergents in those days hey, she giggles.

Elsie had taken the objection at face value, was accommodating, just as John thought she would be. Helen's right, she said, we must all do our best, and once you choose a path you should keep to it, that's what Pa always said. She'd rubbed the top of John's head and said that it was no wonder his hair was falling out. Would he still come to see them, the Fouries? she asked, and he said, Of course, nothing in the world would keep him away.

Your mother was jealous, she says to Marion, because she, Elsie, for all her black husband and children, had risen in the world. They had a car and a detached house with a big garden. So what was the use of Helen and John's whiteness after all?

Elsie rises nimbly out of her chair – she will make a cup of coffee. Mind, she laughs, not to mush the biscuits and swirl it about in your mouth.

Marion says in a thin voice that she can't stay; her face is on fire with shame.

The old woman apologises, she should not have said that. Helen was after all her mother and she had her good points – clever, but also kind, of that Elsie was convinced when she first met her, and without Helen's strength Marion would not be the lovely, successful person she is today.

Marion flushes; she has never felt less lovely or successful. She no longer knows what success means, but she is persuaded to stay.

Helen's instinct about Elsie had been right. The Fouries had turned out to be impossible, in fact, major trouble. On the front page of the *Cape Times* there'd been a photograph of coloured men waving defiant fists, and Fourie in the centre named as a prominent Unity Movement rebel. They'd led a procession through the streets of Cape Town, congregating on the Grand Parade, where Fourie and others had spoken against the new laws. Disgraceful, making spectacles of themselves, Helen had said to John, as she'd read out the report of coloured people marching through the streets of Cape Town; no more than a disorderly mob, when everyone knew that they'd get nowhere with protests and processions. There was no stopping Prime Minister Malan, and really, what Elsie should have done with that man of hers was to emigrate.

Another headline in the *Times* had announced that two hundred and forty coloured families were leaving for England. Helen and John had considered emigration when they first met, but unlike Fourie they hadn't had the means. It had been so much easier to reclassify, just a question of taking the initiative, and besides, she'd feared they would've been no better off in England. If the English were snobbish here, how much more so would they not be there in the old country? No, it was here at home among the devils she knew that she would carve out a better life, turn Malan's plans to her advantage. If only Elsie had followed their example. John had tutted, It's too bad, too bad that Elsie should have got herself mixed up in such a mess with Fourie.

Yes shame, Elsie explains, they were so convinced of the importance of skin, so pleased with their paleness, that they just couldn't understand the real world. John did his ouboeta bit and tried to speak to Vernie about the dangers of politics, but Vernie put him in his place alright – said he was welcome in our house only on condition that he keep the stupid Boer ideas to himself. A very good husband Vernie was, and he didn't mind me inviting John to family gatherings on Sundays, because shame, your poor father had nothing: no people, no politics, no wife to speak of, and because he thought of skin as the alpha and omega, he grew stupid and couldn't think properly about the world beyond passing for white. Of course, Elsie giggles, he has you, a beautiful daughter; that must now be his great joy and comfort. He used to call you his little mermaid.

Yes, that I am – grew up stupid as a mermaid.

Marion is amazed by her own utterance, if not by its bitterness, and Elsie stares at her pensively, as if to weigh the truth of those words. But Marion must deflect; she wants to know why the siblings lost touch, if they were so devoted to each other.

The late seventies were terrible years. One just didn't know whether you'd see your children alive the next day. Our John didn't go to university until he turned thirty; Bella was in the military wing, away for years all over Africa; and our youngest, William, shot dead on the border. I'll never forget that day, when a young woman from his cell brought the news about my boy, already gone two weeks, but for me that was the day of his death. Come to think of it, she was a relation of your mother's – Patricia Williams, a cousin I think, now something of a big shot in the new government. But of course Helen wouldn't have had anything to do with them.

No, your mother need not have worried. Vernie and the children didn't want your father here, told him to his face what they thought of him, and if the truth be told I felt the same. It seemed almost as if he were responsible for William's death. Vernie worried about him being a BOSS agent, not that I thought that he would sink so low, but we couldn't trust Helen. Those were bad times, my child; it may not have been fair to John, but then this was a place of black and white, not a place of fairness, no room for concessions. Such a relief it is now that things have calmed down, the wretchedness at last over. I'm just grateful that Vernie had a couple of years of the new, of seeing the regime brought to its knees and all this racial nonsense finally put paid to. Vernie passed away last year, a month before the elections. A heart attack, you see, just like that, sitting in his chair watching television, shouting as he always did at the politicians of the New South Africa on the screen, and then the shout turned into a seizure, which only goes to show, hey …

Elsie's laughter has dried up. A last trickle, passed through the machinery of memory, comes out as a cluck, the sigh of a guinea fowl ready to roost. Marion agrees to move to the sitting room where the late light now simmers, unhindered by lace curtains. The blinds are up and there are deep cracks along the corners where the walls strain to part. On either side of the mantelpiece there are large pictures in ornate oval frames of people who must be Elsie's parents. Her father's parents. They are in their fifties or sixties – it is impossible to tell with people of another era – and look uncomfortable in formal dress. Marion's grandparents. The grandfather is dark with smooth hair parted centrally and plastered to his scalp; he wears a bowtie. There is the hint of slave blood in his cheekbones, or perhaps it is

Khoi. The grandmother seems lighter, more European looking, although her eyes are slanted; her hair is grey and wavy and rolled into little sausages pinned above her ears. She is not unlike Elsie.

These must be my grandparents, Marion says, and Elsie smiles, confirms, They are your grandparents, your Ouma Isabella Fortuin and your Pappa John Campbell. They say my Oupa Campbell was English or Scottish, but I remember him only dimly as an angry, senile old man who spoke not a word of English. Such trouble I have hanging on to these pictures you know, my John and Bella can't wait for me to die so they can squabble over their grandparents.

Marion goes up to examine them more closely. The pictures are of uncertain genre, neither photograph nor painting, and there is an otherworldly quality about the subjects. The ouma looks feverish. Her cheeks glow with a rouge that a plain country woman would surely not have used. Her husband's darker skin is skilfully daubed with colour that could represent light bouncing off the planes of his angled face, but that also hints at a whiteness straining its way through time. Both their noses are artfully shaded, slimmed down to bladelike proportions. Each has a background of unnaturally deep-blue sky, except for the aureola around their heads, where the colour pales into a celestial glow.

Marion asks about the pictures. Not only are the subjects weird looking, but it also seems improbable that simple country folk should have had their portraits painted. Elsie explains that she found her parents' identity cards after their deaths. The practice was quite common then: a photographer would blow up the image and touch it up with a paintbrush. She'd found the portraits disturbing at the time, had not anticipated that he would touch up the pictures according to his own ideal of beauty, of whiteness, she supposes. Yes, they look strange, she concedes, but the children, who didn't know their grandparents very well, rescued the pictures from a cupboard and had them framed. Now she is pleased, no longer minds the transmogrification, since this is the only likeness of her parents. Except for the identity cards, and she giggles: they ought to have framed the paintings with the cards inserted in the corner, now such a before-and-after look would have been a good representation of the folly of the past. But, Elsie adds soberly, I would not want any further tampering. They are my own Ma and Pa; they are not for display.

So they are and are not Marion's grandparents; they are strangers who hint at a connection with her father. No memories rise out of the past of a Pappa whose clippety-clop knees take the child riding; she has no claim to these people. She will not be there when the young Fouries squabble over the glazed idealised portraits, now ablaze like pictures of the annunciation in the last of the evening light.

*W*hat happened to Annie Boshoff?

Marion doesn't know. She hasn't even thought about Annie for years, which only goes to show that Annie is of no consequence. But having dismissed Brenda's question, its shadow remains, and Marion doesn't know. Helen must have known, but she is exhausted by the idea of Helen, by the bits and pieces she has had to put together, by the construction of a sci-fi monster of moulded steel plates, ill-fitting bolts and scraps of rusted corrugated iron, like the sculptures made by township artists; she has seen a programme on television about such stuff, called transitional art. Her mother has been bolted together and then undone as new information comes to light, but what else could one who hedged her bets expect? The self-made woman, unmade and several times over reassembled. Marion will have to start again, work harder at garnering information from her father.

Have you read *Frankenstein?* Brenda asks.

Marion shakes her head impatiently. Brenda's questions spell trouble. She has told Brenda about meeting Elsie after all. Should she tell her father? He is old and frail and would prefer not to see her burdened with the knowledge of the past. He has sealed off that past so that the cold spotlight of the present does not flood its pointlessness, the silence and lack of colour that makes up his whiteness. His mantra of we-did-our-best-for-you is infuriating, typical of a generation who bullied their children and believed that they could mould them in their own images. Like God. Marion recognises as cruelty the desire to hack open that past for him, to rub his nose in it; she is shocked both by her distaste and her desire to punish. Perhaps she ought to take him away for a weekend to the sea; it would be a good excuse not to see Geoff, who is beginning to lose patience with her. He has too many questions and suggestions. Can she not be left to do things at her own pace?

John says no, he would rather not go to the seaside; he sighs ostentatiously. It is too much effort, packing up, getting ready, and then the journey to the coast and back again. He is being difficult. Of course he must go, she argues, he loves being by the sea, and besides, she's the one who'll do the packing and lock up the house, drive, do everything. The pained expression doesn't go away. It shifts to self-pity, and Marion realises that he is not prevaricating, that going away even to his favourite village by the sea promises no pleasure. He would rather stay at home, comfortably, and have a nice lunch together on Saturday as they always do. A nice bit of pickled fish from Shoprite in Mowbray. Marion does not particularly like pickled fish; she has never brought him any for lunch. He has rolled back his life to an arbitrary point in the past over which he now crouches defensively, diminished, his hands held out in pathetic supplication.

Marion wonders whether to feel guilty. Has her probing deprived him of his pleasures? But this must also be about growing old, about the world shrinking around him just as his gums have shrunk, so that the false teeth clatter and threaten to slip out. He must be used to the prospect of pleasure falling away like rotting fruit.

She remonstrates with him for threading a tie through the loops of his sagging trousers. Pappie, that's the new silk tie I got you on your birthday, she complains. But he can't find his belt; someone has stolen his belt – the neighbourhood is teeming with skelms. Not only is his physical world shrinking, his utterances too are repeated from a dwindling stock of prejudices.

OK, pickled fish it'll be. We'll party here instead, she says briskly.

Food is the game that they are pressed into playing. He feigns enthusiasm, smacks his lips like a greedy child. Providing food is what is left of her filial duty, even though she knows that he has lost interest in eating and can barely distinguish between sweet and sour. Good girl, he says, just the two of us, like it used to be.

It's nice when his Marion doesn't argue and go tekere like these city girls, like the tart across the road, who struts about with a cigarette hanging from her painted red mouth. He drops off before she leaves, but wakes seconds later with the word Good-girl still on his tongue, a boiled sweet on which he sucks for consolation.

When Marion gets home, she sits out on the balcony. Robben Island is a faint smudge of light. To the left, Table Mountain looms darkly; the tinselled city winks without conviction, and soon the cloth of cloud spread along the top of the mountain will roll down to engulf it all. It is cool. She reaches for the shawl on the back of the chair and wraps it around her shoulders. This must be loneliness, this vast emptiness before her. She has not felt lonely in the past, at least has not recognised the condition as such, too busy, she supposes, being her father's mermaid. Growing up on her own, in blankness and silence, meant that she had no expectations of the world, no patience with what she called the pampered, female world of feeling. Now that she has a past, a family, no matter how distant, something like loneliness has crept in. At least the terror of the Williams face stretched on the water is dissipating, dispersed into family history. The history of the country, too, has slid from the textbook into the very streets of the city, so that these landmarks that constitute her world – Robben Island, Table Mountain – are no longer the bright images of the tourist brochures. Nothing is the same. Next time the image appears, distorted on the drapes of her bed or stretched on the water, she must not bury her head and blubber; next time she will try to look squarely into that face and meet its eyes.

The trick is to keep your head above water and to settle on a course of action. What will she do about Geoff? The stories of her parents' lives have taken over. There is no longer excitement about seeing him; it wouldn't matter whether he calls or not, or so she believes. Marion is jealously guarding her new life; she does not know why she cannot share, as he calls it, with him who waits so eagerly for her news. Although that is precisely it – his eagerness is alarming, his notion of sharing inexplicably embarrassing, even shameful. Marion decides to call Geoff and invite him to lunch with her father. For all his curiosity, his indignation at her lack of interest in his family, he has not once asked to meet her father.

It is too cool to sit out. She goes indoors, drawing the woollen shawl closer around her shoulders. Waiting for Geoff to answer the phone, she weaves her fingers through the tangled fringe, all along the edge and back again, separating the strands.

No, she does not want him to come over tonight; she'll meet him at her father's tomorrow.

The shawl through which her fingers are threaded is green; it is the very one in which she wrapped the dead guinea fowl. She did not expect Maria to launder it, to return it to the balcony. Why had she left the bird for Maria to dispose of? What had Maria done with it? Soup for her family of ten, fifteen? Her fingers catch in a stretch of snarled fringe – she knows nothing of Maria and her family. In fact, she hasn't actually seen Maria for months. Now that everything has changed, perhaps Maria too has become a paper-thin, arthritic old woman with snow-white horns of hair peeping from her doek, a frail creature steered by a Hoover across Marion's gleaming floors.

$\mathcal{A}$lthough John thinks from time to time about a grandchild, something diminutive to bounce on his knee and whose little arms would be the reins of a clippety-clop horsie, the image invariably shifts to the Swartberg Pass: the high black peaks, the distant, empty valley below. The grandchild transmutes into an image of himself as child, which these days he finds unspeakably moving.

He does not know of any man Marion has been out with; he does not associate her with the roughness of men, like the ouens in khaki with Harley-Davidsons between their thighs. She is after all a mermaid, her legs fused all the way down, sealed in the elegant lines of mother-of-pearl fishtail. So that when she rings from the agency to say that Geoff will join them for lunch, he is confused, alarmed even. Ag, liefie, he says, the place isn't so tidy, he isn't feeling very well, and the garden is a mess. The boy she sent round was no good at all, held the spade like a piece of cutlery, so that he told him not to come back.

But Marion soothes: it doesn't matter, she's got some nice pickled fish and a bottle of Oude Meester and her friend, Geoff – no, he is an Afrikaner – Geldenhuys – yes he's a business associate – he wouldn't even notice the untidiness. And no, he isn't interested in gardening.

The house smells of piss. Her father smells; he must have pissed himself, dribbled down his trousers, but he refuses to change; he changed his trousers only a couple of days ago. Marion alights on the only solution: they are having a guest, she reminds him; he should wear his uniform. No, it is too hot to wear the full uniform, the trousers and a pullover will do. If he is not mistaken, it is the pullover that Lenie knitted as a birthday present before they married; she was deft with a pair of needles. Marion does not say that she bought it from Woolworths last year. The house still smells faintly of piss, but it can't be helped; she has no time to clean the lavatory. The doors and windows are now flung open and the southeaster, the old Cape Doctor, will have to do the job.

She has brought along some smoked salmon as a concession to Geoff, who won't want the pickled fish, but John is insistent that they all have at least a taste – best thing the Cape has to offer. There is no trace of him being unwell; he is full of bluster and bravado. He has poured tumblers full of brandy for the boys, ignoring the fine Nederburg that Geoff has brought. Marion leaves Geoff suffering for a while, sips with mischievous relish from her wine, before she comes to his rescue with a glass. John is voluble: it is nice, he says, to have a visitor for a change; they used to have lots of visitors on the farm, on nagmaal Sundays when the neighbouring farmers would pop in for cake and coffee in the afternoon. Yes, Ma was the prize baker of the area: bread, cake, melktert, you name it; the willowy young girls in short sleeves – so lovely they were in the late afternoons, gliding through the trees where the trestle table groaned with coffee and cake – were always asking Ma's advice on baking.

Very good tobacco country too, he explains, and boasts about his horses that thought nothing of taking the harvest across the mountain pass. His father had once thought of giving up the farm, when things became difficult with the drought, but fortunately kept faith. It was the best piece of fertile land you'd find in the Karoo; they were so lucky with the river, having a supply of water is a rare blessing.

Geoff is a good listener. He tells of his family's land in the Free State – cattle and mealies were what they farmed; but he says apologetically that he doesn't have an interest in farming, not even as an investment. He has become a city man through and through.

No, it can't be helped, John sympathises, if you want to advance in the world you have to be citified and certificated. Did Geoff say Geldenhuys? Well, who could have a better name than that, and only in the city could you keep making a houseful of money. But when you marry – and he winks meaningfully, for he has registered the guest as a suitor – make sure that you have a patch to garden. We Boere can't mos survive without land, even if it's just a little bit of earth like a basin of dough in which to knead our fists.

Marion laughs. Not so long ago she would have been mortified, would have groped around in embarrassment for words with which to erase her father's, but she is curiously detached. She is, however, astonished by his chatter. It is as if nothing has happened, as if the last few weeks did not exist. Marion does not remember that her discovery is not his. Now, as if he were he no longer her father, she does not feel responsible for what he has to say.

Before they go, they have to look at the garden, which turns out not to be a mess at all. The man she sent has cleaned it up nicely; Marion says she'll ask him to come again. She'll bring red dahlia bulbs, it will soon be time to plant, and right on cue her father says, Don't waste money at these newfangled nurseries; you can find a good bargain on the Parade.

Geoff says he'll wash the dishes, but John is outraged. Ag no man, he says, it's not a man's job. Marion will do it. They'll have a nice brandy, and even though he's never taken the tobacco himself, he does not mind another man having a relaxing smoke. Helen wanted him to smoke – not a pipe of course, she said cigarettes were more sophisticated; but no, you have to have the right temperament for all that slow puffing.

Geoff hovers uncomfortably. It is not worth arguing, Marion says, we won't win.

She is in the kitchen when someone knocks loudly on the open front door. Her father calls out, Who's there? and tries to get out of his chair. Geoff reassures him that the security gate is locked, but he shouts anxiously, Who's there?

A male voice replies, Nobody baas.

Just shut the door, John tells Geoff, It's these donnerse kaffirs.

Please, great sir, the voice whines, I just want some food. Please grootbaas, can I wash your car for some food?

I'll give him some money, Geoff says, but John is adamant: No, and you mustn't let them touch your car, these spiteful skelms will scrub it with steel wool. Marion appears with the leftover pickled fish in a Tupperware container, and he complains, Don't give my things to these lazy kaffirs.

Christ, Pa, she says when she shuts the door, don't you have any manners? It wasn't a kaffir, it was a hotnot – she shouts the words at him. We Campbells can't mind hottie se kind, can we now? she says threateningly. She would like to say, hotnot, like me and you, but takes pity on the old man, who clutches at the chair with both trembling hands and says that his head is spinning, that the Oude Meester is not as pure as it used to be, and that he'd better sit out in the garden for a while to clear his head.

Marion is relieved that they have travelled separately. They'd talked about going to an early evening movie, but Geoff is considerate: they need not go out, he is sure that Marion must be exhausted. She laughs; do her father's antics bring just the catharsis she needs? Something she does not recognise in herself drives her to say, No, she would like to see a movie. She is also her mother's child; she will let neither Geoff nor herself off the hook.

Do you realise how much you laugh these days? It is a kind of hysteria, don't you think?

Marion shakes her head and laughs. She wonders if she's been trying to emulate Elsie's running-water laughter. No, I feel fine – a personality change perhaps? Perhaps it's what the touchy-feelies call finding myself.

The film is one of those frightful, arty French things about intense relationships, with rain and infidelity, high heels on cobbled streets that gleam in the rain, meaningful dialogue from averted faces in half light, and sex. Hideously dark interiors of patterned wallpaper, antiques and modern art that quite make Marion lose her lust for talking things through. She is no longer interested in a post-mortem on the lunch party. She outlines her plan: they get on well together, have been good friends, so that there can be no reason to stop seeing each other. But only as friends, for a while at least.

Geoff says that he is devastated, and indeed his eyes have a wounded look; however, he will not try to persuade her otherwise.

Marion sobs herself to sleep, dreams of dark interiors, but wakes up quite refreshed. Perhaps if Geoff has nothing better to do this evening he'll come over and she'll try to cook something, the sooner they try out being just friends, the better.

But Geoff is already disporting himself elsewhere. Christ, he says brusquely, I can't. He is out fishing with old friends; he'll have dinner with them, the day's catch, he hopes.

What will she do with herself? It is as if she has just arrived in a foreign town; she must do something.

Marion arrives unexpectedly at Brenda's house with Outa Blinkoog's lantern. It is not yet dark but they should light a candle to show Mrs Mackay, who pulls her nose up at what she calls junk, how lovely the coloured glass will look in the light. There is no candle to be found in the house, but the babbie will still be open – they could send Neville. But Neville has mysteriously disappeared, and the women must go to the shop themselves. Mrs Mackay says it's too late, it's dangerous, at least they should drive. But that's ridiculous, the shop is literally round the corner. On the way, Brenda says that coloured people never walk anywhere, that Marion will have to learn to drive ridiculous distances of a few yards – which earns her an elbow in the ribs.

Mr Mahmoud is ecstatic. Any friend of Brenda's is his friend, because Brenda is a fine educated girl who appreciates a rhyming couplet or two. Marion may have come across some of his poetry in the bad old days of the struggle, there was the big rally at the Athlone stadium after the Trojan Horse affair, and of course he knows they had the support of other UDF communities against the iniquitous system of apartheid; he knows that people like Marion too have sacrificed much in that struggle. Marion smiles stiffly; she has no idea what he is talking about.

Well, that old stuff is passé now, Mr Mahmoud says, it's all the rainbow-nation poetry that's in vogue. But he believes that the past has not been properly raked over, thus he is working on a series about the San people and their dispossession. If the ladies have a moment, he could give them a sampler, because now that rap is all the rage he should be practising his delivery. One must keep up with the times: it's not called poetry any more, he explains, it's spoken word stuff – that now is his forte.

But Brenda is firm: they have to get back, her mummy is alone at home and besides, it isn't exactly safe walking the streets in the twilight.

No man, you're giving the lady quite the wrong impression, Mr Mahmoud complains. It's safe as houses lady, you can take my word for it. Hey you! he shouts at a group of dubious-looking men loitering on the stoep, you must keep a lookout; these ladies must get safely home. Mr Mahmoud shakes both their hands enthusiastically. Never underestimate the common people, the salt of the earth, he says. These humble people, for all their orientation towards crime, have a feeling for spoken word, and Marion, whom he can see is also an art-lover, is very welcome in Bonteheuwel, any time. He sends them off with an ululation peppered with San clicks that make the skollies clutch their stomachs with laughter.

Nay, moenie worrie, one with low-slung trousers slurs, we'll keep a watchful eye on youse goosies.

Should I give them money? Marion asks.

For God's sake, Brenda spits, and looks at her reproachfully. You'll never make a decent coloured person.

At home, they have to wait before turning off the television. The evening service is in full swing and Mrs Mackay, who is singing along in respectful vibrato, pauses to say that it isn't right to cut off the voice of God. Besides, that bit of junk looks like it could do with some help from above.

The candlelight glows green, red and blue through the rough shapes of glass, spreading a magical warmth. Brenda's cry of delight is silenced by her mother, who turns from the screen to hiss but cannot help smiling her own admiration. They sit in awed silence, like children around a Christmas tree.

Marion is grateful for the grave voice of God that prevents them from speaking. She has brought the lantern over on impulse and now, under the warm insistent light, an inchoate thought flickers and writhes into being; when Mrs Mackay finally turns off the television it is fully formed, and she knows precisely why she has come to see them.

I'm going away, she says, overseas for six months, so you'll have to look after Outa Blinkoog's lantern.

Mrs Mackay concedes that the light is lovely through the coloured glass, much nicer than one would imagine such an old thing to be, but firstly, she doesn't think Marion ought to call the person Outa, nobody is called that any more, and secondly, if she's leaving her house empty there's no reason why the thing couldn't be left there, it's no kittycat that needs feeding.

But Brenda disagrees. It should not be left on its own; besides, they have been given it as joint owners, so it's only right that the lamp should spend time with her.

Where will Marion go? Marion isn't sure. To Western Europe, she supposes – England as base, Scotland and Ireland, and she might as well take in a few capital cities: Paris, Berlin, Rome.

And what about the business? Marion says without hesitation that she will sell up, that it's time to move on, that MCTravel might as well be swallowed up by the corporate syndicates that have been hovering like wolves over the past few years, determined to squeeze out the small business. She has no idea where this thought has come from, and once it has been uttered, she marvels at the ease with which she accommodates it.

Back home, however, she sees that there are adjustments to be made. There is no time to sell up; she wants to leave immediately. And three months rather than six, for how could she leave her father for so long? How could she leave him at all?

It is three in the morning and Marion sits on the balcony with a cup of rooibos tea and honey. The sea is mottled with moonlight; a cold wind churns the water and the waves throw up broken images that she strains to put together. At first she thinks that Patricia Williams has returned, but then it seems to be a mermaid, holding like any mother a baby to her breast. The wind wraps strands of wet hair around the lump of baby, then when it grows fiercer the mermaid somersaults, clutching her child, and with her tail whips the water into a moonlit froth in which she disappears. Marion would like to think that it is the sea mammal who suckles her young, the dugong, whom sailors thought to be a mermaid, but the Cape is too far south for that. Thus it is, she says aloud, a figment of her imagination.

When Marion's car turns into Station Road just before dawn, John manages to manoeuvre the last of his cardigan buttons through its hole, and without the help of his stick hobbles to the door where he awaits her, beaming. She has brought a basket of nearly thawed scones to bake. As the aroma of coffee rises, he panics: he has not chopped any wood, for there in Ma's kitchen, with pale stars crammed into the window, the log basket is nowhere to be seen.

It's alright Pappa, Marion soothes, I've turned on the electric oven; we'll manage without the stove today. It will take just a couple of minutes.

A mixture of melted butter and fig jam drips onto his cardigan; the kitchen door squeaks to the briny southeaster, and his heart leaps for his Marientjie, who tosses a paper towel into his lap. He is amenable, foresees no problems, is happy with her suggestion that she'll ask Maria to come in every day for a couple of hours, and after all, she will be in touch by telephone. He knows that she has forgiven him, that her heart has softened like butter, and so nothing will give him greater pleasure than seeing his mermaid across the water, visiting the places where his ancestors came from, somewhere in Scotland – which, if he remembers correctly, is the northernmost tip of England.

$\mathcal{W}$ould it have been better to visit the European capitals with someone, a friend, even Geoff? Marion wonders. The world here is aslant and all must be converted to a level when she returns, exhausted, to her room in the evenings. As a child, watching her father's clumsy efforts at carpentry, she was fascinated by his spirit level, by the spirit of failure that sent the bubble of greenish-yellow liquid lurching to the side. Now, in the evenings, it is she who has to be very still, as if a liquid bubble tilting drunkenly must be brought to rest.

She has sent postcards to Brenda: the Eiffel Tower, the Reichstag, matrons in extravagantly ethnic dress brandishing tulips from Amsterdam, Michelangelo's David, Buckingham Palace, cards that take pride of place on Mrs Mackay's sideboard. Marion has been to none of these places, but then her cards make no such claims. Having a lovely time, that is what they say, and that is true. Also: Wish you were here – once, on her first day in London. Geoff would like to hear from her, of her inevitably revised view of travel and how her mind has been broadened, but she'd said that she would not be in touch. What would be the point of writing about that which he already knew? How much he'd wanted to tell her of a little hidden chapel, a square that he'd discovered off the beaten track, a café hidden in a narrow alley where she absolutely must have a cappuccino and a pastry after absorbing the beautiful Fra Angelicos. But no, she'd held her hand up; if it was about discovery, then she should surely be doing her own.

There is nothing of the breathless excitement that Geoff and the guidebooks promise, but wandering through the cobbled streets of European cities, avoiding the landmarks and especially the tiring museums, Marion surprises herself by taking comfort in the traveller's reprieve, the wash of time that blurs the bars on the clock face. When she is bored and tired of looking and the new begins to take on the aspect of the old, flagging its affinities with the familiar, the weariness does not carry over to the next day. Instead, all is washed clean with time.

On a wet day in Berlin, she succumbed to a museum and wandered through an interminable exhibition of international art, reading the labels, which, if truth be told, felt no different from being caught up in an expensive shopping mall. Except there was a room filled with photographs of farmhouses, and she could have sworn it was the Karoo: poor-white or perhaps coloured houses, and in one of them an image of a young man in profile, holding a set of handles of something that has already disappeared around the corner of the building. Drawn in that stark, unambiguous light, the figure made her think of her father, pushing an absent wheelbarrow. Marion found tears trickling down her cheeks. She would have liked to linger, but the attendant, who was conducting a private survey of the ways in which punters consume visual art, stared with such undisguised delight at her old-fashioned tears that she was driven away without having read the label. But that too, the light and shadow of a father's muscled forearms, tensed over the handles of a wheelbarrow, soon washed over with time, belonging to another day in Berlin.

It is in the assumed familiarity of London that she is invaded by the virus of loneliness. It is here that Marion experiences the world in reverse, feels the topsy-turviness of being in the wrong hemisphere. On the red buses and in the orderly queues, the otherwise silent English speak loudly on their cellphones about their whereabouts and arrangements for dinner; they close conversations with Love you. She wonders what degree of love is needed for this declaration; she would rather say Love you to a ripe avocado pear, and then only after having eaten it, since an avocado too, for all its promise, can disappoint. Are people expected to say it in face-to-face conversation? Marion trusts that it would never be required of her. Some seem to say it sheepishly, but all must suspect that Love you is revolting – why else would they leave out the I?

Geoff has given her the telephone number of close friends of his, smashing people, whom he's warned of Marion's arrival, but now that she is here in London, Marion cannot bring herself to call them. She has an irrational fear of nervously ending her own conversation with Love you. Perhaps it is the alien word, smashing, which Geoff accompanied with the inverted commas of curled index fingers, that makes her nervous; it makes her think of shards of china, of the cacophony of crockery thrown at a cold English grate.

Believing that at some level she knows the country, or the language, she is shocked to find herself a stranger, so very different from the natives, although the motley crowds about her can hardly all be natives. The sensation of a hole, a curious, negative definition of the familiar emptiness, develops in her chest, and she feels compelled to see a doctor. But there is nothing wrong. Indigestion, the doctor suggests; Marion should think more carefully about her diet, and drink less. Ignominy then, that is the word for her condition. And is it not also the northern darkness? Although it's summer and the tiny front gardens are bursting with flowers, the light is a thin gruel, doled out parsimoniously; there has not yet been a day when one could take a blue sky for granted, depend on it. Perhaps it is the absence of light that makes her cry. She washes dishes at the sink in the refurbished attic room she is renting, and tears spill over her cheeks; she goes out for a walk in the park and her shrivelled organs rattle like dried peas in the hole of her chest, heralding the tears. On the heath, among dog-owners and mothers who have eyes only for their charges, it shouldn't matter, except she is jealous of that devotion, and the tears flow afresh in self-pity, pity for the grown woman who wants a mother. She admonishes herself: what if someone were to see her tears and say, Love you? That would serve her right.

Marion resolves to immerse herself in something; perhaps she should start reading the novels that the handsome woman at Clarke's Bookshop chose for her. South African novels – if Marion hadn't read any there was nothing wrong in reading them abroad, the woman said briskly; you have to read them somewhere. *The Conservationist*, that is what she advised Marion to start with; the British gave it the Booker.

The novel is hard to follow: often she can't tell who the characters are, who is present in a scene, whether it is her misreading, her own delusions, or Mehring who is delusional. What's more, it doesn't stop the tears – for the man who doesn't know what's up, for the boy who can't speak to his father, for the absence of a mother, for her own ludicrous identification of the black farmhand with her father. At the end she is racked with sobs. For the anonymous girl biting into a meat pie paid for by Mehring. For the grease patch on the brown-paper bag from which pastry, marked with the half-moon of her bite, peeps. For the too-tight shoes she has kicked off. Tears of humiliation scald Marion's cheeks. Reading over and over the description of the girl, she is able to elaborate on it, fill in details of dress and manners from the streets of Cape Town. The hole in her chest seems to fill up with words.

Is this what reading is, or should be: absorbing words that take root, that mate with your own thoughts and multiply? Is identification with a character inevitable, required perhaps? Marion knows she is not that woman, the play-white girl with coarse features, cheap make-up and a give-away hairline of frizzy roots, and yet she is drawn to the scene. Is the girl not, at some level, a version of herself? Of her mother? Marion is not sure of the story, of what happens at the end, but it is undoubtedly the scene with the girl that drives Mehring away; it is the encounter with the play-white that winds things up.

Has the hole in her chest perhaps been there all along? Did it not assert itself, if momentarily, when the brisk English voice recommended a couple of novels from each decade, saying that that would give an overview, an idea of the country's history? As if it determined her choice, the woman at Clarke's looked her straight in the eye, took in the length of her person before plucking the books deftly from the shelves. Had she recognised Marion as Mehring's girl? Marion wonders how many versions of herself exist in the world.

A couple of days later, she revises the question: how many versions of herself exist in the stories of her country? She is in the grip of something like a fever, a delirium that fixates on the-handsome-woman-at-Clarke's, whom she does not know from Adam. She must persevere with the books; she will not let the woman down. Or no, she will defy her expectations of an uncultured Afrikaans girl. On the other hand, if the woman had no idea how unsettling she would find Mehring's story, she need not read the rest. Perhaps the woman had no view of her at all, had all the while been thinking of boerewors and a glass of good red wine as she cast her eyes over Marion.

Thus up and down inquisitorial steps she scuttles, offering various clever replies – humble, defiant, cold, apologetic – to the woman who rakes her fingers, beautifully, nonchalantly through dark hair, until finally, drained of esprit de l'escalier, she is rid of the image of the-handsome-woman-at-Clarke's. Or at least of her fine English voice. Marion decides to carry on reading, to get to know those dark decades when the Campbells were playing in the light. As for the crying, she decides to put up with it as one does with a headache; she wipes away the tears with the back of her hand, no more than swatting a fly, and finds herself smiling at the multiplication of words.

It is summer, but for an hour or two only per day. The mornings start with promise, bright blue skies with buttery orange streaks of sunlight that slowly, invariably turn to grey, and before you know it, rain is energetically driving in. Day after day. Marion gives up on sightseeing; she spends hours listening to rain on the roof, watching it on the slanted skylight. In this old house turned into bedsits, the window is modern, a single pane of glass, so that the greyness above her is inescapable. Some would say that she might as well be in Cape Town, reading novels indoors, but there is something about being cocooned in a single room, about the bleakness of the days, that must be endured, like sitting an examination. It is a place in which to cry. Wantonly – for Helen, the mother, and for representations of herself, which are of course not herself and thus permissible. In this room, with a rug across her knees like an old woman, the world imprints itself on her afresh; her days are rinsed in rain.

It is halfway through her stay, in the early evening, that she looks up at the wall to find a rectangle of light projected opposite the window. There is still some rain, but the sun has struggled through and holds its own. (Jakkals gaan trou, her father used to crow with delight at the combination of rain and sun; and the child conjured up an image, no doubt culled from *Die Jongspan*, of a vixen bride in white lace, resplendent and groomless.) On the wall, light seems to come to life with a shiver, and Marion watches, mesmerised. The rectangle is a painting, or rather, is painting in action, of white light on the white wall. It is a picture of time, a projection of rain drilling into the angled glass, rolling down the pane, translating itself into a dance of light on the wall. It is water silk come alive: a mother's hidden aquamarine gown, its forbidden, sumptuous folds dragged by the child into ludic light.

Held within the rectangle of the reflected window frame, the liquid patterns form and dissolve. Only as the rain abates does the light trickle lazily, pearl here and there into a knot that disperses once more, into a new abstract image. The trembling of a drop on the pane is a pattern of quivering light on the solidity of wall. When the sun fades, the frame wobbles; light lurches at its disappearing edges, then drains into the wall's blankness. It is gone. Marion stares bereft at the mute surface. Tears stream down her face. What an old crier, she berates herself.

When the sun comes out again, briefly, the rectangle has elongated, grown into a trapezium whose base just rests on the skirting board. Marion hastily drags away a chair that's in its way. For a second, the painting is streaked with water at rest, before a gust of wind outside refigures the brushstrokes of light into a restless beading on the wall. The light teases, conjures first a corner of the frame before the whole trapezium returns in a flash, framed in almost black lines, announcing its death by drowning. An after-image of raindrops, smudges of trembling shadow – the delicate imprint of birds' feet across wet sand – then all is gone.

Has she dreamt the painting on the wall? She has never seen anything so wonderful, she supposes, although the word is hopelessly inadequate, this word that she has used in the past to describe baubles – a silk scarf or a pretty necklace. In the house in Observatory there were never any pictures, no reproductions, only picture rails. In the sitting room, oddly, two brass picture hooks hung throughout her childhood above the sideboard. Marion never asked why they were there; she cannot imagine what her parents had in mind. Throughout the house, below the picture rail, the walls were a dental pink. John would have found gallons of bargain gloss paint at the Parade, would have thought the colour a modern departure from whitewash.

The chair on which she sits is not unlike the one on her balcony in Blouberg. She has even found a green shawl to drape over its worn back. The play of water in the light has left her dry-eyed and alert, as if the very air in the room has been charged with the grandeur of light. It is summer, and it takes hours for darkness to fall. In the twilight, Marion hears guinea fowl squawking in the trees. She knows there are no guinea fowl in England, but the sound is unmistakable; one bird's cry soars above the others. She cannot move, does not draw the blind against the fading light, against the outcast bird that may well want to escape from the others and perch on the window frame of a compatriot, but the birds settle down, mutter for a while like babies satiated at the breast before growing silent. The attic window frames the curious marmalade brown of London's night sky, and the sound of traffic eventually dampens to a dull thunder. Marion sits in the gathering dark with her thoughts. It is late. For hours she sits with an after-image of the trapezium, now framed by darkness, watching the light move in a forest of hieroglyphs.

It is a moment past midnight when the thought comes boldly, with the old-fashioned sound of a typewriter, a headline being printed, letter by clacking letter: The Betrayal of Annie Boshoff.

The newspapers were full of it, or so her mother said, for Marion would not have read the reports. Mr Boshoff caught with his pants down on top of a coloured girl, his buttocks white and frozen in the policeman's torchlight. In the very backseat of the Chevvie where Marion and Annie bounced about with the dog on Saturday-afternoon drives to Milnerton

Beach. But the photograph in the *Argus* was of the girl, her face caught in torchlight, distorted with terror. Helen could not understand what he saw in the little trollop. These coloured girls may not be oil paintings – the girl's mouth was distinctly African – but they certainly knew how to tempt a man, to ruin his life.

Annie was off school that week, and when Marion phoned Mrs Boshoff's faint voice explained that Annie was ill, couldn't speak, that she would be back in class before long. But that was before Mr Boshoff made the scandalous public statement: he would not be charged under the Immorality Act; he loved the girl and had every right to love her; he was himself coloured, a play-white who now wished to be reclassified once more.

And poor Mrs Boshoff, Helen wondered aloud, betrayed by that rat – or had she known all along, herself guilty of immorality? In which case, the family deserved the scandal, the just deserts for unlawful behaviour. They had all been betrayed by the Boshoffs, the whole community, and Helen was sorry to say that there was no question of Marion ever seeing Annie again. Besides, Mrs Boshoff would have to move, she could surely not stay in that respectable area with her brood, who were, of course, strictly speaking, coloured, and strictly speaking should be taken away from her. Unless it turned out, and Helen pursed her lips, that Mrs Boshoff herself was coloured, and thus would also be reclassified.

Marion sat with her fingers plugged into her ears. She and Annie loved each other; they were more than sisters. They owned a joint scrapbook with their favourite pictures of ballet dancers and film stars and things. Helen said to forget it – that family would never live down the scandal, the shame of it all. The Campbells could have nothing to do with them.

It was early on a Sunday morning. Marion knew, seconds before the quiet knock, that it was Annie; she jack-knifed out of bed and tiptoed past her parents' room to open the front door. The children stood facing each other through the security gate. They wore identical pink nighties from Woolworths, with chains of white daisies embroidered on the yokes. Annie must have run all the way; she was out of breath and her cheeks were flushed. Behind her, Devil's Peak was purple-pink in the dawn light.

They did not speak; their eyes met briefly. Annie held out the scrapbook, passed it through the bars of the security gate, and turned to leave. Marion shut the door. Before returning to her bed, she dropped the scrapbook into the dustbin in the backyard.

Marion was eight years old when she betrayed Annie Boshoff.

It is well past midnight. She has been sitting in the dark, enveloped by the past, shivering with cold. When the shawl drawn tightly round her shoulders would do no more, she'd risen to light a candle, then lit the small gas fire and curled up on the hearthrug. The central heating has long since gone off. Marion sits dry-eyed, hugging her knees; she traces the pattern of stylised leaves on the pink-and-green Victorian tiles. It is a small fireplace: six tiles on each side make up a floral design of stems that cross from tile to tile, with straying tendrils looping back to a tile below. Like bindweed. In Rome, at one of the excavation sites, she'd stared at flowering bindweed, looped in a deathly embrace around an ancient stump of marble. The shallow, white porcelain bowls of the flowers, delicately rimmed in pink, tilted shamelessly towards the sun, greedily consuming the light, their pretty calyxes turned into begging bowls.

It is with the image of a begging bowl, of coiling, looping memory, that Marion falls asleep on the hearthrug, drained by her midnight meditations. When she wakes at dawn, for she had not drawn down the blind, her body is sore and stiff as any heroine's. But it is not cold: the old-fashioned gas fire hisses quietly and the candle has burnt down, its wax draped on the tiled hearth. Lying on her back, Marion stretches her limbs by the fire. The square of morning light above is a subtle hue of English lavender-grey. Her eyes traverse the space: a small room, with a row of bells high in the far corner, possibly the only remaining evidence of the building's origins as a townhouse. This would have been the room of a servant girl, from the countryside perhaps, and therefore rosy-cheeked, who would rise at dawn and be ready for a summoning bell. How odd, to take a tea tray from lily-white serving hands.

$\mathcal{H}$er friends have kept their word: they do not ring her, and Marion has not called anyone at home. Except for her father. When the phone rings she therefore assumes that it is John, or about John, that the worst has happened. She panics, she cannot find the bloody thing – but there it is shrieking and twitching on the draining board.

Oh good, she says, how good to hear from you. Surprise is displaced by relief. It is Vumile Mkhize, whom she'd had to call hurriedly from Cape Town airport to cancel a meeting. Brenda would deal with the panel-beater's bill, she explained.

But now he is on business in Scotland; he's noted the pleasure in her voice and so does not beat about the bush. He thought that she might well be in Scotland – the place is awash with Campbells, he laughs. He hoped they could meet, have dinner or go to a movie together. He does not say that he is sick of being on his own, that the hours after business are long and dreary.

Marion hears herself saying that she is about to leave London, that she will be catching a train to Edinburgh the next day. Vumi turns out to be in Glasgow, not that this is a problem, the cities are close together, virtually nudging each other; Marion too sees no problem in deflecting to Glasgow. What about her ticket? No, she has not yet bought a ticket. It does not occur to her that Vumi Mkhize might misinterpret her willingness, her enthusiasm even, to meet with him. And he does not know how eager she is to get out of that attic room with its deceptive light. Will every place she inhabits lure her into memory?

Settled in the train with her bag of padkos – not only because the rand translates into worthless copper, but the British sandwich can be a terrible thing – Marion looks forward to starting the next novel, *In the Heart of the Country*. She finds the title inspiring; she chooses to read it as her country having a real, live, throbbing heart. In this alien world, it pleases her to think of South Africa as her country. She is a colonial at heart: it is with pride that she takes the book out of her bag (she has already read the first page), examines the back cover with its accolades and the photograph of a kindly author smiling encouragingly at the timid reader. The stylised image on the front cover is of an odd-looking woman staring into a mirror. Marion supposes she will be lured into identification with the one-eyed woman, she must resign herself to that, but at least she would never be caught wearing such an awful frilly garment.

At Peterborough someone comes to sit opposite her. Huffing and puffing, with a face red as beetroot, a woman lowers herself into the seat and, as if Marion had been waiting for her, as if Marion were not struggling with a heroine's numbered thoughts, she pants, Well, I almost didn't make it, and it were Martha's fault this time, couldn't find the keys. The two of us, and she shakes her head indulgently, we're a right pair; we seem to take turns in making each other late. Martha's me daughter. She lives with me, came back after five years with the bastard who wouldn't marry her. I says to her, it's now or never, just ask him straight, and cool as cucumber he told her he weren't getting married ever and don't want no kids like and that's what give it to our Martha. Just like that, like a dose of the clap. That's why I can't be hard on her 'cause she's got the – and she lowers her voice, looks about furtively – the cancer you see. Then she looks pointedly at Marion's chest and nods. Are you alright pet? she asks, as if her X-ray eyes had spotted blemishes deep inside those shapely breasts, but she doesn't wait for a reply. Folk say it's nothing to do with the worries, but you take it from me, pet, it's the worries alright, our Martha's always been the one for the worries, even when she were a schoolgirl like, and five years with the bastard must've kept her on tippy-toes, worrying all the time if she were doing things right. If you're a worrier there's no point in being told not to worry, that just makes things worserer, so I kept mum, didn't say a word. But then when I spotted things weren't right no more, I had to say something like. The bastard said I were an interfering cow but he would, wouldn't he, missing his hot dinners 'n all. She flushes with a fresh dose of indignation.

The woman fans herself throughout with a folded tabloid newspaper. All these are good for, she says, you got to buy it like for the headlines, but you know it's only good for the heat. She doesn't notice Marion's scarf, her jacket buttoned up to the throat.

Marion's left hand settles on the corner of her book and her thumb riffles slowly through the pages, not too eagerly, or too deeply into the page; it is the blankness of the edge that soothes. She has been smiling, nodding agreement, understanding. Would she now be able to open her book? When would she have her sandwiches?

But the woman senses her withdrawal. You wouldn't know, pet, about them things, but it's the hot flushes you see. Martha don't like me talking like this; she says I'm not to talk about her business either, but as I always say, there's no harm in it, no harm if you're the injured party like. Gets it off your chest, then you don't have to do all the worrying by yourself – like them cannibals in the South of America. Them primitives know a thing or two. I seen it on telly: they tell their worries to tiny little dolls, voodoo dolls I suppose, so they just don't get the … you know – and she lowers her voice again – the cancer, you know. So, to get to my point: hot flushes, it's no joke, but no need yet for you to go worrying, pet. They come and go like, except for my friend Tilly, well into her sixties and she still gets them. But that's from drinking, as I told her: Tilly, the drinking can't do you no good, but Tilly believes everything these things say, and she swats the paper vigorously against the edge of the table, so that Marion starts. A Guinness a day keeps the doctor away, that's what them papers say, or perhaps it's the telly. Eh pet, has the drinks trolley been round yet?

Marion seizes upon it – a Guinness a day keeps the doctor away – a refrain that goes round and round in her head, innocent and soothing over the woman's blather. The woman makes her feel foreign: here she doesn't know the signs, can't tell, as she would at home, whom to give the cold shoulder, whom to cut short. Now it is too late; she has nothing to resort to other than riffling with her thumb through the margin of the book, while looking out of the window at the fields of acid-yellow oil-seed rape. She feels this is less rude than reading her book, but again she's got it wrong. Martha's mum has no wish to impose; if her stories are not appreciated she'd be the last to foist them on anyone. She composes her face with the haughty look of Janice in *Coronation Street*, straightens up and flicks open *The Sun*. When she gets off at Newcastle, she doesn't so much as nod at Marion, who wonders if she should call after her, Love you.

Vumi meets her at Glasgow station and they take a taxi to her hotel. What about a bus, or the underground? she asks, but he is flash in his formal suit and briefcase. It is also clear that he is in a rush; he has a business meeting and won't be able to see her until later in the evening. He's booked a table for dinner. The taxi waits for him as he escorts her into the foyer. Taxis, he explains, are cheap here; they are for everyone, even the poor take black cabs. She can't imagine the down-and-outs clustered around the lamppost, too drunk to beg with conviction, hailing a cab; she has watched the meter anxiously.

Vumi is forty minutes late for dinner. No problem, sir, not on a week day, the waiter says snootily; they are stared at by staff and expensive clientele alike. Marion finds it intolerable but Vumi laughs; he is used to it. Does Marion think they wouldn't be stared at in Cape Town? He speaks of his business, about being a member of the Petroleum Board, of the EU delegation to South Africa, which is how he met his man from Glasgow. Glasgow's shipping industry is over, he explains; it's the oil and gas discovered on our west coast that interests our friends here, and Cape Town's set to become *the* ship- and yacht-building centre. Man, we've got some business to do with each other. He apologises for having to attend more meetings tomorrow; he thought that he'd clinched the deal, but no, he hadn't read the Scottish negotiators correctly. He loves Scotland: the people are generous beyond belief, and also like Zulus in other ways –

immodestly keen on their own culture and traditions. Perhaps a bit more cautious than they claim to be about investing in South Africa, so who knows how long it will take, but he can meet with Marion most evenings; he'll try to keep those clear. She might even like to come to dinner with the investors; it would be an opportunity for networking.

Marion is not tempted; plain old working sounds more attractive. She says that he shouldn't think of her as his guest, that she is perfectly capable of looking after herself. She will be the good tourist: there are the sights of Glasgow to see, a daytrip to Edinburgh with more sights, and who knows, she might even do a train journey into the Highlands to see a loch or a ben-something. He laughs. Of course; he has no doubt that she is capable of anything she chooses to do.

Not so long ago, Marion would have resented Vumi for being at the receiving end of what's known as fast-tracked black economic empowerment. She tells him, and again he laughs; he has endless supplies of good humour. Of course you would, he says, but only when you're back home. Vumi is warm, cosy; in one evening he extracts information from her about her childhood, love affairs, the business, details she would normally call intimate. She finds herself relaying the words of the woman in the train, trying to do the northern accent, and they giggle like girls.

When they leave the restaurant, they are decanted into another world. The rain has stopped. It is late, eleven o'clock, but the northern light lingers; the night sky is still flushed with the memory of sun, and the blonde sandstone buildings hum with an eerie pellucidity, as if it is there, from the denseness of stone, that stored light is being released. It has been like this throughout her stay: dull summer days, with the sun making a languid, yawning appearance in the evenings. They walk back to her Travelodge through streets thronging with young people in skimpy dress, the white, white skin of near-naked girls, phantasmal in the stubborn, time-tricking twilight that will slip, as she later discovers, unnoticed into dawn. Vumi has taken her hand, or perhaps she has taken his; she can't remember, being tipsy on impossibly expensive wine, weaving through the honeyed Scottish vowels in the gloaming. It is good to be so far away, to be with someone from home, and she wouldn't mind if he kissed her goodnight. He does, fleetingly, on the left cheek.

Garnethill, Glasgow. How has she landed on the very crest of this jewel-named hill with its mixture of old and new? With no desire for crossing boundaries, or none that she knows of, she is a traveller who has stumbled into another country. She imagines that fanciful Brenda would want to wind her way around the contours of such a place, would prise her way into the inner chambers of any pomegranate hill, hold its jewelled seeds up to the evening light. But the streets are a grid and Marion zigzags through them, covering every inch of the garnet hill. She peers into tall windows of tenement houses, where blinds or curtains are not drawn against the dying light, where young people with haloed red heads clink glasses and laugh; they are actors in a silent film. It is a place where citizens sleep in, even in the week, exhausted no doubt by the bright nights. Nothing comes to life before nine. If only the people of Garnethill knew that their summer mornings are like Cape Town's: blue skies with the reddish-yellow blush of pomegranate rind where the sun rises. The light stays for almost an hour before cloud rolls in for the day, only retreating before the late-afternoon sun. She watches the sunrise from her hotel window.

It is not easy to be out on her own late at night; that is the time for couples and for eager, fearless, red-headed youth. Marion sits in cafés and watches them with wonderment, with envy; she has never been young. On the second evening, she waits for Vumi to call; then, realising that she doesn't actually want dinner, turns in for an early night. Vumi has taken her at face value; he does not get in touch. She might be hurt, but actually his phone call to London can be seen as no more than a geleentheid, thus she will not allow her spirits to sink, will not return to being a crier. Should she ring him? No, no point in coercing someone into being your friend; besides, he is virtually a stranger, and she has found another way of thinking about him – as the messenger, the one who has brought her to this town. That is good enough; that will have to do.

The woman on the train said that Scotland may not be the place for weather, but it certainly is the place for landscape, that the lochs and mountains are incomparable. Far more beautiful than Switzerland even, she said proudly, or so she believed – she had of course been to neither. With a family like hers ... But Marion finds that she is not interested in the landscape. This city, or even Garnethill, is quite enough for her; the project she has set herself of combing each street thoroughly, working her way meticulously through the map, takes longer than one would think. She has found an Italian café where it is not so difficult eating on her own in the early evenings, and then there is the reading, which becomes slower and slower as she devotes more time to it. *In the Heart of the Country* proves to be even more difficult than *The Conservationist*, the character more delusional than Mehring. She started reading greedily, eager for the story that kept on sidestepping just beyond her grasp, but the voices at the end are too hard, the words are indeed in stone. Now she has started again, slowly, drawn into the crazed thoughts of Magda, a hole crying to be whole. Marion tosses the phrase in her mind, but she does not identify with Magda; that father is not her father. So Garnethill, she thinks, is also a place where she learns to read, and who knows, perhaps this time Magda's stones will crack open to reveal meaning in pearly, red pomegranate seeds.

When it doesn't rain, and when the children are not yet out of school, she sits reading in a little park or garden she can see from her guesthouse. It is a magical place of grass and pebbles and flagstone that follows the slope of the hill. From a tower-like structure for children at the top, a stream meanders down to an amphitheatre of hewn stone, where it splits and gurgles its way over pebbles. An old man whom she has watched feeding the birds tells her that it is a lovely day. She supposes it is; there is no rain. He is delighted by her accent; he too has family in South Africa, marvellous place, but he believes it's all been messed up now. Murder, rape, knifings, all kinds of atrocities, he says, rolling the r's with bloodthirsty relish. Mind you, everywhere is being messed up, look at Garnethill where he was born and bred, full of Pakis with their wee curry shops. Marion, who has been hounded by esprit de l'escalier for too long, says it's a pity that he should use such uncivilised language. The remark may not be clever, but at least she will not spend the night recasting this conversation.

Oh no, Paki, he says, it's just short for Pakistani. That, you see, is where they come from. In droves, with all the other refugees and asylum seekers and suchlike, to Glasgow, where the Council has conveniently forgotten about their own Scottish poor. And the English, too, they've bought up all the properties here in Garnethill, sent the prices sky high. See, we've been an oppressed people for centuries, but it won't stop us. Och yes, we're a humble people but we've got our traditions; it'll take some armies of immigrants to turn us from our culture.

Well then, Marion says cheerily, you've got nothing to worry about.

She's done her bit; it is not her place to take on benighted Europe, she decides. She tells him that her father wants her to look up the Campbells, find out about their Scottish background, and Dougie, as he insists she call him, launches into a complicated history of Highland battles and treacherous Campbell murders, for which she is not ungrateful. She would have had to invent something for her father, and Dougie's version will do nicely. But the heritage business is too ethnically charged for Marion's taste; she steers him away from the battles of the distant past.

Dougie shows her the flagstones where stories about people's lives in Garnethill have been carved into the stone, and reads out his favourite with the delight of one who hears it for the first time. He reads slowly, reverentially:

Living in the main door flat at 150 Renfrew Street in the 1940s I was ill in bed with the flu. Suddenly I heard this loud bang and clatter ... the wall collapsed and a digger with a man on it came through the wall. They were demolishing the house next door to make room for the new playground, so the story goes. Folk said that was one way of getting a man anyway.

Dougie says that he knew the lassie, a bonnie redhead she was, and one who had no difficulty in finding a man, oh no, none at all; he himself fancied his chances like – and he winks, tilting his head rakishly. They stand over the gurgling stream and he tells her about the Scottish water spirit, the kelpie, that takes particular delight in drowning travellers, and that assumes various shapes, often that of a horse.

So not nice then, like a mermaid? Marion asks.

Well, sometimes, kelpies have been known to help millers in trouble; they keep the wheel going by night and so get the work done, like the wee elves and the shoemaker, but he, Dougie, would say beware. If folk are no longer as good-natured as they used to be, then he wouldn't bank on the spirits either.

Marion asks if they are visible to humans. Oh aye, Dougie has himself seen the kelpie in his time, browsing by the lakeside on the verge. The kelpie, he teases, patrols the borders, keeps an eye like on youse travellers.

When Dougie leaves for his tea – See ya the morra hen – Marion wonders about the stories written in stone. Why did she find them charming? Do the storytellers like the idea of people, travellers, strangers, reading about their lives? The recorders would no doubt say how good it is to *share* your life with others, how your story ought to be heard. But would such good folk like to see their own stories printed in stone in a public place? Marion shudders at the thought of her life laid out in lines, carved into a stone tablet for a tourist to bend over, bum in the air, and read. And if, she wonders – in a drunken state, say, or old age – she were to be lured into telling her story, which part, which anecdote would be selected to bear the weight of presenting her to the world? How sure you'd have to be that the story you tell is indeed of the you that will prevail. Might Dougie's bonnie lassie not, a couple of years later, have shook her head with incredulity – well, I never; who would've thought? – not recognising herself at all as the subject, the person who lay ill in bed as a man on a digger burst through the wall? Not for nothing the disclaimer: so the story goes. No, Marion decides, the stone tablet cannot be for the ephemeral lives of people; it is for gods, with their messages or commandments. When she turns to her book she is cheered by Magda's fictionality and the flimsiness of paper. This is what helps her to persevere with Magda's mad murders and phantom couplings: they are preferable to the stories of real people coming through walls, and what's more, they have nothing to do with Marion.

It is not until the seventh day, as she is thinking of getting back to London, that Vumi rings from the oilrigs of the north, near Aberdeen. Things have been hectic but now he really is free, the deal's been clinched, and what a pity she won't be there to celebrate with him – surely she can stay another couple of days.

Marion sees no harm in changing her plans once again: another geleentheid is how she looks upon it. She has just finished the book again and cannot face a third attempt. Together they could try the tourist thing. Oh yes, she enthuses, she'll show him round Garnethill, the School of Art and the Mackintosh House in the West End, places she has not yet got round to seeing.

Vumi the businessman is buoyant with success, an unlikely candidate, perhaps, for mythologising as messenger, but Marion must keep an open mind. It is lovely to saunter with someone through the late, lingering light that does not simply cast its aura over this time, this place, but rather seeps into everything, keeping yesterday aglow. Vumi buys champagne, speaks enthusiastically of the far north, where he clinched his deal. Last night he was taken to a businessman's club, with glamour girls called hostesses. He tells of his desire to see, no, to touch fiery-red pubic hair. Vumi is a talker. In between swotting up on the guidebooks and planning where they will go and what they will do, he speaks of his childhood, of having been brought up as Victor McKee in a coloured neighbourhood where no one was fooled by the family. They called them kaffirs, he laughs, and not only behind their backs either. His parents carried on pretending that no one knew they were Zulu; they threw parties that the family could ill afford, plying the lighter-skinned scum with expensive whisky. But at home, with the doors shut, they made sure that their children knew about their forebears, their Zuluness, and they, the children, would never have dreamt of complaining about being bullied at school or being called kaffirs.

Marion clucks sympathetically. Parents, hey, what they put their children through.

Oh no, he says, mine were okay; people do what they can to survive. And then when apartheid came to an end, my mum just took her wig off, right there among the coloureds, and now they're living nice and comfy in a black neighbourhood. I just love their impertinence – he laughs uproariously.

How do you know what to call yourself? she asks.

You mean why not Victor? Because in the bad old days, Victor was just a code. V for Victor he simpers; imagine doing business with such a name. Might as well be called Nike, after a shoe.

Marion takes Vumi to the park in Garnethill, where they find Dougie feeding the birds. She hadn't been the day before, and he is delighted. He just knew that she wouldn't leave before saying goodbye. Another traveller, she announces, and Dougie is taken aback for no more than a second or two. He is pleased to meet a real African, he says, and Vumi pumps his hand mirthfully as the old man congratulates him on his English. In the amphitheatre, where they sit under a grey summer sky, Vumi and Dougie teach each other their folk songs. Marion is disgusted, but is inveigled into providing the soprano. They spend the rest of the day together in bars, so there is no time to do the tourist sights. Dougie wishes they could be there for Burns night, when the whole of Scotland is ablaze with song and poetry and of course whisky and the haggis. Do they know Burns, the best poet in the world? It rings a bell, Marion frowns – and then she is transported to primary school. Yes, the father of Afrikaans poetry, Reitz (another F.W., as it happens), wrote the first Afrikaans poem after Burns's Tam O'Shanter, except his Tam is a coloured man called Klaas. Dougie says that's a crying shame, but when Marion recites, clapping her hands to the demonic dance, as they did at school – Aleksander Klipsalmander / Trap hulle algar met malkander – he recognises the iambic beat, the guttural g's and rolling r's. Still, he hopes they'll be back to hear the real thing next year.

Before they leave, Dougie fishes two packages from the bottom of his Tesco bag of breadcrumbs. One is smartly wrapped, for Marion's dad: a tie in Campbell tartan, and the other is for her: a haggis – MacSween's, because no other brand can be trusted. He knew that she wouldn't leave without saying goodbye.

Dougie will not join them for dinner; he has no stomach for fancy food. Neither has Marion tonight, but she has no choice. After the restaurant, Vumi walks her back to the guesthouse. It is late. The sky is still streaked gold and pink with the memory of sun. Sauchiehall Street is a catwalk for the young sashaying in and out of bars in the seductive northern light. It is her last night. Can it do any harm, asking Vumi up, spending the night with him? Shall we see if there is a bar in the guesthouse? she would have to say. Vumi would be surprised, but businessman that he is, he would not want to miss an opportunity, would acquit himself energetically. But then, perhaps not, perhaps he would think of her as mad, guilt-ridden Magda.

$\mathcal{B}$renda and Geoff are at the airport to meet her. They struggle with the luggage across the car park, against the wind and the driving rain; they say how well Marion looks, how radiant. A word reserved for brides, she thinks, drawing her coat closer. It is bitterly cold; she does not remember Cape Town ever being so cold, but they say that the temperature is not unusual.

When they get to the car, Geoff realises that the keys have been locked in. Excitement, he says bitterly; he has never in his life done anything so stupid. He hates looking the fool, and goes on patting his pockets, although the keys can clearly be seen dangling through the car window. It is the man driving up and down the aisles with a luggage buggy who comes to their rescue. He hums and ha's; he would not give such information to any Tom, Dick or Harry, but finally discloses that there are wire hooks hidden in the stanchions of the shade netting – if not in the one above their car, then a few stanchions along. In a matter of seconds he unpicks the lock and lets them in. He looks disdainfully at the ten-rand tip that Marion offers, turns without saying a word and zooms off in his clattering buggy.

It is all planned. They will drop her at home and then Geoff will get Brenda back to work; in the evening the three of them will have dinner together. Brenda supposes that Marion will come in to the agency later that morning, but no, Marion will go and see her father, see what the old boy is up to, and then if there's time perhaps … Is everything okay at the office?

Brenda looks at Geoff, who says, Yes, all is well. He looks appreciatively at Brenda: she has done a brilliant job; there'll be no reason for complaint.

Marion smiles; she didn't think she would find any. At home, from the window, she watches them walk to the car, watches Geoff open the door for Brenda, who looks up and smiles and says something, so that leaning on the door, leaning towards her, he lingers before going round to drive. Marion does not turn away to put on the kettle until the car is out of sight.

She would like to put the old rattan chair with the green shawl back out on the balcony, but the rain is being driven in by a wild west wind and the sea is brown with churned weed. The flat seems dark, unwelcoming, unfamiliar; she ought to do something about the dreary bedroom. The bed, stripped of its muslin drapes, is bizarre; it will have to go. She can't imagine ever having wanted it.

In Observatory, John Campbell can't believe his ears when he hears the Mercedes speeding along Main Road. It is the silver Merc for sure, even if she does sound somewhat asthmatic, and he stumbles out of his chair; he'll have to get the kettle on. How could it be so late? He's only just had his breakfast, and no one told him that Marion would be coming. He staggers off, forgetting to take the stick, and must reach out for the sideboard to help him on his way. But he misjudges the distance and falls. God-God-Gotallah! he calls – for Helen, he knows, is not there to hear the forbidden oath, and in any case this is a proper pickle. John hasn't fallen before. Whatever will Marion think, finding him on his back, waving his arms and legs like an insect? He turns, inches forward. There must be some purchase on the solidity of the sideboard – if only the blarry thing had legs – but there is nothing to grip; he can't haul himself up. Tears of humiliation blur his vision, blur everything. Ma will have to help; Ma will come and just say, Get up, in her no-nonsense way. No one disobeys Ma, so he'll find himself rising, jisso, like dead old Lazarus, a little dazed but soon revived with a nice cup of coffee and a rusk at the ready for dunking. That is what he must focus on: the comfort of a soft, coffee-soaked rusk.

Marion knocks. If only he had half a minute he could get himself up, but now there is no point in trying; he does not call out.

Marion lets herself in and finds her father stretched out on the floor, for all the world as if it were a bed of feathers. She is distraught. Putting him back in his chair, she strokes his hand. He smells strongly of pee; he has clearly not changed his trousers in all these weeks. Ag no, he says, please could he now be left alone, he's been badgered quite enough about changing his clothes by Maria and also by Brenda.

Brenda, Marion exclaims, what has Brenda got to do with you?

Oh, a very nice girl really; it's only lately she's been bothering about his clothes. She's been coming round to see him and so enjoys talking about the olden days. A very good listener, and he has no objection to helping her; he thinks she might be lonely.

John had phoned the office a number of times – clean forgot that Marion was away. And Brenda, taking pity on the old man, came to check up on him. Marion gets the story out of him piece by piece. He'd run out of brandy and that impertinent Maria refused to go to the bottle store. Imagine, she said haughtily; she didn't go into sinful places like that, and in any case Marion would not approve of him drinking so fast. He tried to reason with her, said he could now practise drinking more slowly, but what a stubborn, stupid old hotnosmeid. Anyway, he phoned Marion once or twice to complain, to insist that the girl be sent away. He had of course given her notice, told her to go, but she just turned up all the same; and when he wouldn't answer the door she let herself in, brazenly, having stolen his key. Thank God for Brenda, who came with a bottle of brandy and some decent mutton bredie, enough for two, so that they sat together nicely and chewed the fat over a good plate of food. Brenda also had a word with that blarry Maria, sorted her out alright, so now she knows her place, knows her job is to clean and to leave him alone. It's just this morning that she started up again, interfering with his clothing.

A clean pair of trousers lies crumpled on the floor. Marion has brought along Dougie's tartan tie. She tells him about the friendly Scotsman and gives a version of the story of the murderous Campbell warriors, who misbehaved in their hosts' castle way up north in Glencoe – to which he smacks his thigh appreciatively. Jisso, so that's our people hey. Marion says they will have to photograph him in the ancestral tartan to send to Dougie, but first a bath before he may try the tie. This Dougie, he says, Marion ought to have paid him; he'll want his money. They'd better send some with the photograph, for the Scots, he pronounces, are a stingy people who won't part with a cent. Marion explains patiently that that is nonsense, that one should be wary of so-called national characteristics, that it takes only one Dougie, who parted voluntarily with a great deal of money for the tartan tie, to prove that John is talking rubbish. To which he nods sagely: yes, he has been catching himself out lately, thinking rubbish thoughts.

She runs a bath, helps him take off his shirt, and is shocked by the topography of that ancient chest, its lumps and folds, and the sickly colour of aged, thin skin. There are blue-black bruises all over. It's nothing, he says; no, he hasn't fallen before, bruising comes with barely brushing against the wall. So that is how enduring blood behaves in the old: protesting, frothing obscenely just below the surface, ready to spurt, to abandon ship. Papery flakes of skin fly from the grubby vest.

The smell is overpowering and Marion is relieved that he refuses help with his trousers. From a chair by the side, John should be able to lever himself into the bath. In the meantime, she changes his bed, where he has been lying inch-deep in a ghostly rustle of flaked skin. It was not so long ago that her father would recite his cleanliness-is-next-to-godliness maxim. Why, when all the other clichés spring as readily as ever from his lips, has this one fallen into disuse? Can it be reinstated? Is the elderly's aversion to changing their clothes, their tolerance of dirt, as physical as the onset of rheumatism, a preparation for the body's demise? She will have to supervise at least a weekly bath, and grit her teeth to tackle his toenails.

If truth be told, Marion is apprehensive of going to the agency, but with her father cleaned up and ready for a nap – like a baby, he thinks despairingly – she has no reason to delay.

The men in the car park are delighted to see her. They serenade her with a drunken song; they have thought of her every single day. Her welcome in the office is equally effusive. Both rooms are festooned with flowers, and Tiena blurts that now they can have the cake; they've been waiting all day. Tiena has dressed up in nautical white and blue for the occasion: over her jersey she wears a striped vest, and on her head a jaunty cap with the legend Hello Sailor in gold lettering. Marion says dutifully, Hello Sailor, which sparks a discussion: Boetie thinks that it is they, the readers of the words, who are being greeted as sailors, to which, frankly, he objects. But Brenda is of the opinion that the words carry a say-after-me force, that Tiena is identifying herself as sailor. Tiena settles the dispute by saying that they work in a travel agency, thus none of them are sailors; the cap is just fashion, its words being just words that would mean the same if it said Hello Tailor.

Boetie reports on everyone: Tanya's bout of flu; Brenda not doing too bad a job running the office, although there has been a sticky patch or two – it's been a sharp learning curve for one so young. Tiena has also experienced a learning curve: she's had to learn that giggling will get her nowhere in a well-run establishment, and nor will inappropriate dress, he adds.

And now, Brenda says, I'm pleased to report that Mr van Graan has acquitted himself with efficiency and dignity, and cannot be accused of having messed about with learning curves.

Boetie shouts, Yip-pee, punches the air and cuts the cake.

When Marion sits at her desk, it's as if she has not been away. She doesn't know if that is good or bad, but she had imagined this as the moment that would reveal whether to keep the business or not. Brenda, too, appears to have no difficulty adjusting to the boss's return; if the old routine had been disrupted, it is quickly re-established. Could things really be so different, and also be the same? Will she have to resume her old life as if nothing has happened? But then, nothing has in fact happened.

Something will have to be done about her father, but she will think of that later. Marion leaves with everyone at five.

When Geoff collects her for dinner, Brenda is with him, bustling with carrier bags on the back seat. Something is the matter, but she will not ask, not yet. It is not until they are on the highway and Marion looks down at the curve of the bay, the twinkle of ships' lights, that she realises they are driving away from the city. They come to a halt at her father's house.

It is a surprise: a party for her, Marion, who has never had a party. Candlelight, from dozens of candles, douses the dreariness of the sitting room. Not only is her father spruce in his tie, busily conducting with his stick, but in the kitchen Mrs Mackay and her father's sister Elsie, of all people, are fussing over pots.

You didn't tell me, Pappa, Marion teases when they are alone, and he says anxiously, Didn't I? I must have forgotten. But he drops the mask and laughs, I'm not beneuks; it was meant to be a surprise. Then he whispers, nodding towards the kitchen, It's not the same you know; Elsie's turned out so very different, not at all like my old sussie. Of course I was pleased when Brenda first brought her, even if she does laugh too much, but it's a cover, you know, covering up for wanting to bully me, to tell me what to do as if I'm not her ouboet. Don't you think this party is going to be too noisy for me? I'd rather it was just me and my mermaid.

But Marion says that it's going to be fine, that they both love parties, and indeed he is reassured. He sings tunelessly: Afrikaners is plesierig dit kan julle glo / Hulle hou van partytjies en dan maak hulle so – conducting with his stick and winking conspiratorially at Geoff.

Ag no sis, Boetie John, don't go spoiling the party with Boere nonsense, Elsie says, bearing a tray, and he laughs uproariously, tapping her behind with his stick.

Man, in this New South Africa we can play at anything, mix 'n match, talk and sing any way we like. Because of freedom, he explains.

In the small sitting room, where no guest has ever been, they bump into each other around a table laden with food. Lekker coloured food, Mrs

Mackay says, urging Geoff to try her lightly curried tripe and trotters with beans. The vegetarian dishes, which Brenda has brought from the new delicatessen, she pushes aside. Geoff says that he is a country boy and thus partial to offal, at which they laugh good-humouredly: it is a party, and everyone is allowed to talk nonsense. For Marion, who is the guest of honour, Mrs Mackay has tied brains in a pouch of honeycombed tripe that makes her stomach heave; she insists on sharing it with Auntie Elsie, who is as much a guest of honour. Which sends sprightly Elsie to her feet to propose a toast. Her speech, woven through with laughter, starts with Nelson Mandela and works her way down to Brenda, who in her own humble way is an agent of reconciliation; she even has a gracious word for Helen, now sadly departed, whose beauty, like her melktert and crunchies, was unrivalled.

All they need is Patricia Williams to wind things up, Marion whispers to Brenda. Oh, and what a pity Vumi is still overseas.

Brenda whispers back that Williams, poor thing, was in the news last week; she has been appointed as South African ambassador to some place like Finland.

Later, Marion announces that this may well be a farewell party; she is thinking of buying a new place, so that her father can live with her. She must have had too much Pongracz; she is as surprised as the rest of them by the announcement.

John's head has been lolling for some time but he perks up to say, Not over my dead body, and tugs impatiently at the napkin Elsie has tied around his neck.

Then, Marion persists, we'll have a housewarming party, and Geoff says, yes, they'll have to have another in order to look at her photographs from overseas. Marion holds her glass aloft by way of assent. She doesn't have any photographs; she does not even own a camera, but this is a party, where one does not disappoint with the truth.

*B*renda is disappointed. Marion has thanked her profusely for everything, brought her a book on modern art from the Rijksmuseum with wonderful colour plates, and a beautiful necklace of amber, is unfailingly civil, but has made no arrangement to see her on her own. Are they not supposed to be friends? So it is she who invites Marion out to Kirstenbosch on Sunday: they can have a walk and lunch, although Marion will have to come all the way to Bonteheuwel to pick her up.

It is a lovely day of brilliant sunshine and clear blue sky that tells of spring being on its way. As they set off, Marion has another idea: a walk by the sea, and why not just go back to Bloubergstrand? They could pick up something and have lunch at her place. Brenda would like to get a bottle of bubbly; she is surprised to find that one can't buy drink on Sundays, which in turn surprises Marion. It is warm and they wear their trousers rolled to saunter along the beach in bare feet, shrieking when the icy water creeps up, lapping at their ankles.

Back on her balcony, they admire the classic view of Table Mountain. That is one good thing about going away, Marion says: seeing afresh how lovely the sea and mountain are. And the clear, unambiguous light. But she will be moving to the city soon; Blouberg is too far away and she no longer enjoys the isolation. Besides, she'll need a bigger place when her father can no longer manage by himself. It is from the kitchen, where she is opening a bottle of white wine, struggling with the cork, that she calls out to Brenda, Are you going to tell me about your relationship with Geoff?

So that's what it's about, Brenda says, you're jealous. You dump Geoff but don't want him to have a relationship with anyone else.

Nonsense. Isn't that why you've come out today, to tell me all about it?

As it happens, no. I was under the impression that we were friends, and friends spend time together, tell each other what they are doing and thinking, chew the cud. I have nothing to tell about Geoff because it's you he's interested in, you he wants to talk to me about, and that because he thinks we're friends.

Brenda steps out onto the balcony, stands with her back against Table Mountain. They say it's history, centuries of history that comes between people, but I don't buy that. I can't be your friend because I'm too dependent on you. Right now I'd like to leave, but see how I can't flounce out, holding aloft keys slipped through my index finger like a movie star. I have to ask you to take me home. She pauses. Actually, that's not true. I could ring someone to fetch me, flounce out without the keys, and then face the ignominy of waiting outside.

Stop being childish, Marion says. And as for history, I'm glad you've dropped that old chestnut. It's true that I've been uncomfortable about you and Geoff, disappointed, because there is so much I wanted to tell you but couldn't while I thought ... it's irrational, I know, but there you are. So let's drink to friendship.

How peculiar that Marion has no idea who Brenda would call. Who would come out all the way to Bloubergstrand to fetch her? Unless it is the Tiki or Ricki person she has spoken of.

Brenda laughs. Let's drink, then, to learning about friendship, she says. We're all novices when a new person comes along – not so different from falling in love.

They chat until late in the night, and Brenda phones her mother to say that she'll stay over.

The next evening, Marion gives Brenda a lift home after work. She'll collect Outa Blinkoog's lantern, and then meet Geoff later in Claremont to see a movie. She has decided to take him seriously as a friend; she'd never really thought of friendship in relation to a man before, and perhaps that is why things with Geoff have not worked out.

Brenda says that she will miss the lantern, that it has brought good luck. All her life she has wanted to write, and literally could not get as much as a sentence onto paper, but lately, in the last few weeks, it's happened, and she has made good progress. Nothing brilliant, of course.

How do you manage in that noisy household? Marion asks.

It started by lighting the lantern in the bedroom while her mother and the others watched television. Just staring at it seemed to drown out the noise so that, well, lying on her bed she just started writing.

In that case, Marion says, you ought to keep the lantern.

But no, Brenda is not dependent on it. She hopes Marion doesn't mind, but in her absence she's been spending weekends at the office, doing second drafts on the computer.

Marion doesn't mind at all, indeed is pleased for her, but why didn't she say anything last night?

Brenda clears her throat. This isn't easy, she explains, and her voice catches. It's all thanks to your father. He kept on phoning, thinking you'd be there. I felt sorry for him, took him a bottle of brandy and he just couldn't stop talking. About the farm, his childhood, meeting your mummy and all that, it all came pouring out, and I found when I got home . . . you know what it's like, all your life you want to write and you sit there chewing your pencil, not knowing what it is you want to say – well, I found that your father's was the story that I wanted to write, the story that should be written.

Should be? Marion swerves, pulls off the road. Her voice is cold with rage. So in the guise of a do-gooder, you went back to prise more out of a lonely, senile old man who was grateful for your visits? Sis. How dare you! Why don't you write your own fucking story?

I know it's a rhetorical question, but let me answer all the same. Writing my own story, I know, is what someone like me is supposed to do, what we all do, they say, whether we know it or not, but Christ, what story do I have to tell? I'm no Patricia Williams, with adventures under my belt. Mine is the story of everybody else in Bonteheuwel, dull as dishwater. Or my sister and Neville, treading the boards between the television and their double bed – why would anyone want to write about them, invent

217

something around such tedious lives? So that tedium can be converted into something improving? That, I say, is the business of God. So that such lives, too, can be known about? I say they are known only too well; the people in Mr Mahmoud's shop will yawn and skip the pages in the hope of something beyond poverty and television and coloured people's obsession with food, something at least to laugh about. Now your father, there's a story – with his pale skin as capital, ripe for investment . . .

That's enough. Get out. I know my father's fucking story.

Actually, Brenda says, I suspect you don't.

She keeps her eyes averted as she gets out. Her thumb flicks at the lock before she shuts the door with a quiet click.